# THOSE THAT WAKE

### JESSE KARP

HARCOURT

HOUGHTON MIFFLIN HARCOURT

BOSTON    NEW YORK    2011

For information about permission to reproduce selections from this book,
write to Permissions, Houghton Mifflin Harcourt Publishing Company,
215 Park Avenue South, New York, New York 10003.

www.hmhbooks.com

The text of this book is set in 12-point Garamond No. 3.

LIBRARY OF CONGRESS CATALOGING-IN-PUBLICATION DATA IS AVAILABLE.

ISBN 978-0-547-55311-5

Manufactured in the United States of America
DOC 10 9 8 7 6 5 4 3 2 1

4500280634

*To Zoe and Verity.*
*You give me hope.*

And hope is but a dream of those that wake.
　　　　　　　　　—Matthew Prior

# PART 1

# MAL

MAL LOOKED IN THE MIRROR and saw a road map of mistakes. Scars traced a fractured route down his face, splintering across his torso. The worn paths were interrupted by fresh welts and discolorations, the result of his most recent misstep: three rounds, bare knuckles, with a guy who had ten years' experience on him. That was good for the deep yellow around the eye and the welt on the forehead. But it had been a sorry-looking mug to begin with, scarred across the bridge of the nose and along the cheekbone, crowned by dark, somber eyes. It fit poorly over the seventeen-year-old face; instead of lending it wisdom, it robbed it of something vital. Beneath

3

the blue veins riding up his arms in relief and the taut flesh of his chest, the muscles were tight, but they ached with the echo of fierce impact. It wasn't a promising picture, so he smiled at it, showing teeth over his hard jaw.

A crack ran through the reflected smile, making it into two dislocated halves of good spirit sloppily sewn together by some depraved surgeon. The mirror hadn't had a crack when he left just a few hours ago. It was just the mirror's time, he supposed. Like the glass, his smile cracked and then fell away.

He touched the tender spots on his torso, figured he'd wrap his ribs with medical tape. He slipped from the gloomy little bathroom, down the short hallway. The limp he had just acquired did not help much in keeping quiet past the door of his foster parents' room. Were they light sleepers? He hadn't been with them long enough to know. His foster parents, who were named Gil and Janet Foster. It was ridiculous, but of all the foster parents in all the world, some of them had to be named the Fosters, didn't they?

He made it into his own claustrophobic little cubbyhole without incident. He pulled the first aid kit out of his bag, but found he just didn't have the strength for it. He put it back in and dropped himself into bed.

Sleep, ornery and evasive, eluded him. It was in the second hour of shifting position in the darkness that he turned and saw the message LED blinking on his forsaken cell phone.

Already an ancient model at two years old, he had never bothered to learn how to employ most of its features, thus didn't have the cool, polite female voice to inform him that he had a message waiting. He'd slipped out of the apartment for the gym at 11:30 and never carried the phone with him to a fight. The call had come between then and his return at two a.m. No one called that late unless something awful had happened.

He reached out and keyed for the message.

"Uh, hey." A face he didn't recognize flickered onto the screen. "It's Tommy." Mal sat up straight in his bed. Tommy. His brother. Whose face he no longer even recognized. "Where are you at one o'clock?" Tommy paused for a long stretch, uncertain. There was the sound of strong wind, or something rushing, maybe water, but the image on the small screen was grainy and dark behind the face. "What am I doing calling at one o'clock, right? Maybe . . . ah . . . maybe you could call me when you get this? Doesn't matter what time it is. Okay, so . . . you can give me a call." There was another long pause, but instead of a goodbye, the image flickered out and the cell voice informed him that the call had come in at "One. Twenty. Two. A. M."

The geolocator app was being blocked from Tommy's end, which left no way to see where the call had come from. He dialed the number that showed on his screen and let it ring twelve maddening times before he keyed off and dialed again, this time giving it only six rings.

He stared out the grimy window and listened to a garbage truck rumble away down the dark, dirty street. Far in the distance across the water, a large insectlike shape blotted a small part of Manhattan's silhouette of glittering lights. There was only one person who would know how to get hold of Tommy. So he got back in bed, because he wouldn't call anyone else at three in the morning. And he wouldn't call her anyway. Tommy hadn't seen Mal in over two years, had done just fine without him for a lot longer than that. Tommy would do just fine without him now.

But if that was so, then how much trouble must Tommy be in to call a brother he hadn't seen for so long now, in the middle of the night?

Mal sat up again and picked up the cell and stared at it. He gripped it so hard that his fingers and knuckles turned white, bringing the dozens of nicks and scars into wiry relief. He keyed the goddamned number. It rang twice and he closed his eyes tight when it picked up, the small screen lighting with a man's surprised and disheveled face.

"Hello?" The face was dulled by sleep and the voice was thick and rough.

"George, it's Mal," he whispered, for fear of rousing the Fosters, just a slim wall away.

"What? Who is this?" George was squinting angrily into the screen.

"It's Mal," he said stiffly. "I need to speak to Sharon."

George's face gaped exhaustion, then shook in disbelief and moved offscreen. There was heavy breathing and then shifting and muffled voices. An ad for a sleeping pill, now available in extra-strength form, scrolled along the side of the screen.

"Mal." Her face was heavy with more than just fatigue. Her voice was hoarse and he couldn't help wondering, despite the hour, if she was exhausted or hung over. Whatever the case, the syllable of his name came out with the same old mixture of impatience and barely contained disappointment.

"I need to find Tommy and I don't have his number," he said without preamble.

"You need to find Tommy at three in the morning?" Even pulled from sleep, her disgust with him was evident.

"He called me up and asked me to get back to him as soon as I could, but he's not answering at the number he called from."

She glared at him. He could see numerous responses cross her features.

"Hold on," she finally said. Her attention shifted downward while she searched the cell for the information. George asked her something and her face turned. They went back and forth for a moment and his final comment was loud and wheedling. Mal watched as the advertisement shifted, now offering medicated bandages that "soothed as they healed." There was more movement, and then she was back. "I have his number here." She gave it to him.

"That's the number he left me," Mal said. "But he isn't there."

"Well, that's the number I've got."

"Have you spoken to him lately? Is he okay?"

"I haven't spoken to him in months."

*"Months?"* He hadn't meant to sound incredulous; certainly not, considering how long it had been since he'd spoken to Tommy himself.

"He and George . . ." She sounded more tired now, in simply pausing, than she had when she first got on the line. "He and George had some trouble. He left, and I haven't heard from him but twice since then. Once to give me his new number and address and once to tell me that he was going to come by work and see me, but he didn't." She didn't seem very impressed with Tommy or, for that matter, with George.

"He left?" Mal's voice was hard and accusatory, and he didn't bother trying to hide it.

"Yes, Mal. He left. Figured he could do it all on his own, just like his brother."

They stared into the screens at each other, far more distant than the miles of space that separated them.

"Give me his address," he said.

"You're going to go there now?"

"No. In the morning. I'm sure he's fine."

"Sure. He's always fine." She gave him the address, and they didn't bother with goodbyes.

He slammed the phone down, punching it into the bed as hard as he could. He got dressed in the same jeans and hooded sweatshirt he had worn to go fight. Sneaking out of a foster home twice in the same night was no record for him, not even close. Now he was bone tired, of course. If he closed his eyes, he'd be out in a second. He took off.

Getting to the address cost a long subway ride deeper into Brooklyn, but when Mal walked out onto the sidewalk again, there still wasn't a hint of light in the sky. It was a crumbling neighborhood of intermittent lighting and staccato bursts of human sounds from a doorway, around a corner, down a shadowed block. He kept his head up and walked as if he knew exactly where he was going; not a stranger, not out of place, not prey.

The building was a wreck, and the lock on the gray metal door had been ruined long ago. The hallway was dirty; not heaped with junk, just dusty, grimy, not looked after. There were no bodies in it, though, no homeless wanderers who had lucked upon an open door and a night's refuge.

Mal walked up the stairs, his feet whanging with uncomfortable volume from the thin metal planks. His thighs ached fiercely from the fight a few hours ago. Down the hall, lit by two dim bulbs, were three figures standing before a door that would surely turn out to be Tommy's. They saw him arrive and followed him with their attention as he walked over, making a cursory check at the other apartment numbers on the chance, the one-in-a-million, cut-me-a-break chance that they weren't standing at Tommy's door.

He came to them, looked between their heads, and saw the number in fading black on the door: 302. Tommy's apartment.

"Hey," he said.

They were younger than Mal, dressed in massively baggy jeans and shirts that came down to their knees and jackets that swelled their bodies to three times their actual size.

Mal noted how the wood near the doorknob looked rough and splintery, and his eyes shifted around to their faces. They looked back at him, committing to nothing.

They watched him with an unnatural stillness. Mal knew guys like these, went to school with them, trained with them, fought them. Even sitting in a corner looking sullen, their aggression usually burned like hot coal. But not here, not now.

They looked at him, not aggressive, not even curious.

"Well," he said, "don't let me break it up, I just need to get inside three oh two there." He gestured at the door.

"You can't," said the spokesman in a voice of quiet authority. No challenge, no verbal shove, nothing characteristic of his appearance. Just final, certain refusal.

"Oh. So, you live here?"

"No."

Mal pushed out heavy air. He was bigger than they were, but there were three of them, and who the hell knew what they were hiding inside the vast clothes they were buried in? His knuckles, crosshatched with scars, were still red from earlier tonight. There were no sounds coming from inside the apartment—calls for help, clatter of a fight—but something in there was important enough to post three guards at the door.

"I have to get in there," Mal said, tired of analyzing his odds.

"You have to?" the spokesman asked, his features still indifferent, but his body coming to attention. His two companions shifted at the announcement. The hallway felt different now. Inexplicably changed from quiet, dim squalor into something . . . *imminent.*

The door to 302 opened then, and Mal flinched at its suddenness. The dark apartment produced another guy, his scalp covered in a tight cloth. His stark white eyes passed over

Mal with no particular interest, and he stepped aside, clearing the doorway.

Mal nodded, stepping carefully between the four of them and into the apartment.

"'Scuse me," he said, closing the door on them harder than a peaceful man would have. He stood on the other side, unmoving, wanting to hear their footsteps recede down the hall. After a moment, hearing nothing, he leaned up to the eyehole and looked through.

All four of them stood in front of the door, staring at it. Staring at the eyehole.

Mal pulled his head back.

"Jesus," he whispered to himself. "What the hell?"

A minute of silence passed. The lock fixture had been decimated, and without being able to lock them out, he felt like a hostage in this small place. He turned, gave up the door, and addressed his prison.

It was a tiny place. There was a kitchen alcove, a sink piled high with dishes, and a refrigerator filled with cans of beer and soda. One corner of the apartment had a table with two chairs, and another held a bed with a lit lamp near it and a window with a spider web of cracks in it. Tommy's apartment, his own apartment where he lived by himself; no Sharon, no George, no Fosters. A fleeting squeeze of jealousy tightened Mal's heart.

The last Mal knew of Tommy, he was charged with anger and it kept tripping him up. Tommy could always push things too far, but he could never stick with them; could always pick a fight, but always backed down when trouble really started. Mal was frankly surprised that Tommy could get it together to find and keep a place of his own.

Tommy was not here to explain it, but a picture of him with his arm around a pretty girl at the beach was propped near the lamp. When Mal came to it, he couldn't take his eyes off it. At eighteen, Tommy was barely a year older than Mal, and he had Mal's young face, but without the mask of scars over it. Tommy's wounds were inside his head. He had Mal's dark hair, too, though it was long and shaggy on the older boy. But he'd never had Mal's ability to contain his anger and *use* it. Even without the scars, even with the boyish hair, Tommy's face looked hard, challenging, even in that moment, which must have been a happy one.

The place wasn't exactly tidy, but it wasn't trashed, either. No one had overturned furniture or plowed through drawers. It meant those guys hadn't been looking for something Tommy had or something he owed them; they were looking for Tommy himself. This, in turn, meant that it was good Tommy wasn't here after all. Imagine, Mal thought, just imagine coming in and finding Tommy's ruined body. Mal's face grew hot, thinking about that.

He stormed back to the door, pulled it open hard, clenching his fists. But the hall was empty, and in their wake they had left only the quiet squalor.

He could go after them, see what they wanted with Tommy. But that would just get him into the fight he'd managed to avoid in the first place. He was here for Tommy, but all it took was a tick of the imagination and he was ready to throw down; eager to, even. And what good would that do Tommy? What good would it do Mal? Less than none, considering his condition.

He closed the door, went back, and sat down on the bed a minute to think about it. He could wait here; maybe Tommy would turn up. Maybe that would mean not being back when his foster parents woke up. Go looking for Tommy now? Where did he hang out? Where did he feel safe?

Mal hadn't seen him in two years, hadn't even really *known* him long before that. He couldn't answer those questions any better than he could come up with the name of the pretty girl in the picture. He looked back at the picture and smiled at her and Tommy. She was a nice girl, he would bet. Maybe she was what kept Tommy together, if he still couldn't manage it himself.

He pulled his aching body off the bed and went back to the Fosters' house, where the guilt could eat him alive in peace.

# LAURA

WHEN LAURA'S EYES OPENED, they were looking at the small pink clock on the table by the side of the bed. The hands of the clock said it was 4:20, though light streamed through the shades and lit the corner of the room behind the clock. If it was 4:20 p.m., then she had slept something like sixteen and a half hours. If it was 4:20 a.m., then—

She shot bolt upright, crawled over the bed to the dresser, and grabbed her watch from the top of it. Her clock had broken at 4:20 a.m. Her watch told her it was 9:35.

She was showered and dressed by 9:50, and only four minutes after that she was in the family car, speeding down the highway faster than her parents would ever have allowed. This left her one remaining minute to cover ten miles, find the right street, then the right address, and report for her interview.

It took her twenty-five minutes before she stepped into the dry, climate-controlled outer office. The lady behind the desk was sour, aged beyond her years, dried out by the artificial, regulated air.

"You're late," the lady said. "You're going to have to wait for the next slot."

"Of course. I'm so sorry." Laura bowed her head low as she said it. *You old bag* was how that sentence ended in her head. She didn't bother making excuses; this wasn't the person to make them to anyway, and excuses to the receptionist would just make her appear tense.

It wasn't as though her entire college career, and thus her entire future, rested on this interview. It wasn't as if her parents had chosen the worst possible time to take their annual long weekend in the city. It wasn't like if her mother had been at home this morning she would have been certain to rouse her on time. Come to think of it, had she slept through her parents' good-luck phone call? If not, this would mark the first time in her life that her parents had not kept their full focus on her until the very last second before an important event. And strange timing, if they had chosen this moment to ratchet up her independence: just when she didn't want them to.

Laura sat down and did what she could with her hair in the camera app of her cell. The receptionist let two others in while Laura stewed and shuffled through the files on her cell: high-school transcript, application form, recommendation letters. Attached to one of them, on the Post-it app her father used for these small surprises, a message: "Don't forget to tell them about the college courses!" A little more than half an hour later, the receptionist deigned to look her way again.

"Laura Westlake," she said, "you can go in."

Laura rose, absently touching her hair, and went into the office. It was larger and brighter and greener than the reception area, thanks to the lime carpeting and matching trim. The man behind the desk was as slim and sharp as a razor, polished with a cold fastidiousness, right to the stiffness in his collar. It was just plain remarkable, she thought as she took a seat across his desk, that some people looked exactly like the part they played in life. The plaque on his desk said he was "Martin Stett."

"Ms. Westlake," he said, fingering the touchpad of the screen on his desk that contained all the information Laura had sent along. He looked at the screen with his eyes but didn't turn his head toward it.

"Yes, sir." She smiled, willing her already bright blue eyes to light up even more.

"I like your grades and extracurricular activities," he

said, clearly scanning them for the first time. His eyes found her suddenly. "You know, our last intern was a young man."

She looked back at him, more surprised that he paused after the statement, waiting for some kind of response, than she was surprised at the statement itself. *Well, a man will do in a pinch.* She almost said it.

"That's interesting," came out instead.

"Mmm." His eyes flicked back down to the file.

He was quiet long enough that she began to tussle with the idea of offering an excuse for her tardiness. She opened her mouth with the first word of it just as he looked up and spoke. As they interrupted each other, he stopped and actually scowled at her.

"I'm sorry." She motioned with her hand for him to continue.

"I see you've applied to Yale," he said. "My son attends the law school. Why Yale?"

"Their psychology program is ranked among the ten best in the country, and I'm very serious about pursuing psychology as a career." Did she sound too proud about it? How could she soften it a bit? "It's also just a few hours away from home."

"Yes, I hear it's an excellent program. Do you suppose they particularly mind if you're thirty minutes late for all your classes? Or, later, when you have a private practice, do you think your patients will mind if you show up after half their sessions are through?"

Shocked by his unpleasantness, she blinked very slowly and reigned in the response held just behind her lips.

"I'm terribly sorry, Mr. Stett." It sounded just a little tight. "My father is out of town, and my mother came down with something very harsh last night and I had to get her to the doctor rather unexpectedly." *Too many details,* she scolded herself. Cramming in details always weakened a lie. "I'm really never, never late like this."

"Well," he said, taking his eyes off her once again, "that's provably false, isn't it?"

She held her tongue for a moment longer, debating whether or not her entire future actually *did* rest on this interview.

"You understand this is a six-month internship," he said, "specifically for our hospital statistics study. What do you think you could contribute to this study?"

"I've done three years of advanced placement work in psychology," she said without preamble, prepared to move on if he was, "and last summer I took a psychological statistics course at SUNY Stony Brook."

His eyes began to wander as she spoke, to a note on his desk, a picture on the wall.

"I've been a volunteer at the Stony Brook Medical Center

for three years, too," she soldiered on, "and I know they figure prominently in your study. And I believe very strongly in the purpose of your research." He was through. He didn't want her from the beginning, either because she was late or because she wasn't a young man. It was plain now as he considered her flawless qualifications with squinting unkindness.

"I don't think so, Ms. Westlake." He finished it like a hit man firing a bullet into the back of a head, quick and cold and without a glimmer of remorse. "We're looking for someone with a more dynamic variety of interests."

"More dynamic. I see," she said to that stream of nonsense. She stood, but rather than strolling casually out, held her position.

He stared silently, waiting for her to disappear and the world to resume its natural order. She had so much to say to him. She could feel it bubbling in her stomach and trembling at her jaw.

"Was there something else?" he asked, begging her, *begging* her to say it.

She didn't.

Sitting in the car, numb, she called her parents. She was shocked to have the call go straight to her mother's voicemail. They knew exactly when her interview was. Why would their cells be off now? Why, in fact, had there not been a message from them waiting on her own cell?

But it was *their* long weekend, and if that was more important than *her* interview, Laura could grudgingly, albeit confusedly, grant them that. She voice-texted something artfully vague and drove herself home.

Mookie bounced around manically as she came into the house. In Laura's rush this morning, she had failed to feed him, and now she paid the price as he whined and slobbered at her feet. She stripped off her nice clothes and stuffed them angrily into the hamper, then pulled on the frumpiest sweatpants and sweatshirt she had. Then, and only then, did she saunter into the kitchen and unload a can of the meat slop Mookie favored into his bowl.

Standing in the kitchen, she began to fume again. Despite wanting to yell at Mookie for no reason, to scream at her parents for good reason, to jump up and down and throw a fit, her reputation as the calming voice of reason and harmony among friends and family haunted her even when she was alone. She pulled out the soothing peach tea instead and opened the cabinet to fetch her mug. As she pulled it out, her eyes caught on the long jagged crack that had formed, spontaneously it seemed, down its side. The mug, shaped into a lumpy surface by her own eight-year-old fingers once upon a time, had the words "I LOVE YOU MOMMY," with hearts standing in for all the Os, carved into its rusty brown surface beneath a shiny glaze. She had created it in art class as a gift for her mother, but by the time she got home and spent a month hiding it, it became clear that it had to be her own. Finally, tearfully, she confessed her terrible secret. Since then, it had been holding her milk, orange juice, and tea every day of the intervening nine years. But not anymore. The crack was so deep, she could see light through it if she angled it properly. The glaze was flaking away around it, and shards of hard clay were already crumbling from the surface.

So Laura cried it out, leaning over the sink, the poor maimed mug hanging shakily off her finger, with Mookie dumbly munching away by her feet.

If her parents had been here, this would not have happened, that was for goddamned sure. Even her mug would probably be okay if her parents had been here, because then she would have been up on time and had orange juice this morning and that would somehow have saved her mug; it wouldn't have felt abandoned, forlorn, and thus given up the ghost.

Of course, didn't her parents always take this long weekend on their anniversary every year? Hadn't they, in fact, had their reservations long before the appointment for this interview had even been a possibility? Had it not been Laura herself who insisted they keep their date when they realized it would mean their absence during the interview? It had been a mad push for the independence they sometimes seemed so reluctant to give her that had now blown up in her face.

And what was more frustrating, really: that her parents weren't here or that she so desperately wanted them? It was as if no accomplishment was real until they had acknowledged it; no failure could be confronted without them to hold her hand. All this talk about giving her the independence to make her own way . . . when was she going to learn how to forge that path?

As the last tears began to dry on Laura's face, Mookie started thumping against her shin with his shaggy head.

She knelt down and rested her forehead on his and rubbed the sides of his belly.

"Sorry, dude. Just because the rest of the world is filled with assholes doesn't mean you have to live with one."

She got his leash and put on sneakers and let him lead her, racing, out of the house and onto the road.

She called her parents again while she was being tugged along, and though the phone was clearly on, because it rang several times before the message this time, she still got no answer. Amid the shadowed trees, the familiar houses snug behind their neat lawns were a hallmark of the quiet affluence and security of her life. She passed them by unnoticed as she checked her own messages and found not only that her parents hadn't replied to her text, but that there were no messages from Rachel or Cheryl, either, who both knew she'd had the interview this morning, though they at least had the excuse of being in school today. Laura had taken the day off as one of her allotted college days, with the assumption that it would be noticed by her interviewer as a sign of her commitment. So Rachel and Cheryl would be at the end of pre-calc now. She could voice-text them, or wait the ten minutes until lunch and call them. But she felt hollow at the idea of talking to them before talking to her parents about this. For all their double-checking, their last-second notes, their wholesale and often frustrating investment in practically every step she took, wasn't this exactly what parents were for? She didn't need them to tell her how to do everything right; she just wanted them there when things went particularly wrong. Which, as she recalled, was where they had always been until now.

Back at home, she took a real shower, dressed in a tight light-blue T-shirt and her jeans skirt, and put her black hair in a ponytail, tugging her father's old Mets cap around it. She sat at her dad's desk and unfolded the cell screen to its largest size. She enlarged the touchpad and spent the next hour web-numbing her brain.

By the time she was bleary-eyed and bored, her parents hadn't called back in three hours, and it was surely enough to worry a person. Given that her mother still told her to put her seat belt on every time she got into the car, was it any wonder that dreadful thoughts would spring to Laura's mind? Not that the other explanations were so wonderful, either: that they had forgotten her interview was today (not possible, given how long she had been blathering on about it) or that they didn't care (not possible, given how long *they* had been blathering on about it).

What the hell was it about New York, anyway? After all the crap that had been heaped on that place, why would two people want to spend a vacation there?

"Screw this," she said out loud.

She turned music up louder than ever would have been permitted in a parentally supervised house, cleared her mind of this useless nonsense, and got down to work.

Just because the internship she'd been planning on—had, in fact, assumed she'd be getting, given her much-vaunted credentials—had fallen through didn't mean there weren't a thousand others waiting for her elsewhere. She started looking and found that, in not having bothered to look around, she had missed others that interested her just as much. Two of them were even through the Medical Center, where she already knew people who would, she assumed again, be happy to help her out.

Her eyes wandered to the message indicator.

Still no call.

She put the music back on louder still, too loud for Mookie, anyway, who darted out of the house through his dog door and started rooting in the yard. She retreated to the laundry room and ironed what was waiting in the dryer while the next load was going, then ironed the new stuff. She folded it and brought it to its proper places and had the knob of one of her dresser drawers crack off in her hand as she slid it open. Like the mug, it was done, but unlike the mug, it could be replaced.

Still no call.

With a high-pitched shriek of frustration, she gave in, snatched up her cell, and keyed her parents. Expecting to be frustrated once again, and not sure whether to present herself as happy or furious if she did get a response, she was immediately surprised to have the screen brighten with her mother's face after one ring.

"Hello?" Claire Westlake said, looking quizzically at the screen.

"Mom!"

"I'm sorry?" her mother said. She was focused right on the screen, and Laura could see the generic décor of a hotel room behind her, so the cell was clearly working properly.

"Mom, it's me." She took off the Mets cap; though, if anything, the hat should have made her *more* recognizable.

"I'm sorry," her mother said. "Who's 'me'?"

This whole day of not calling and refusing to answer in service of some half-assed joke? That was not like her mother, and it was definitely not like her father.

"Mom, what are you doing?"

"I'm sorry, young lady, but I don't know you. Have you"— her mother stumbled, obviously troubled by this exchange herself—"have you checked the number you're dialing?"

"What's wrong, Claire?" her father's voice came from off the screen, and her mother shook her head without looking away.

"Mom," Laura said again, because, really, what else was there to say? "It's *me*. Laura."

"I'm sorry, Laura," her mother said. "You seem to have the wrong number."

"I . . ." Laura's voice trailed away, her mind suddenly stupid and her fingers numb.

"Try again," said her mother, not unkindly. "I'm sure you'll get who you're looking for." She looked at the screen quizzically for one more moment, then keyed off, leaving behind a scrolling ad for reduced train fares to New York.

Laura stood immobile in the middle of the living room, her body stiff and her eyes dizzy. Dazed, she looked down at the empty screen.

"Mom?"

# ANNIE

MAL'S EYE WAS PURPLE and yellow. It didn't hurt as much as his knuckles, which always stung fiercely the day after a fight; nor as much as the back of his torso, where he'd taken a kidney punch; nor his wrist, which had hyperextended in a clumsy block. Nevertheless, it was the eye that Sharon noticed.

"What do your new parents say about that?" she asked, and maybe her voice was smug, or maybe that was how she always sounded. Mal couldn't remember. "I'm sure they love it, knowing you're coming into their home with other people's blood on your knuckles."

"They get me an ice pack," he said, "and ask me if I'm okay." A lie. He had gotten out of the house before the Fosters had even seen him.

Sharon was a tired woman, washed out and wasting away, scrubbed at by a rough and bristled life. It was the same thing Mal thought he saw in the mirror; something strong in his face worn away, the defining and striking sharp edges dulled until strength had become sorrow and a gleam in his eyes had become a dull flatness.

"And do they care that you aren't in school?"

"If they do, that's their business now. Not yours. I'm here to talk about Tommy. Or are you finished with him, too?"

Her jaw hardened. She bit something back, then nearly spat out her next words.

"I told you already, I haven't actually *seen* him in months." As she sat on the edge of her couch, her face wasn't softening, but her fingers wouldn't stay still, searching for a smoke, or something more powerful. "Tommy always talked a good game and dropped the ball as soon as things got hard. He barely graduated, then he couldn't find work." She snorted. "I hounded him about it, but what the hell good did that ever do? He'd make a halfhearted try, then never follow up. George arranged an interview for him; more than one. Tommy didn't even bother showing up for the last one. George yelled at him, said it made him look bad; said Tommy had to pull his weight if he wanted to stay. Tommy said he'd pull his weight." She laughed, her eyes looking inward. "Pull his weight right out of George's house. And he did. Only solid decision he ever managed to stick to."

Mal nodded. He had never been to this apartment, tiny and crowded with the objects of a life he had nothing to do with anymore. No light found its way in here, through the grimy windows. A bulky shadow loomed outside, cutting off the sun. He had not been in the same room with his mother more than three times since his father had marched out, pulling Mal behind him. But his mother still had the same harshness in her look, a look of perpetual accusation.

"So he got a job, found a place," Mal supposed out loud.

"I guess so," Sharon said. She didn't sound convinced.

"You don't know what he was doing, nothing like that?"

"Christ, Mal, at least I had his address. When's the last time you saw him?"

"I didn't mean it like that." He *had* meant it like that. "What about his friends? Do you know any of them?"

"Well, sure, there's Danny and Miles and Tony. Oh, you mean their *last* names, don't you? So we could, like, look them up and ask them about all this?" Her unpleasant sarcasm was also something he remembered well about her. "You're not the only one with a brain in your head, Mal. I never spent much time with his friends. I doubt I'd have been welcome to if I'd wanted to."

Mal nodded. She was steamed, and he was only making it worse, which was their classic dynamic playing out beautifully to form. He saw it among guys at the gym again and again. Some climbed into the ring just because it meant a couple of bucks or some recognition or a chance to punch an anonymous face. Other fighters had it in for each other specifically, and it had nothing to do with a shared history. It was purely chemical. Mal and his mother had a history *and* they had that chemistry. They suffered through it, at each other's throats for the first eleven years of his life, when Sharon was sober enough to pitch a fight and wasn't bothering to have one with Mal's father.

"How about a girlfriend?" It was all he had left. "A blond girl, real pretty." Sharon was shaking her head.

Mal's eyes wandered around, and finally he nodded and stood up.

"Okay," he said, instead of offering anything reassuring or hopeful. What did he owe her, exactly?

"So, what, are you going to go back to his place?"

"I guess I am. Maybe he'll show up."

She led him to the door but stopped in front of it and held her place.

"I think we should call the police," she said.

What he thought about the police, generally, was that you shouldn't call them. But Tommy was actually *gone.* Not missing like he went for an unexpected walk, but missing like he had called for help and there were people after him. At least that would explain why Tommy was blocking locator apps when he made his call to Mal.

"Okay."

She looked up at him, letting her guard down just long enough to show him she was frightened, then shut it away again. What did she do about her fear these days? Did she still go on week-long benders, or had George cured her of that? And why should Mal care, really?

He blew off school for the rest of the day. Would anyone realize he wasn't there? He wasn't good enough or bad enough for teachers to care one way or the other. There were people who knew him, of course, but no one who particularly sought him out, unless it was for a fight, because he had a certain reputation in some circles. He didn't make a habit of ditching, but he did it when he needed to. Sometimes they called his foster parents, sometimes they didn't. What would the Fosters say if they did? He had no idea. They were nothing but a pair of faces to him at this point.

He sat in Tommy's apartment again. The place was nothing new in the daylight, though the hall outside was noisier. Music played too loud through one of the doors, and two different sets of people yelled at each other in two different languages from behind two other doors. Smells of spicy food filled the hall and seeped into Tommy's place.

He poked around, embarrassed when he found some condoms and surprised when he came upon a sketchpad filled with rough pencil drawings of things and people. The sketches made something funny happen in Mal's chest. At first they made him feel as if he were seeing something about who Tommy was, but as he flipped through them he started to feel as though he was searching through a stranger's life. He left the rest of the apartment alone and just waited. Pacing, he kept finding himself in front of the picture of Tommy and the girl at the beach. Important enough for Tommy to take a hard image off his cell and put on display. Was Tommy the sentimental sort, or had the girl in the picture made this choice? Was she the reason Tommy had stayed out of George's house without crawling back, had managed to keep an apartment of his own for months? Mal looked at the photo intermittently for minutes until he finally convinced himself he might need it to show their faces around. He removed it from its frame and slipped it into his back pocket.

He played the last half hour of a movie about an alligator terrorizing a city, beaming it from his cell onto a cracking wall, and was into the last rounds of the week's *Blood Match X-Treme* finals when he started to wonder if he was going to be here forever. When he'd decided to wait, he figured it could be for as much as two or three days, but now, just two or three hours started to seem interminable. He abandoned the ball game and went to the window. Outside, the world looked gray. He felt as if he remembered a time, as a child, when there was a sun and people looked up at it instead of down, embroiled in a conversation on cell, or into the palms of their hands, surfing as they walked, their minds on anything but the gray world around them.

And there was a knock at the door.

He limped hard to the door, adjusting to the stiffness that had set into his injured body as he'd been sitting there. He hesitated, remembered looking through the peephole last night and seeing those four faces staring weirdly back, right at him. Cautiously, he checked the peephole again and saw a young face framed by blond hair. It had five thin silver rings in the left ear and a tiny silver stud in the left nostril. It looked worried, and sweeter because of it.

The door had no functioning lock left. Mal wouldn't have been able to get in if it had. It was pure luck—or something harder to explain—that the place hadn't been cleaned out last night after he'd gone. He pulled the door open, and the girl looked happy, then surprised when she ended up looking into a chest instead of the face she was expecting to see. She followed the chest up and seemed to relax once she got to the head.

"Um, hi," he said, guilty about getting caught in a place he didn't quite belong. "I'm Tommy's brother."

"I know." She smiled. "Mal; you're kind of . . . uh . . . *big,* for a little brother. It's hard to tell in the pictures."

"You've seen my picture?"

"Sure. Tommy has pictures of you in his cell."

That was shocking enough to keep Mal staring dumbly for too long.

"I'm Annie," she said, trying both to be polite and to look behind him into the apartment at the same time. "Is Tommy back?"

"He's not, actually. Why don't you come in?" He let her pass, closed the door, and followed her back to the couch. With her here, he felt like he was the guest now. She sat down and, obviously sensing the same shift, gestured for him to take a seat.

"So, do you know where Tommy is?" she asked.

"I don't. Do you?"

She shook her head, looked down somewhat darkly.

"No idea?"

She shook her head again without pause. She'd obviously been over this on her own.

"When was the last time you saw him?"

"Yesterday afternoon," she said. "I haven't seen or heard from him since."

That wasn't such a long time, Mal thought, but she was talking about it like he had been marching off to meet his doom.

"Where was he headed?" he pressed a little. He felt foolish doing it. He wasn't a cop or a truancy officer; he wasn't even Tommy's brother in any way that really counted. But what was left to do? He had taken up a mission of some kind, and he'd come back here for these answers.

"Tommy had a little . . ." She searched for a word that would get the urgency across but not betray Tommy. "A little trouble, I guess you could say, with some people."

"Yeah, I met them."

"You did?" She looked up, her eyes showing doubt and hope, fused together.

"Sort of. Weird bunch."

She shook her head, not understanding.

"They were street, but they were kind of missing the attitude."

"Street kids? No." She shook her head. "I never saw him, but Tommy said the guy he met always wore a suit.

Tommy said he was . . . what? Like, kind of cold. Quiet, but you knew he didn't think much of you. That's what Tommy said, like he was just a tool to this guy."

"So he was never into trouble with any street kids?"

"No." She didn't waver for a second. Tommy was her open book.

"So what about this guy? What did Tommy do for him?"

Her eyes wandered away, fell on the sketchbook that Mal had put back in its place on a windowsill.

"Look, Annie, I'm not trying to find Tommy to make trouble for him. I think I'm probably enough trouble for him when I'm not around. He called me last night and said he wanted to see me, and he sounded a little scared. I wasn't there when he called, and when I finally got here, he was gone. I just want to find him and help him if I can. That's all I want."

"Then we both want the same thing." Annie was almost crying. He could see the tension in her face and neck as she tried to hold it back. She took a moment or two before she went on. "I don't know exactly what he did. Carried things sometimes, I think. He was well paid for it. I'm just not sure."

Good pay for carrying something around meant only one thing to Mal. He knew kids who'd taken that kind of work. Most of them lived high on the cash for a little, then the consequences came crashing down on them. Which, unfortunately, sounded like Tommy to a T.

"Do you know where he does business, this guy in the suit?"

"I know where Tommy used to meet him."

"Show me." He stood up and offered his hand to her, which she promptly and gratefully accepted.


Rain came down from the gray sky in cold needles. Cars had their headlights on and steam rose from the streets, and it made it look like nighttime even though it wasn't. They descended into shadow, pushed through the scanners, got on a subway, and went downtown.

The attack on Con Edison some years back, a day that the national voice had christened Big Black, had ostensibly been the work of that ubiquitous scapegoat of unforeseen disaster: the terrorist attack. A few said that this was merely a story given by authority in an attempt to mask the real, though more mundane, cause: negligence. Other, more cynical voices said it was the corporations, seeing that they could sink their profit margins into the necessary rebuilding. Whatever the case, Mal remembered hearing the explosion from across the river. He remembered the darkness the city had been plunged into for nearly two weeks afterward; riots, looting, murders, residents too terrified to step outside and buy candles to light their pitch-black homes. Mal even remembered what the faces of people looked like before that fear had set in permanently, before so many who lived or worked in the city realized they had lost someone—a neighbor, an employee, a sister—in the incineration of the four blocks surrounding the power plant. Faces that used to look up, determined, now looked down, into cell screens or at their own feet. Anywhere, anywhere but ahead, anything but facing what else might be coming toward them. Not just the people, but the city itself. In the wake of Big Black, the city, already under the strain of the nationwide financial collapse, had allowed several public services to be taken over by private concerns.

And so, the subways. Scanners, installed at every access point, inspected your metal when you pushed through the turnstiles. Some people said that they scanned the MetroPass feed on your cell, too, and told the corporations what stations you were leaving, where you frequented and spent your time and money. The trains themselves: instead of repairing or maintaining the cars, the private concerns had left the structures to languish, acquiring tears and blemishes of rust, seats cracking apart, the walls collecting a miasma of graffiti. Rather, the corporations removed every window and installed in their places HDs in every car, locked behind high-impact plastic that cost more than the entire train itself. Now people gazed emptily at flickering ads for businesses passing by high above, the same ads scrolling down the sides of their cell displays, so they could key in and learn more. If you did not want to fix a thing, then what you had to do was make people ignore it.

What the city did contribute to its subways, all its public transportation now, was the watchful eye and the drab gray uniformed figures of the MCT. The Metropolitan Counterterrorism Task Force posted two officers at every station, the scanning lenses of their security goggles burning into everyone passing by, falling on surprised individuals and finding on them the offending set of keys or leg brace or new model of cell. This was the environment that travelers faced every morning, every evening, every ride in between.

"Did you get that when you met the kids you thought were after Tommy?" Annie asked Mal, her back to the HD and her empathetic eyes locked on him.

"What's that?"

"Your eye." She gestured and grimaced a little.

"No. That's, well, that's from a weak defense on the right."

She nodded as if she understood, or more importantly as if she didn't have to understand for it to be all right.

An MCT officer walked through the car, swinging the reflective circles of his goggles back and forth like a searchlight. Mal and Annie both instinctively looked down. Meeting the eyes of the gray sentries always bought you sharp and suspicious attention, sometimes worse. Better to look at an HD or down like you were working on a cell, even if you weren't. Better to appear absorbed in anything but the real world, until the officer passed. He did, inevitably, and left deeper silence in his wake.

"Have you and Tommy been together a long time?" Mal asked when the officer had moved into the next car.

"What's a long time? About four months. It feels like longer. In a good way."

Mal wanted to ask what Tommy had said about him, what picture she had seen, but it seemed desperate. He was getting a good sense of his shortcomings as a brother. He didn't need to put them on the table for everybody else to shuffle through.

"So Tommy sketches? I didn't know he ever had an interest in that stuff."

"No, the sketchbook is mine," she said, and a little piece of the picture Mal had been putting together of his brother disintegrated, leaving what felt like a larger blank than had been there before. "But," she went on, "he's interested enough when I do it. He won't sit for me." She smiled softly. "He could never stay in one place long enough for that. But for my birthday, he took me to the museum to see da Vinci's sketches. That was a good day."

"Your sketches are very good. I mean, I think they are. I'm no expert at all." His face creased a little. "The sketchbook was just lying out. I thought it was Tommy's."

"Oh, that's okay," she said, but her cheeks reddened. "I'm glad you liked them."

The subway rumbled on. He stole glances at her reflection in the window across the way, as though looking at her could tell him more about Tommy. She seemed young, though she was probably Mal's age or older, if she was about Tommy's age. Maybe it wasn't about age, maybe it was more that she just looked happy. Worried, sure, but somewhere between seeing her picture and now, Mal had decided she was a happy person. Tommy never seemed like a happy guy, exactly. And no wonder.

Maybe it made her happy to fix things, because that sounded like what she was doing to Tommy. *Trying* to do to Tommy. Mal reminded himself why they were here.

The subway stopped in midtown, and she rose and pointed at their stop. He got out with her and glanced at his watch as they went up the steps. He looked at it, squinted, shook it, but it had died. It made him think of the crack in his mirror. Was the entire world starting to fall apart? He shook his head and followed her out.

The buildings here were massive and shining, and even the thick gloom couldn't quite kill the sense of self-importance about them. In some ways, they seemed like the only real, solid things in a world of ghosts.

"There." She pointed. Mal followed her finger.

"The one with the planters in front?"

"No, next to it. There."

"I don't . . ." He shook his head.

She glanced up at him queerly, then gently took his chin in her fingers and pointed his face just a little to the left.

"Right there," she said.

And there was the building, all reflection, breaching the gloom above and disappearing into the dirty white of the rain clouds. He wasn't sure how he could have missed it.

"We'd stop by here, sometimes," Annie said, "if I was with him when he needed to pick something up. I'd always wait outside, but he'd never be more than five minutes or so. I don't think he ever even had to go upstairs or anything. I think he just went into, like, the lobby or the lounge or whatever's right in there."

Funny thing. Mal didn't while away his hours in mid-town, but he wasn't a stranger to it, either. He couldn't remember ever seeing this building before. True, many buildings looked alike around here, and it was so crowded with them, one seldom noted any building apart from another. But this one was so tall and composed of nothing but reflection. Even at the ground floor, the doors lacked address numbers or even a name plate. They were just two long rectangles of dark mirror, reflecting the droves of passing people hunkered down in their own worlds, and the street beyond them, and, across that street, Mal and Annie.

"What kind of trouble did Tommy say he was in with this guy?"

"He never said specifically. He never even said he was in trouble exactly. We were just talking about getting together and I knew he needed to come by here, but he said he wasn't going to. I pressed him a little, but he just kept saying it was nothing. But it was something. It's easy to tell when Tommy is nervous."

Was that true? Mal wasn't even sure.

"Okay. You can take off if you want to. If you want to give me your phone number or something, I'll give you a call later on."

"No, I'll wait here for you."

"I'm probably going to be more than a few minutes. It's raining and all."

"I'll be right here. I'm not going anywhere."

He wanted to pat her on the shoulder. He would have if she were a guy. He nodded instead, then turned and looked at the building.

"Be careful." She touched his arm. "That sounds silly, but be careful anyway."

He nodded again and jogged across the street. He stood for a moment at the front doors, looking at himself looking uncertain, then pushed.

The doors whooshed open onto a massive lobby. There was a security desk before him with space for three or four people. There were cubbyholes for coffee shops and newsstands in the walls. A bank of elevators sat in two huge columns in the center of the room, with more lobby hidden beyond them. But it was all unfinished, form without façade. No guards at the desks, no stores. It was all metal and concrete, grays and more grays. Someone had made this lobby and stopped short of giving it a personality. And it was empty; massive, open, capable of containing and occupying hundreds of people at a time, but utterly barren of those people.

He stood still as the doors whooshed closed behind him, cutting off the sound of the street completely, leaving him in a cold silence. He turned around, foolishly, just to check that the street was still there. It was, sure enough. People hurried by, unmindful of what was in here, blind to the strangeness of it.

He craned his neck to see beyond the twin bank of elevators and stepped forward to move around them. His muffled footfalls practically boomed in here, open as it was. He hurried along, sliding more than walking, trying to stay flatfooted. He went around the elevators and saw more lobby on the other side. There was a lounge of sorts, a large space for small tables and chairs spread out so that people on their lunch break or visitors to the various businesses above could sit and look out on the small garden or fountain constructed at the lounge's center. Except there was no fountain or garden, there were no tables and chairs, no people on their lunch break, no visitors. There was just a space, filled to the brim with nothing.

A ding from just behind gave him a start, and he saw the indicator light over an elevator glow stark yellow. He hurried back around the other side of the big central columns, hidden from view. He heard the elevator doors open and one pair of feet step off and head toward the lounge. It was one person, he was sure of it, though he couldn't see. Once he stopped walking, there was silence.

Mal waited, hearing his breath and afraid that anyone would be able to hear it, an illusion perpetrated by the all-encompassing silence.

There was a whoosh, then, from the front, and the booming footfalls of a person coming in a hurry. The person went from the front door, past the other side of the elevator bank and over to the lounge. Mal heard the arrival shout a greeting, which was unreturned.

The acoustics and lack of competing noises made hearing the two quite easy.

"Take this to the library on Forty-Second. There will be

a woman at a table on the third floor, looking at a book about fairy tales. Give it to her." It was an odd voice, not like a normal speaking voice at all; large, but somehow hollow. Mal recognized the voice, almost. Not like the voice of someone he knew, but a tone or a timbre that he had heard before, maybe many times. "This is your money," it went on. "I won't need you again until Friday."

"You got it." This voice was nervous and a little breathless. It sounded younger, but old enough to know better than to do this. Whoever it belonged to hurried out.

As the arrival's footfalls boomed away, Mal moved across and peered around the front of the elevator bank column to catch sight of the departing figure. He was worried—more than that, even, he was pained—by the idea that if it was his brother, he might not even recognize him from the back.

He knew instantly that it wasn't Tommy. It was a young man in jeans and a sweatshirt, which was what Tommy still favored himself, for all Mal knew. But this guy was taller and much thinner than Tommy, almost scrawny. He had a wrapped package in his hand and he pushed through the doors and took off.

No sooner had the doors whooshed closed than the footsteps in the lounge padded back to the elevators. There was another ding and elevator doors opened and closed, and Mal was alone again.

He went out to the lounge and made a quick circuit of it. There was nothing more to see, nothing to indicate where the two had stopped to speak, or even that they had been there at all.

He went back to the elevators and stood before them, deciding just how far into all of this he was going to plunge. It seemed like a big step, going up, maybe running into someone, but he'd committed to this last night when he heard Tommy's voice on the machine. He had even come here intending to confront this man or one of his associates, though that had been before this turned out to be something very far from what Mal was expecting.

He stabbed the button, and a door dinged open instantly. He poked his head in and found a dull metal interior that reflected only a vague, misshapen silhouette of him. He got in. There were two rows of buttons, the last one numbered eighty. There was one button beyond that, though, a single circle of plastic crowning the two rows, but it was blank. A penthouse, perhaps, or a maintenance floor. He pushed a button at random: thirty-two.

The speed of the elevator put pressure in his ears. In seconds, the door dinged open.

He had expected a floor like the lobby, embryonic and empty. Maybe some cubicles, maybe some offices around the sides, awaiting inhabitants that might, in the end, never show up. More remotely, he thought he might end up playing the fool again and walking out into some crowded business, a law firm or a publishing company, the self-important eyes of suited men and women turning to look at the bruised kid who obviously didn't belong.

It was a big empty room, its walls lined with doors. There were dozens of them, with less than two feet of wall between each. They were gray metal, unmarked, with dull silver handles.

He stepped partially out, making sure the elevator didn't close on him, and looked around like a man looking at a world turned on its head, the familiarity of its parts making it all the stranger.

There were something like thirty of them, and while his vision of the building from the outside was not photographically perfect, the size of the room seemed to rule out the possibility of the doors actually leading to anything but wall.

With a look of distaste, he abandoned the elevator and walked up to one of the doors, again at random. There was not a single thing about it but its place in the line to differentiate it from the doors on either side of it or, for that matter, the doors on either side of those.

He put his hand on the knob and turned it. There was no keyhole in it, and it was not locked. It opened up and showed him a white hallway, a gurney pushed against a wall, carts of medical supplies stationed in two different places. There was a patient on a gurney and an orderly near her, his back to Mal and the door. A medicinal smell, like the smell of a hospital, pushed out of the place.

Mal quickly threw the door closed and stood staring at it. He went to the next door to the left and pulled it open. It was dank and poorly lit, obviously a basement of some kind, yet somehow here on the thirty-second floor. He could hear the hum of the boiler and feel the heat within. Far down from the door, beyond rows of boxes and other doors, seemed to be a metal stairway. Mal yanked his hand away from the doorknob, letting the door swing closed, failing to note that it remained slightly ajar as his eyes shot wildly around the room. There were thirty doors in here. Did all of them lead to a place as large as these last two?

He rushed back to the elevator, and to his profound relief the door opened as soon as he pushed the button. He got in and pushed another button, nineteen.

The door opened on an identical floor: thirty more doors so identical to the ones above that Mal wouldn't even have been sure he'd left the last floor had he not felt the motion of the elevator.

He looked back at the buttons. His eyes fell on the top one, again, blank and isolated from the rest. His finger twitched, the idea crossing his mind to press that one, go to the top. But his hand didn't move. It couldn't. The muscles suddenly locked, and his heart was beating too fast. He was afraid, choked with fear, in fact; paralyzed by it. The button put fear in him. No, not the button, exactly; the idea of *using* the button, of where it would take him. He remembered this kind of unreasoning, screaming fear from long ago. Growing up killed it; reason made it empty and silly. But he had known it as a child. Everyone had.

He didn't toy with the notion of fighting it. He hit the button marked *L,* and when the doors opened, he ran the hell out of the place, his heart not slowing, his breath not coming evenly until he was back out on the crowded street. Some passersby noted him without more than cursory interest and went on their way.

He stood, blinking away the last of the strange fear that had taken him, then straightened up and looked across the street to find Annie.

But Annie wasn't there.

He ran across, looked up and down the block, into the windows of a jewelry store and a restaurant and an upscale clothing store. Annie was not here anymore.

He whipped the picture of her and Tommy from his pocket, worried suddenly that she would have disappeared even from that. She was still there, pretty as could be, Tommy's arm around her. He looked up at the people going by. Their faces were blank, often lit by the cell screens they gazed into. He could show them her picture, ask if anyone had seen her, but even though their bodies moved along this street, they were absent from it, enclosed in their electronic shells. They walked alongside one another, but each was completely alone; they were no more likely to see those around them than they were to spontaneously drop their cells and offer their assistance. This had become a city of phantoms.

Even if Mal shook one from his fugue, asked him if he had seen Annie, no one would have. Mal was sure of it. He looked back across the street at his reflection in the doors of the horrible building. He saw himself, standing there, alone amidst the phantoms. Before the fear could take him again, he ran off, up the block and away.

# MOM

IN THE DARKEST HOURS of morning, Laura found the old flash drives under her mother's quilts and loaded the home movies onto her cell. Images, years, flickered by on her cell as the process sped itself through: a first day of school, a trip to Disneyland, a birthday party in the park. She snatched the emergency credit card from the kitchen drawer, along with her parents' hotel information and the roll of ten emergency twenty-dollar bills her parents always left her when they went away for a weekend. She used her cell to book herself a seat on the next train leaving Stony Brook for the city, left a full bowl of dog food in the kitchen, and marched into her room to change clothes, because a skirt was not something you wore on a mission. Jeans were something you wore on a mission, because you could run and jump and shout at people in them. She got into jeans, a sweater, sneakers; put the money, the credit card, and the pictures from the album into her wallet; stuffed the wallet in her back pocket and her cell in her front pocket; and pulled her father's old Mets cap on her head.

Mookie raised his shaggy head in sleepy concern for the commotion. She approached, and he rested his chin back down and watched her with expectant eyes.

"Don't . . ." she began and then lost her thought, or maybe didn't have the strength to say it. So she got down and rested her head on his for a minute. She left him sleeping in the dark.

The train ride took an hour and a half, the landscape, lit by tired dawn light, becoming increasingly grayer, more crowded with decaying edifices and pallid people. She sat next to a creaking old man breathing out hot, wet air, who told her she was lucky.

"How's that?" she nearly demanded of him.

"We're coming in from underground," he said, leaning closer. "If you come in from above, you can see the dome. You know what's *really* under the dome?"

Everyone knew what was under the dome. That didn't stop him. Apparently, he knew something no one else did.

"9/11 shook this city bad, but Big Black's what tore it down. There's no life left in it, no *real* life. So the corporations hide the damage. You know it was the corporations who caused it in the first place, right? So where the explosion went off, blew apart a chunk of the city, they put that big gray bubble over it, four blocks long. Looks like a giant insect with that wire framework inside, squatting over the ruins like they're eggs or something. The corporations are trying to hide what they did and what's left under there, but you see that giant bug every day, walking by it or when you come in on the bridges or fly over in a plane. They tried to hide it, but they made it worse."

The man was becoming increasingly agitated, his rheumy eyes lighting up with paranoia. Laura held her face still.

"And you know what's under the tent? Poison. Just like after 9/11, all the metal and concrete and chemicals disintegrated into the air, and they're keeping it trapped in there. Everyone knows. They walk by it every day of their lives and they know that if that tent ever rips, or if anyone ever gets through the MCT and cuts it open—"

"Jesus Christ, would you please leave me alone!"

He started at the revulsion that had burst onto her face. He blinked twice, and the sick light went out of his eyes, and he remained silent—but for the heavy breath coming from his open mouth—for the rest of the trip.

Gray MCT officers wandered through Moynihan Station, moving slowly, further congesting the already hopelessly crowded train station, further infuriating already frustrated travelers. The officers' heads swept back and forth, occasionally stopping and focusing the bulky goggles they wore attached to heavy battery packs at their belts. It simply wasn't feasible to check every bag coming into the city, so this was what they did instead. Laura had once put on a pair of them during a civics demonstration at school. The boys wasted no time in training them on the girls, pretending at obscene revelations; but through the lenses, the world became gray and ghostly, super-dense plastic showing a smear of dull blue, metal in dark blue and incendiary chemicals becoming burning lumps of bright red. The mechanism of the packs also became unbearably hot rather quickly, however. Her civics lesson at school was followed that night by an economy lesson from her father on tax money and inefficient, wasted resources.

Laura stormed from Moynihan Station at Thirty-Fourth Street and Eighth Avenue to the Grand Mariner Hotel at Fifty-First and Ninth, refusing to notice the city around her: the cracked sidewalks, the once-grand façades dwindling and dirty, the sky a gray block bearing down, disintegrating in a cold drizzle. The city for its part refused to acknowledge her. She may as well have been a lamppost or a mailbox to the people scurrying around her, conversing on their cells, plugged into a song they used to shut the world out, as far away from where they actually were as possible.

Who did pay her attention were the MCT officers, now a significant percentage of the city's already enlarged law force. They scanned her as she passed, sensing somehow that she was out of place, that there was something wrong.

Something wrong.

Two years ago, at fifteen years old, Laura's friend Rachel got a summer job in a pizza place. Friend Cheryl doubled up on her baby-sitting schedule. Laura volunteered in the children's ward at the medical center. Cheryl ended up raking in the most cash, though Laura's parents had supplemented an already generous allowance when she'd decided to carry out this heavily encouraged plan. Rachel came home every night with a fresh pizza pie, Cheryl with various bumps and bruises, frayed hair, and bleary eyes. Laura came home with unforgettable stories every night, some harrowing, few uplifting.

One of the stories was of a young boy, seven according to his chart, who was in psychiatric care. He swore from his down-turned mouth with two new teeth growing into it, beneath his tight, tense blue eyes, beneath his bright blond hair, that his parents were not his parents. There were no signs of abuse, physical or mental, and Laura had seen the parents many times, coming in for consultations, respectably dressed, showing convincing signs of secondary trauma, as she'd heard the doctors say. She watched from afar for the most part, her heart aching for the boy, but also scared of him in a most instinctive and primordial way. He was the embodiment of a nightmare dredged up from her own younger life, the product of a too-early showing of *Invasion of the Body Snatchers* by an overeager father who had caught hell for it from a sleepless mother for the rest of the week.

One evening, as Laura was departing, the boy was sitting on the old couch outside the therapist's room by himself. His eyes wandered around, looking at the hospital hall as if it were an alien place, confusing and cold, even though it must by now seem as recognizable as the home he no longer lived in.

Laura stopped mid-stride, hypnotized by him at first, struck still by his wandering, helpless eyes. Those eyes found her, and she smiled back at him and walked over and sat down.

"Hi," she said, putting on a bright smile for all she was worth. "I'm Laura."

"Hi," he said in a voice as timid as anyone would have imagined. "I don't have a name anymore."

"What? What do you mean?"

"My real parents have it. They took it. They took everything about me with them."

The Grand Mariner Hotel was a tall brown building, its awning and windows once blue and sparkling silver, but now dulled with a patina of soot. A tired doorman in an incongruously grandiose overcoat let her into the lobby with a forced smile. Inside was also silver and blue, somewhat better preserved, with high ceilings and walls adorned with antique paintings of ships at sea. Laura walked around the tinkling, central fountain growing from the well-trodden tile, past the restaurant, and up to the desk.

"Good morning," the man at the counter greeted her with a big blond smile. "Can I help you today?"

"Yes," she said, managing a smile. "My parents checked us in this morning, and I'm supposed to meet them. Unfortunately, they're not answering their cells and they didn't tell me the room number."

"I see." He met the problem head on with his can-do smile. "If you tell me the name, I'll ring the room and let them know you're down here."

"They're actually out at some museums. I'm supposed to meet them there with some things that are up in the room."

"All right. What was the name?"

"Westlake. Ron and Claire Westlake."

His fingers brushed across the touchpads on his screen for a moment.

"May I see some ID?" His smile didn't waver.

"Of course." She fetched her cell, and when she looked back up he had the phone in his hand and had dialed the room. Little blond punk. If her parents answered and were told that a daughter they didn't think they had was down in the lobby, that would get her thrown out of the hotel.

"Looks like you're right." The blond man put the receiver down after a moment and accepted her driver's license. "This is in order, ma'am. I can give you the room number, but I can't give you the key."

"If you can't give me the key, then I'm not going to be able to get the things they need."

"I'm sorry, ma'am." His smile made the subtle shift from genuine to fake. "It's policy. I can only give the key to the guests registered in the room."

She gave him the look designed to make him squirm. It worked on mall sales personnel, waiters, and some teachers. It didn't work on DMV clerks or school administration—or hotel clerks, apparently.

"I really am sorry, young lady," he said, the smile straining at the corners.

"What's the room number?" She was done with him.

"Fifteen twelve, ma'am."

*Fuck you, you rat-fucking bastard,* she thought and strode away. She found a seat at the restaurant breakfast counter and struggled back and forth with the idea of ordering liquor. She drank wine at dinner occasionally, had been known to get served a beer when in the company of the very mature-looking Cheryl, and had once thrown up a stomach full of bourbon on an ill-advised date with a college boy a few months ago. She didn't want to throw up now, but she wouldn't have minded the numb-headed feeling the bourbon had given her.

She had a Coke and watched the lobby. Every couple that walked by she followed with her eyes, feeling the calm in herself strain. If her parents could forget her, could she forget them? What if they came in and she didn't recognize them? She fixated on things like clothing choices, strides, handholding, anything that resembled the choices her parents might have made.

Ron and Claire Westlake walked in around eleven o'clock, disturbingly unromantic for a couple on an anniversary vacation. They weren't holding hands, a habit that Laura claimed to find tiresome but secretly thought was sweet. They went straight to the elevators without looking up.

Once in the lobby, she dreaded the elevator ride. Once in the elevator, she dreaded the walk through the hallway. Once in the hall, she dreaded standing in front of the door. Eventually, she stood before 1512, an anonymous length of wood with a handle and a pad for the magnetic key. She stood for so long that two different guests came out of their own rooms and walked by her curiously.

She poised her hand to knock hard, with forthrightness and command, then brought it back down and put her ear to the door. She could hear nothing; not a whisper, not a footstep. She pressed her ear harder to the door, compressing it painfully and still not a hint of anything living beyond it.

Fuck the door and fuck the sound waves for not getting through it.

She pulled away, glared at the door, and knocked on it hard, three times.

Nothing happened, so she hit it again, pounding it, really, then pressed her ear back to the door. Nothing.

She futilely twisted at the handle, then kicked the door and almost yelled through it, but managed to hold that in. She went back to the elevator and down to the .lobby and from the corner stared at the desk personnel. Besides the blond there were two others on duty, both women. She walked across the lobby, relatively close to the counter and glanced casually over as she passed them. One of them, thin-faced with big hair and trying to hide her age with too much makeup, may have been in her mid to late fifties.

Laura went up to her and leaned on the counter.

"Diana," she said, reading the name on the little gold plaque Diana wore on her jacket, "I need your help."

"What's wrong?" Diana leaned toward her, looking worried. She had picked up on Laura's manner, more sensitive than a man would be, and dispensed with the smile and the "ma'am."

"My father is in room fifteen twelve. There was some trouble at home last night, and he won't answer the door. I think he's in bed with his cheap slut girlfriend. Could you please give me the key?" Laura was shocked to find herself able to say such a thing about her father and remain completely calm.

Diana did an admirable job of not looking shocked. Perhaps Diana had not had an easy life with men herself. Laura was gambling on it.

"What's your name?" she asked.

"Westlake," Laura said, producing the digital license on her cell as Diana checked on her screen.

Diana only glanced at the license, but did take another moment to look at Laura's face. Laura tried to think of what she would need to look like for this woman to help her. Would Diana respond to someone who was scared, or someone who was—

"Give me your cell," Diana said. Laura blinked and passed it across the counter. She scanned the code of the cellock into it and handed it back.

"Thank you, Diana. Thank you so much."

"You do what you need to do, honey."

Laura took the card and marched back to the elevators. She walked purposefully to 1512 and decided not to knock. She keyed the lock code in her cell and the cellock clicked and she pushed the door open.

Her parents were there, the two people that comprised her past, defined her present, and delineated her future. They sat at the small table by the window, staring out into space. She had expected a shocked response, anger, and action on her parents' part before Laura could offer undeniable proof of who she was. But neither of them even turned. Only when the door slammed behind Laura did her father turn slowly around. His face was a mask of haggard indifference, a look Laura had seldom seen on him in her life. Once, perhaps, after being passed over for the same promotion the third time in a row. Once, when the Mets finally hauled ass out of the disintegrating city and relocated to Las Vegas.

"Claire," he said, now showing a ghost of concern.

Her mother turned, and here Laura fixated on the twitch of every muscle, looking for a sign of recognition, even unconscious recognition, revealed unintentionally by eyes or lips. There was nothing but flat incomprehension.

Her father stood up and took a step forward.

"Who are you? What are you doing?" He wasn't angry, exactly. There was a pass at it, like he knew he was *supposed* to be riled up, but the emotion just couldn't make it past an uncharacteristic dullness in his eyes.

"Dad," Laura said, her voice going weak. "Dad. I'm your daughter, Laura."

He blinked at her stupidly.

"Are you on drugs?" he said. "Don't you think I'd know if I had a daughter?"

Laura came up and threw her arms around him and he flinched, immediately pushing her away. She wanted him to be angry, to rage at her. *That* she knew how to handle, because she was the family's emotional balance point. Laura was the composed one, who stilled her father's temper and eased her mother's occasional depressions, who nodded patiently and smiled when her day, her life, was eagerly planned out for her.

Dealing with indifference and apathy had never been in Laura's job description, had never been in her parents' repertoire. That's not who her family *was*. And she could prove it.

She pulled out her cell, keyed the movie theater app, and beamed the moving images captured over the years onto the wall over the table.

Claire Westlake had submerged much of her own personal ambition within her role as a mother, and was consequently possessed of ferocious maternal instincts. One of the great family stories was of toddler Laura becoming lost at the public pool and, imagining her little girl tipping herself inadvertently into the water, Claire went tearing through the men's locker room, her shortest path to the pool, shoving brawny, naked swimmers out of her way in search of her daughter. Laura's father often recounted with great delight how it had not been five-year-old Laura who had refused to leave her mother on the first day of kindergarten, but Claire who had had her child pried from her own viselike hug.

Claire Westlake looked up mutely at the snatches of home movies bleeding across the wall.

"Mom," Laura said. *"Mom."* She took her mother's chin and turned it up toward her own eyes. But rather than giving the soft smile that often met her gaze, her mother reached up and slapped her hand away. "*Look,* Mom," Laura demanded. Angry, terrified tears were streaming down her face. "That's you coming out of the hospital with me all bundled up in your arms." She keyed to the next, and the images on the screen flickered and reconfigured. "This is when Dad was teaching me to ski." Her fingers jabbed agan. "Our trip to Disneyland. My first day of kindergarten."

Clare Westlake's eyes were dumb and empty.

"I don't know any of these people," she said.

"*What? Look!*" Laura nearly screamed it. "That's *you,* Mom!"

Her mother's hand came out and interrupted the line of projection, swallowing their history in shadow.

"Please turn that off and leave."

"Mom." Laura's face was soaked in tears and snot. She struggled to make herself understood from beneath her sobs. "You have an appendectomy scar, but you still have your appendix because they misdiagnosed a bad stomachache when you were twelve."

Her mother looked thunderstruck at that.

"Dad." Laura spun around. "This is your Mets hat. You bought it the first time you went to a game when you were ten, and you gave it to me for my tenth birthday."

Her father was shaking his head.

"I don't have a scar," her mother said. "I don't know who you are, but you need help. I'm going to call security."

"No, *no!* Mom. One of your students made a pass at you once and started sending flowers to the house until Dad—"

"This is preposterous." Her father's dead voice belied the claim, but he took her by the arm and pulled her toward the door. With a burst of hysterical strength, she yanked free from his grasp and lunged at her mother. She got hold of her mother's clothes and tore at her shirt and the waist of her pants, trying to reveal the scar she knew was there.

But her father had her by both arms now and pulled her kicking and screaming from the room and slammed the door in her face.

The key code forgotten, she attacked the door with her hands and feet, tears flying from her face.

*"Mom! Mom!"*

She didn't stop shouting until hotel security, in suits and dead expressions, came down the hall and took her by the arms. By the time the elevator doors opened in the lobby, she had stopped the tears. She saw Diana, watching from behind the desk, her face sick with sorrow.

"Get the hell off me!" she screamed at the guards, pulling her arms away and walking out of the hotel and into the gray city beyond the doors.

# BRATH

MAL HAD A DREAM that he was in his apartment. Not the Fosters' apartment, and certainly not the apartment he grew up in, but his own place, which didn't exist but looked like Tommy's apartment. There was a pounding on the door, which was more than a pounding. It was really a slamming, something massive flinging itself against the door.

In his dream, Mal stood, watching the door buckle but hold, again and again, each blow shaking the hinges, loosening the entire structure from its frame. Every time another blow landed, something in the apartment broke, mostly mirrors, which there were a lot more of than anyone actually ever had in an apartment. He stood and watched the top hinge snap and hang pitifully. He watched the lock start to twist just a little and the middle hinge start to lose its screws. Through the slim line beneath the door, he could see a shadow, big and shapeless.

The middle hinge *pong*ed off the door, not even managing to maintain the ineffectual grasp of the top one. The door tilted, near to giving up. Mal shouted with sudden, overwhelming anger and fear. He charged, cutting his feet on broken mirrors, and threw himself against the door.

He pushed it back into its frame and leaned against it, baring his teeth and taking the impact with a shout of rage at each blow. His skull rattled. He wondered if parts of him were going to start breaking. But he wasn't going to let the door come down. No way. It was a fight now.

The bottom hinge gave; the lock cracked and let go. Mal was essentially holding the door in place himself now. Whatever was out there banged, and Mal shouted in response. *Keep banging,* he thought. He was here for a fight.

The banging stopped. He held the door up, waiting for the attack to renew. When it didn't, he unclenched his eyes and looked at the door. The hinges were back on, the lock was fine. It was dented, but solid, a fine door. All it needed was someone fighting for it.

He woke up remarkably tense from the dream, his muscles stiff, as though he'd actually struggled with something in his sleep. He got up slowly, stretched himself out, limped to the bathroom, threw water in his face, and rubbed the short bristles of hair on his head. The cracked mirror showed him that sleep hadn't relaxed him at all.

When he picked up his cell to call Sharon, the night table it sat on promptly collapsed, one of its legs having cracked off for no reason Mal could conjure. Another thing to add to the junk heap when he finally got around to replacing all the stuff that had broken over the last few days. It didn't even seem weird to him anymore. Or it did, actually, but now it was just some extra weird in a giant field of weird, no more strange than a building that seemed bigger on the inside than out.

He picked his cell up from the floor.

"Hello?" Sharon appeared, her jaw tense. Mal realized with a flash of unwelcome familial insight that this was exactly the same way he carried his own tension.

"It's Mal. Have you spoken to the police yet?" He could see beyond her, through her window. The dome loomed; the outline of the metal piping that held it up was dimly visible, perched like a giant spider, stalking her from behind.

"Mal," she said, and then, away from the phone to someone else in the room, "it's Mal. What's going on, Mal?" She was back with him. "Did you find Tommy?"

"No. He's—I didn't—it's complicated." He couldn't even begin. "Did you speak to the police? I need the name and precinct of the officer in charge."

"We didn't call the police. George thinks—"

"George! Are you kidding? Tommy is gone and—"

"Don't you shout at me," she interrupted him, not to be outdone. "I spoke with George, and we felt that we didn't know enough to tell them anything. Who do you think you are, telling me about how I should look after Tommy?"

"You're his mother. Supposedly," Mal said quietly.

"You little shit," she said coldly, and he remembered how her voice rose when she was angry, but when she was furious it became quiet, frigid, and hollow, like a cavern of ice. "Where were you when your father left Tommy and me all alone? Oh, that's right. You went with him. Well, your example never gained Tommy a single thing except to send him away and land him in this trouble."

Mal stammered, working his jaw. This was how it was with her. He remembered, but he hadn't actually *felt* it in years. If she were before him now, he wasn't sure that he could have stopped himself from striking her.

"Nothing to say?" Sharon taunted bitterly. "What a surprise. When it comes down to it, you're just like your father was up to the day he died: a second-rate—"

Her face disappeared and was replaced by another one, a chubby male face with uncomfortable eyes and too much slicked-back hair.

"Mal," the face said, "this is George."

Mal slammed the cell into the wall so hard that the room echoed with the impact. He let it fall away, leaving a spider web of cracks in the plaster. The cell, of course, was still intact. It was sure to be the only thing left after this whole flea-bitten apartment came tumbling down around his ears.

As it happened, Mal had not gone to the police himself. After Annie disappeared, he went back the Fosters' place, thinking she might have gone there, though she'd never been there before. But she knew his name, and his name was online along with his address. She might have gone because she got scared, then found his address and been waiting for him. But she hadn't been there, of course. He'd spent a frustrating half hour with several functions on his cell that he'd never used before. Preposterously, he put the name "Annie" into his cell's city phone book app and, not surprisingly, found thousands of listings. He fumbled through the profiler app, feeding it a clumsy description of Annie based mainly on guesses: her age, height, weight, hair color, eye color. Again, he built a queue of thousands to look at and finally gave up just short of blasting his cell apart against a wall.

He remembered the sketchbook then, and went back to Tommy's apartment. Her name wasn't in the book, though Tommy's was, the letters adorned with flowers and vines and gargoyles. He searched through the apartment in a maniacal quest for something with her name on it and found nothing.

He almost went to the cops. He didn't have her last name, but he did have her picture. In the end, he just couldn't bear giving the picture up. That felt like turning the fight over to someone else, like giving up on Tommy. He could get a copy of it made, but he felt time pressing down on him until it was nearly crushing his brain. The answer wasn't in the photo, anyway. It was in that building with the doors, maybe on that top floor. Just thinking of it made his stomach flutter.

He could tell the cops about that. Then they'd come with him, raid the place on a charge of too many doors.

But he had one line left: Brath. Brath was the sort you were always afraid to approach but who always came through once you had. But he was an opportunity of last resort, because once he started doing something, he followed it through no matter what crashed and burned around him.

"Everything okay, Mal?" Gil Foster was standing in the doorway, his eyes tracing a line from the new cracks in the wall to the cell on the floor, to Mal, standing dejectedly over it.

Mal looked up at him, searching for words that weren't angry or aggressive.

"Sorry, Gil," he managed, barely.

Gil was a short man going thick in the middle, though you could tell from the shoulders and legs that he'd been solid once upon a time. He had a short salt-and-pepper beard and a balding head, and he was dressed in pants and a white undershirt.

"Yeah. We're going to have to—Jesus! What happened to your face, Mal?"

Mal turned his head back down, trying to obscure his bruises again, though it was too late. At least he'd slept in his T-shirt and the damage to his torso wasn't visible.

"I tripped going up the subway steps," Mal nearly mumbled, turning to his bag where he kept all his clothes.

"Subway steps," Gil said, now standing right next to him. "Look, Mal. Look. I understand we're just starting to know each other. But you're going to be with us for a while, I figure. Would you mind a little unsolicited advice?"

Mal did him the respect of turning and facing him, though he remained silent.

"I do know what your life's been like the last year or so, going from one foster family to another. And I know who your father was, of course. Fighting comes naturally to you, and that's probably real good in some situations. God knows,

I been in construction for thirty-five years, and it's filled with tough guys. I see men looking for a fight all the time. And I see what they end up with, too, which is nothing. Sometimes, the best thing you can do is let it all go. Just turn around and walk away."

"Give up," Mal said, no emotion in his face or voice.

"Be a bigger man."

"That's . . . a lot to think about."

"Sure. Take your time. I ain't going anywhere. And neither are you. So maybe after school we could finally get your bag unpacked."

Mal looked at his bag, which held everything he owned.

"Jan's got some breakfast going," Gil said, "or she will once I can get her off the damn cell."

"I'm sorry, Gil. I have to get to school."

"No sweat, Mal. You can take it with you."

Mal's shoelace snapped when he tried to tie it, and the strap of his bag had come apart sometime during the night. As he headed for the door, Gil handed him eggs crammed between two pieces of toast and Janet looked up from her cell long enough to say goodbye, but her eyes didn't linger long enough to catch the bruises Mal wore.

He stared suspiciously at people passing him on the street. It was that kind of tension the dream and then the "conversation" with Sharon had left him.

On the subway, a lady limped into the center of the car and announced that she was looking for work right now but couldn't find any. She was trying to raise two children and none of them had a roof over their heads. The words were misshapen, spoken through a slack jaw. She couldn't be thinking straight or she wouldn't be doing this when an MCT officer could come through at any moment, haul her away to one of the homeless camps that everyone talked about but no one ever saw. She asked if anyone could find it in his heart to give her some money. Anything would do, she said, looking up and down the car with one good eye, the other perpetually staring up and to the left. A quarter, a dime, a nickel; anything at all.

No one gave her money. Few even looked up from their cells or away from the HDs. One or two scowled at her as she went by, her slightly trembling hand held out before her.

Mal watched her as she passed, no money coming out of his pocket, either. She went on to the next car, to pastures that promised to be just as dry and unforgiving or worse than that, if she ran afoul of the MCT.

When the doors opened at his stop, he went out with a few others. One of them, a middle-aged man, seemed to go out of his way to exit through the scanner a young lady was about to enter, thus keeping her from getting to the train before the doors clunked shut.

"Fuck you, you fuckin' bastard," the young lady whipped over her shoulder as she ran for the train anyway.

"Bite me," he said with a dead expression as he disappeared up the stairs.

Mal came up more than half a city away from school. He went the block and a half to the old building that was adorned with a sign that showed his last name, JERICHO'S, in letters so faded that you could only tell what they were if you already knew what it said. He went up the dirty stairway and into the gym with the big ring in the center with the stained canvas and fraying ropes. He passed between a big lumpy bag suspended from the ceiling by a chain and a man spinning through a jump-rope set. He stopped at the display case against the back wall. The glass over his father's old, worn boxing gloves had fissured down the center. He watched it, daring it to crack further while he stood there and watched, challenging it to drive him right over the precipice.

"Mal." A stubby man with a cigar chomped in his jaws leaned out of a smoke-filled office. "No school today?"

"Brath in yet?" he called over.

The man answered with a blunt finger, pointing toward the showers, the only good news Mal had gotten his hands on in a while. He went into the shower room, humid and steamed up from guys done with their morning workout, soon to head over to the docks or the meatpacking district or a construction site.

Nikolai Brath looked like a human sports car: sleek and powerful. His slim body was ridged with tight cords of muscle beneath lacquered skin, up his arms, down his torso, along his legs. His dark blond hair was slicked back, a tight cap on his head. Razor-blade lines—high cheekbones, aquiline nose, sharp chin—made his young face dangerous, and dark blue, ice-chip eyes had frozen opponents in the ring often. He was pulling on his shirt when he saw Mal and reverse nodded at him.

"Brath."

It was just one word, but the sound of it, something in Mal's voice, brought the sharp profile up in a look of concern.

"What is it, Mal?"

"My brother's missing. I need help."

"Sit down." Brath put a strong hand on Mal and pressed him down to a bench. "Say it slow." There was the whisper of an accent on some of his words.

Mal's caution died immediately. Brath was young, only two years older than Mal himself, but his quiet assurance made it seem as if he already knew everything. It was this calm, invincible confidence that Mal always found himself trying to master in his own moments of desperation. So Mal told him: Tommy's call, Annie, the building, maybe drug dealers, but what the hell were the doors? The top-floor button, that was the only thing he didn't mention.

Other people came and went through the locker room, catching only snatches of the story, making of it what they would and clearing out.

Brath shook his head when it was over.

"You did the right thing, Mal. Cops would have done jack." Brath had dealings with cops sometimes. To hear him speak of it, they were either hassling him for no reason, or laying off because he gave them what they liked. The only things he liked less than cops were MCT officers and punks who couldn't control themselves in the ring.

Brath had been among the groups of kids sent in here by city agencies, by parole officers: juveniles edging up on their eighteenth and in danger of doing some real hard time. Work off your steam in here, or end up back in jail. Most of those kids had come and gone. Brath stuck around, got better and better, acquired skill and speed. Mal could never figure why Brath was among those other hotheads sent in here; he was always calm, his vaguely accented voice barely more than a whisper. He had money, too. Not gobs of it, but enough to pay his gym dues, always in cash and always on time; enough to entertain as many girls as he wanted, all without having to negotiate any of it out of the slightly psychotic uncle he lived with. The older brother Tommy never was.

Brath finished dressing. He turned to his locker and pulled a slim, black automatic out of it. It was Brath himself in the form of a weapon: perfectly compact, not a single wasted inch of machinery. The grip was ergonomically curved, the body sleek, all high-impact plastic and feather-light super alloys; the whole thing no bigger than the palm of a large hand. He touched a button, and the clip hissed from the butt. The first time Mal had ever seen it, also in the locker room, he had looked up at Brath and found the ice-chip eyes studying him in return.

"There's more than one kind of fight, Mal," he had said quietly.

Now Mal watched him check the load and snap the clip home, then attach it to the back of his belt along a magnetic strip.

"Why don't you and me go have another look at this building?" he said to Mal.

"You mean you're coming with me?" Mal asked, nearly breathless with relief.

"Yeah, Mal, yeah." He threw a leather jacket on and made the weapon disappear.

"Brath. I really . . ."

Brath nodded, squeezing Mal's shoulder once, hard, to get past the sloppy stuff.

"Sure, sure. Let's get going."

"There." Mal pointed at the building.

"Where?" Brath squinted.

"Right there." Mal stared right at it, the huge, unmissable tower.

Brath squinted a moment longer, then turned to Mal and shrugged.

"See the building with the gold trim on the doors? Look to the left of those. Stop. You're looking right at it."

Brath's eyes locked.

"Oh, yeah," he said curiously.

Mal moved toward the doors, but now Brath held him back.

"Hold up a minute." His ice-chip eyes were hard-focused on the doors. "You said they had people coming in sometimes, runners. Maybe we'll see one."

Mal held his spot. Brath had been the one to go to, no doubt about it. He took charge and knew what he was doing, and he stayed calm. Mal felt his world straightening out just a little bit.

There were morning crowds in midtown now, thick flocks of people hurrying in to work. The building hadn't changed at all, a silent, reflective obelisk; but fantasies of disaster had plagued Mal so often in the last few days, like one where he brought someone back here only to find the building completely finished within, bronze and gilded, with newsstands and security guards and people running to and fro.

"There," Brath said, calling Mal's attention to a figure departing the building and setting a quick pace toward the subway.

Brath went into a swift jog, cutting between cars like a shark headed for prey. Brath was that kind of a machine: he fixed his sights and he went. Mal followed him across the street, would always follow him, for better or worse. Brath wasn't in this for himself. He was the only person Mal knew who would get embroiled like this, no questions, simply because a friend had asked. He was the only person Mal had ever found a way to trust.

Mal followed, stopping at the top of the subway stairs just as the person who had come from the building, a young woman, got to the bottom of the stairs.

They caught up with her on the platform. She was slim and hard looking, carrying a messenger bag over her shoulder, stubborn around the eyes but jittery, all the more so when she saw the two of them approaching. She pretended not to look at them.

"Hey," Brath said.

"Yeah?" she said too quickly.

"The package."

"What package?" she tried, but Brath just looked right through it.

"Open the bag," he said.

"Who the hell are you?"

"How come you're not in school?"

"I'm nineteen," she said. "How come you're not in school?"

"What's your name?"

"I'm gonna tell you my name?"

"Just tell me your first name," Brath said, all reason. "I can't do anything with just your first name."

She looked him over a moment longer. Her eyes flicked to Mal.

"Isabel." She nearly spit it out.

"Look, Isabel. I need to see the package. You can hand it to me or we can do it a different way. Do you want that kind of trouble?"

Her expression didn't back down, and Mal was perversely proud of her for it.

"Why don't I go talk to the MCT about this?" she suggested.

"Yeah, Isabel, why don't you?" Brath met her bravado with a cold gaze. His razor-blade face was still, all its focus collected around the freezing eyes. Maybe the girl had seen that kind of look in her life before and knew what she was dealing with.

"Look, I don't know what it is," she said. "The scanners would go off if it was something dangerous. I got a job. I come pick stuff up sometimes."

"Let's both find out," Brath said, and his hand wandered behind his back, as casually as you please. "I'm not kidding."

She ejected a disgusted *"Pfff,"* and her hand went to the bag and started to pull the package.

"Whoa," Brath said, his own hand moving around to the small of his back. "Just open the bag and show it to me."

Isabel obeyed, and Brath reached in and took out a bundle about the size of a dictionary.

"Where was this going?"

"I'm supposed to leave it on a bench in a playground."

"Where?"

She supplied an address.

Brath looked down at the package, Mal doing the same over his shoulder. Even Isabel, now that it was sitting out there, looked at the thing as if it held something bad, something wrong, something dangerous.

"You know a kid named Tommy?" Brath said, not even looking up, showing her that the answer didn't have any real significance to him. "Around our age, dark hair, dark eyes, does the same kind of work."

Mal was about to pull the picture out, but she was already shaking her head.

"I don't know anyone in this, just the man in the suit who gives me the packages."

Mal wanted to ask her about the man in the suit, about that voice he'd found somehow familiar, but he let it go by him, in fear of ruining the illusion with his uncertainty.

Brath nodded absently at her response, his attention held by the package.

Mal didn't want to see what it held, for fear that it would condemn Tommy to something unforgivable.

"Open it," he said anyway.

Isabel was watching, almost glaring at them now. There was some sense from her, as well, that finding out the contents of the package was of sudden importance, that it held the depth and breadth of her destiny, too.

Brath's sharp fingers tore and revealed shreds of paper within. He sifted through it, letting it fall to the platform at his feet, until he was holding nothing at all.

They looked down at the scraps of paper, shredded to such a degree that only stray words and images were readable: "lost" and "desperate" and "failed"; blurry pictures of a woman's face weeping; the limp arm of a body, presumably dead. Brath stamped on it, making sure he had missed nothing.

"What the hell is going on?" Mal pleaded to him.

"Let's go find out," Brath said, then turned to Isabel. "You're on the next train."

She stood on the platform and watched Brath lead Mal back up to the sidewalk.

"Do you think we should maybe get your uncle or something?" Mal said, his gut churning as they approached the building.

"No," Brath said in a tone that left no room for consideration. "You don't ever want my uncle in on anything with you. He doesn't fix things. Not the way you want them fixed."

Mal let it go. He escaped to Brath's apartment sometimes, to escape his various foster parents, but had met his uncle only once, on account of the bizarre hours he kept. The man had not said a word, regardless of what was addressed to him, but merely stared back with shining eyes that suggested something hideous and barely contained.

They went back to the building, and Brath made sure he got to the doors first, not even pausing before he pulled them open and slipped in.

It was still a blank place. Mal had forgotten how removed it felt with the street noise cut off. Maybe, he thought just then, this wasn't such a good idea after all.

Brath went at a brisk pace past the elevators and looked down into what, for lack of a better designation, could be called a lounge, confirming that the lobby had no one in it. He made less noise than Mal when he moved, though Mal's heavy footfalls negated the accomplishment.

"Let's see these doors," Brath said, his voice always low.

Mal nodded and led him to the elevators and reached out and lit the button. The elevator they were standing directly in front of dinged almost immediately.

Mal had a tall, powerful build, two inches over six feet, with broad shoulders. The figure that came out of the elevator was not only taller, but bigger. Mal had to bend his neck up to look at the figure's face. It was dark and, in this brief instant of action, somehow without detail, and the figure itself swooped rather than walked.

Brath was exceptionally fast, his hand went to the small of his back and whipped out his gun. There was a flash from the muzzle and a crackling hiss of discharge just before the figure's hand swept by and the gun sailed away, echoing a metallic *whang* as it met the door of another elevator. The figure's hand swept back along the same path and smashed Brath's face so hard that his body spun around and he went straight to the ground.

Mal moved fast, too, but before his fists even met a body, the figure's hands snapped around his throat. They were huge hands, encompassing Mal's entire neck easily, and they were strong, compressing his thick and instinctively flexing neck muscles without trouble.

There was no percentage in grasping at the hands, trying to pull them away. Mal threw an abdomen punch with his right and landed hard. There was no give beneath the blow, and the figure remained silent. Mal couldn't find any air. Little explosions of light were invading his vision and— it was shocking in a dull, distant sort of way—he realized his feet had left the ground. He kicked with one of them and believed he landed dead center between the figure's legs. The fingers, though, didn't loosen.

Darkness swallowed him whole.

# GREY

LAURA JOLTED AWAKE from a dream, her heart thumping fast with paranoia and her stomach heavy with nausea. She opened her eyes with effort, sticky as they were with sorrow and sleep, and found herself on the train, the last echo of its horn fading as it left a station. The figures around her were sparse, but she saw their faces turn back down to their cells. She wondered for a nervous moment just what they had been looking at while she slept.

She blinked the remnants of the disturbing dream away, and everything still seemed far away from her, impossible to grasp. She had literally lost her roots, and for the first time was truly, utterly alone. And alone she had never been, even at her worst moments. It had robbed her even of the parents in her mind, against whom she always measured her actions and ideas. She felt afloat, a drowning person with nothing to grab hold of.

Nothing?

She pulled her cell from her pocket with stiff fingers and began to key Rachel's number, when she saw that her cell screen was an inert gray. She jabbed at it, keyed to switch to the secondary battery, slapped the thing hard against her knee, all to no effect.

"Oh, come *on,*" she breathed out in a harsh whisper. She looked around at all the other cells in all the other hands and realized in a flash of sour insight how helpless she felt without her cell, her immediate connection to other people, to the Internet, the world. And she felt the panic; it didn't have its fangs in yet, but it was sniffing around with the sense that it might soon have a meal here.

She breathed deeply and shut her eyes, but when she did, she felt as if she could hear sounds and voices from her dream still, just beneath the hum of the train's motion. So she abandoned her calming breaths and opened her eyes.

Thirty-five interminable minutes later, the Stony Brook station rolled into view. She practically leaped from the train and got to her car in the lot only to realize that with her cell dead, she couldn't activate the damned cellock. She could break in—she would certainly have been happy to break something—but without the cell, the car wouldn't start either. She called from a paycell for a cab to pick her up and used twenty-five of the two hundred dollars to get herself to the front door of Linus P. Talbot High School. The majority of days over the last four years had found her passing through this doorway at least twice, though now what might have been comfortingly familiar was instead loaded with stomach-twisting tension.

Having begun this unbelievably shitty odyssey so early, she had made it here during the second-to-last period. Rachel would be in Advanced Bio, Cheryl in gym, and Ari, ex-boyfriend and all-around scumbag, whom she would barely even consider speaking to in this dire situation, would be either in Statistics, or out at the track field cutting Statistics. Surely if there was ever a situation that called for disrupting a class, this was it. But whatever was happening, Laura was still a product of her upbringing, her social structures, and so rather than cause a stir in a class, she walked directly to the administrative office.

The woman behind the desk looked up and fixed her eyes on Laura. Laura knew she was a mess from a sleepless night and spewing every imaginable fluid out of her face back at the hotel. But if that elicited an extra measure of sympathy, then so be it. She wouldn't turn it down just now.

"Mrs. Greene," Laura said, smiling shakily at the woman behind the desk.

Mrs. Greene nodded in response as Laura came up to the counter.

"I'm sorry, Mrs. Greene," she said. "I'm having kind of an emergency at home, and I really, *really* need to speak to Rachel Parker. She's in Advanced Bio right now. Could you possibly call her down to the office?"

But a sick feeling had already settled in Laura's stomach. She had not shown up for classes this morning, and no excuse had been phoned in by her parents. The first words out of Mrs. Greene's mouth when Laura entered the office should have been a demand for an explanation.

"I'm sorry for your trouble at home, sweetie," Mrs. Greene said in a measured display of both concern and suspicion. "But who are you, exactly?"

"Mrs. Greene," Laura repeated, still trying to smile, though her voice was beginning to fray at the edges, "it's Laura." Mrs. Greene remained blank. "Laura Westlake. We just strung up all the balloons for the PTA potluck in the gymnasium two weeks ago."

"I'm sorry. I don't recognize you," Mrs. Greene said, "and I can't call a student out of class without a request from a parent or faculty."

Laura yanked her cell out, but before she keyed the screen to call up her license, she remembered it was dead. She slapped it on the desk hard enough to arouse the attention of two people seated at desks nearby.

"I'm Laura Westlake," Laura said, and she spelled her last name out slowly. There was no smile left now. "I've been attending this school for four years. You may not remember me, but if you look at the school records, you'll find my name there."

Mrs. Greene accepted the information evenly and bowed toward a screen and moved her fingers about it for a moment.

"I'm sorry," she said after a moment. "I don't see you listed here. If there's some—"

But Laura was already backing away, absolute rage tearing her features apart.

"God!" she screamed, surely loud enough to be heard through the hallways. *"This is so fucking unfair!"*

She ran out of Linus P. Talbot High and ran and ran until she had no breath left to drive her any farther.

Exhausted, her brain aching from endlessly cycling ideas about what to do next, she arrived home. Would her parents be back soon, or did they think they lived somewhere else now? Or, her heart skipping a beat as she realized it, wouldn't they think that *she* lived somewhere else now?

Wouldn't they arrive home to find a teenage trespasser

waiting for them? But there she would have them, of course, because her room was still there, filled with a lifetime's worth of proof.

She forced her aching legs to churn faster. She ran up her yard and through her door to make sure that her room was actually still where she had left it, only to stop short at the sight of two strangers sitting in her living room.

They sat at the edges of the sofa, in the poise of experienced visitors, never in one place for more than a few minutes before having to move on. They both wore unremarkable suits and bland expressions that characterized their professional detachment.

"Ma'am," the lead man said, standing, as he pulled out his wallet and flipped it open for her, "I'm Agent Grey with Homeland Security." His ID card had a gold seal beside his photograph and the name "Grey, Rodney." A holographic American flag leaped an inch off the card, beneath the words "Department of Homeland Security." "This is Agent Deel." The other man stood and held his ID out. "We've received a complaint from a Mr. and Mrs. Ronald Westlake, whose home this is, regarding harassment by an unidentified teenage female. Would you please accompany us to answer some questions?"

She shook her head. Despite what had happened to her in the last eighteen hours, it turned out she could still be shocked. Homeland Security? Responding to a complaint of harassment? Arresting a teenager? What the hell?

She looked from their badges to their faces. They were as nondescript as the suits, as if they were for formal presentation and nothing else. Both pairs of eyes looked identically dull.

"I live here." She looked Grey right in his flat gaze. "And I can prove it."

Slipping his badge away, Grey looked over at Deel and then back at her.

"Ma'am, if you'd just come with us."

*"Come with you?"* This was insane. "Let me see your badge again." She held her hand out. When Grey hesitated, she pushed her hand forward. He slipped it out and handed it to her. She pulled out her cell by instinct, before remembering that it was the most recent casualty of this cosmic breakdown that had been plaguing her. She tossed the useless thing onto the nearby table. "Give me your cell, please," she said without embarrassment.

With no shift in his disinterested expression, he pressed several keys and then put his cell in her hand.

"Department of Homeland Security, how may I direct your call?" came a clean, clipped female voice from a screen that framed a Homeland Security shield. Advertisements for surveillance products—binoculars with thermographic enhance, digital cameras in the form of fake fingernails—began to scroll down the side.

"I want to confirm an agent's name and badge number."

"Hold, please."

She looked up at Grey while she waited for some sign of discomfort. He watched her placidly.

"Special Agent Kingston, may I help you?" said a male voice, the Homeland Security shield still holding the screen.

"I'd like to verify that you have an Agent Rodney Grey working out of your office and that his badge number is . . ." She flipped open the badge and read the number off. There was a pause on the other end.

"Please put the agent on the phone."

She handed the cell to Grey. He lifted it to his ear.

"Grey. Check. Check." Everything was a bore, it seemed from his monotone drone. He held the cell up so that the screen faced him, and a red light from the lens flickered a hazy laser across one vacant eyeball. He handed the cell back.

"Yes?" Laura said.

"Retina scan confirms an Agent Grey, Rodney, badge number as follows." He read it off, and she followed it on the badge.

"And what address has he been sent to?"

"I'm sorry, ma'am, that's confidential."

"But it's *my* home."

"I'm sorry, ma'am."

"Please describe Agent Grey."

"Height: five feet ten inches, weight: one hundred seventy-five, eyes: brown, hair: brown. Hold for image." Instantly, the picture of Agent Grey that adorned his ID replaced the Homeland Security shield.

"Thank you," she said absently, and keyed off. Grey took his cell and badge back.

"Ma'am, please come along quietly."

"My room is right through that door," she said, taking a step in that direction. "Just walk over and I'll show you."

Agent Deel pulled out a sleek gun of hard black plastic and pointed it right at her.

Her eyes went wide, the muzzle of a gun something inconceivable to her, utterly disassociated from her life. Neither of the agents' eyes changed. They were as lifeless and dull as they had been when she first saw them sitting and waiting. Deel looked as if he was fully prepared to snuff her out simply to spare his partner and himself the trouble of further argument.

"Ma'am." Grey's hand lashed out and had her by the arm as swiftly as his other hand had produced a hypodermic.

"What?" Laura cried, incredulous. None too gently, Grey thrust the needle through her sweater and into her arm.

"Mookie," she tried to yell, but it came out choked and quiet. She wasn't expecting him to come charging around the corner, to leap up and bite the agent's hand until the gun fell and she could run for her life. No, she just wanted him to appear so she could see one thing she loved.

But he didn't appear, and in the fleeting moments before darkness saturated her vision, she wondered if it was because Mookie was confused by the call of a stranger's voice.

# MIKE

MIKE BOOTHE WAS a tall man who slumped a little in the shoulders. With the exception of small and suspicious eyes, he had a big-featured face, from his forehead to his nose to his teeth, and dark hair that had been bright blond when he was a child. He carried around fifteen more pounds than he wanted, and rather self-consciously at that. Most of his shirts were from before he'd put the weight on and so tended to accentuate his bulges.

He came down the basement stairs, his heavy footfalls echoing off the metal steps and announcing his arrival through the dark, humid concrete halls that held the boiler and the circuit breakers and the maintenance equipment.

And the English textbooks. Which was why he was down here. As head of the English department, all five faculty members of it, he had, lo, those many months ago, been charged to find a place to stow the new textbooks. These days, cells were loaded with the material and students did their schoolwork, as they did everything else, on their cells. Problem was, no one had overhauled the budget, so now, in addition to purchasing one current textbook program to be loaded into all the cells, the school continued to purchase hundreds of useless textbooks. Textbooks that needed to be stored so that they could molder and gather dust pointlessly.

Modern public education.

And of the infinite array of reasons Mike resented storing the books, the primary one was that he was responsible for doing a useless job that required more time than he could spare and most assuredly more strength than his back could comfortably accommodate.

He had argued against keeping the books at all—it was his way—starting with the principal, who said that textbooks on view were bad when Board of Education inspection time came around. But they couldn't be trashed, because if anyone questioned the budget, the money that had gone to buy them would have to be justified. Mike then argued with the English department about exactly where to store the books. They said the basement was the obvious place: it was out of the way, so the kids couldn't get to them and burn them as they had the history textbooks in the upstairs storage room the year before, in what some faculty were still calling "the Book Burning of Storage Room Twelve."

Finally, Mike argued with Manuel, the maintenance chief, who said that storage space in the basement was only for maintenance supplies, and if he let the English department store books there, he was going to have to let everybody do it. For that one, at least, Mike called in the principal and got his basement storage closet.

He lugged the books down, the first spine-wrenching box of twelve boxes, because apparently it was the head of the department's duty to transport them. Ironically, he had accepted the head position in the first place because he was under the impression that such a move would exempt him from many of the more menial responsibilities. Manuel, still smoldering over his loss of precious closet space, informed him that the maintenance staff was not responsible for lugging the English department's textbooks around. Manuel's glare challenged him to go to the principal again, assaulting the very notion of how a "man" acted. For the sake of what was left of peace, Mike sacrificed his spine and lugged the books.

Down the steps, along the hall, around the boiler room, back near the rows of pails and mops and detergents that had been hauled out and lined up in the hallway to clear space for the books was the closet door.

Except that the closet door wasn't alone. There was the closet door, the one he and Manuel had stood in front of, arms flailing and gums flapping at each other. It was wood, heavy and old, seams running through it from the humidity and banged and cracked badly from years of collisions with rolling buckets and janitor feet. On every visit Mike had ever made down here, there had been that door and only that door. That was part of the problem, really: not enough doors leading into not enough closet space for his damn textbooks.

Yet now there appeared this second door, as sometimes happened in life, when a thing could not possibly be so but was so nevertheless. Like keys that are not where they're supposed to be one instant and then are, as soon as you turn back around. This second door was only three or four steps away from the closet, though it could not have been further away from it in type. It was matte gray metal, stark and impenetrable, with a metal handle so clean and bereft of age and wear that it managed to collect and reflect even the dim twinkles of light in this dirty, smelly basement. It was slightly ajar, pushed in just a few inches, and there was a pale white light burning just beyond.

Mike looked over his shoulder, knowing he would find no one here, thanks to Manuel, and not sure what he would say to them anyway. *Hey, did you know there's a door here?*

He plunked the box of textbooks down where he was, groaning with relief and damning his body for getting older and fatter, as he did many times each day. He stood in place, looking at the second door and finally stepping toward it.

The closer he came to the door, the more it didn't go away, or prove to be a trick of the light, or explain itself at all. Once at it, he stood, waiting for it to do something other than be. It was cracked open just enough that a white line burned down its side, but not enough that he could see anything of what was on the other side of it.

So he pushed it open.

There was a room there, lit by a cold, fluorescent light. There was an elevator off to one side, its surface as reflective and unblemished as the door handle, showing him the room again and his own face peeping out of the door. One of many doors. There must have been about thirty or forty of them, maybe ten or fifteen on each of the other three walls, all matte gray with their shiny handles, all closed except this one.

This was really, really not possible; not possible in the most extreme way, which was actually not *possible* instead of merely undesirable or unthinkable. The room with the doors was big, far too big to be encompassed within the school basement. Indeed, it extended off to the left with gray door after gray door into the space where the controversial maintenance closet should be. *Should* be? *Was.* It *was* right there. He could pull his head out and see it there. He went the four steps over to it and opened it up and, sure enough, there had not been any major construction on the foundation of the building that no one had heard of or seen or known about. The maintenance closet was right there, containing only cleaning supplies, dirt, and a bad smell.

He went back to the other door, and the huge room of doors was just as much there. In the same space.

"I don't . . ." Mike said. "What's . . . to . . ."

Something dinged. It was the elevator on the fourth wall, which meant, he realized only now, that there was an elevator extending either up or down—or both; yes, why the hell not both?—into solid ground below or a school with no elevator in it above.

A man in a suit stepped off the elevator.

"Excuse me," Mike said, his mouth feeling sort of numb and his voice far away in his ears, as it had been once when he had broken his ankle playing basketball in high school and again when a mugger stuck a gun in his face. "Could you tell me . . . ?" He couldn't come up with an end to that sentence. He just couldn't conjure any words that seemed to do the situation justice or encompass exactly how much there was to explain.

The man was looking at him. He might have been looking at him when he'd gotten off the elevator, or he might have just noticed him. It was impossible to tell, because the man's face was dead, empty, not like a face at all but more like a computer approximation of a thing called "face." Even his eyes, which should have widened or blinked in surprise, were flat, lifeless. Dull.

"I'm sorry, I didn't mean to scare you," Mike said, not handling any of this to his own satisfaction. "I just don't—"

The man had barely missed a step. He stepped off the elevator, Mike had spoken, and now he was walking toward Mike. He was coming quickly, not running, but moving in a way that was instinctively clear to Mike how malign it was. It was the way a high school principal walked with intent upon seeing a student breaking into a locker or tearing pages out of a textbook—if that high school principal intended to murder the student.

Mike flung the door closed. He heard it slam, though he didn't see it. He was careening back around the corner through the basement, nearly tumbling over the box of books but catching his awkward weight, running madly past the boiler, back through the hall, and back up the basement stairs.

He came out into the lobby and smacked right into a

student. The student stumbled backwards, and Mike bounced off of him and into a wall. Four other kids and one teacher who happened to be walking by stopped and stared.

"Hey, mistah," the student said, a foul look on his face, "where da fire?" He looked resentfully at Mike, and if Mike had been another student this would have been only the start of it.

"Sorry, sorry," Mike said, the buzz of madness still alight in his head. "Get going." The student stayed and looked sullen. "Get going!"

The student hissed in disgust and went on his way.

"You okay, Mike?" The other teacher came up to him. Mike stared at him, a shorter, grayer man who took a tie and jacket very seriously, even in this environment. "Mike? What's wrong?" He took Mike's shoulder.

"There's a door in the basement," Mike said, ready to be quiet and reasonable now.

"Yeah?" The other teacher was waiting for the answer to his question, unaware that it had just been given to him.

"Come with me." Mike disentangled his shoulder from the man's grip, took his arm, and nearly propelled him toward the stairway.

Mr. Craig of History and Global Culture Three squinted through his glasses down into the basement. In his sixteen years on the faculty, he had never actually been down to the basement. There was plenty he'd never done here, including raising his hand at the wrong time in a faculty meeting or being noticed in any way. That, really, was the only way to survive as long as he had in a school like this.

Mike led him down into the basement, around the corner, and down the hall. Long before they reached the end, it was apparent that there was now only one door there: that of the maintenance closet. This didn't take Mike by surprise. On the contrary, it was exactly what he had expected.

He went over to the wall where the second door had been and touched it. Mr. Craig was looking at him.

"Everything okay?" he asked, glancing about himself with mild interest.

Mike shoved past him and went back to the stairs. Mr. Craig followed behind.

"Mike?" he said as Mike walked back into the lobby and toward the offices.

"Yes!" Mike snarled. "Everything's *great.*"

He pushed into the administrative offices and found Manuel making work for himself, in back, standing on a ladder and dealing with light bulbs.

"Manuel," he said, coming to the foot of the ladder in what he hoped was a threatening manner.

"Yes, Mr. Boothe," Manuel singsonged in an effort to be as condescending as possible.

"Come down here, please."

Manuel took his time coming down.

"Where does that other door in the basement go?" Mike demanded. "The one right next to the maintenance closet?"

"What are you talking about? The only other doors down there are to the boiler room and the server room. They're nowhere near the closet."

"Good," Mike said, jutting his head forward as he did so, causing Manuel to flinch back. "*Exactly* what I wanted to hear." He fumed away, storming by the principal's office, its door slightly ajar.

Mike sat in his office amid the other boxes of textbooks, his head in his hands, staring down at the desk. There was a knock at the door, which Mike patently ignored.

"Mike." The principal's voice came from beyond, and then the door opened. Mike looked up. Principal Tate, as primped and tidy as ever, was more a businesswoman than an educator. Just beyond her stood a man Mike didn't recognize.

"This is Jon Remak," the principal said, an unmistakably cautionary tone in her voice. "He's with the Mayor's Task Force on Education."

Remak nodded in greeting. He was athletic underneath his bland suit, in a short, compact way. His hair was short and spiky and black. His eyes were curious and intent on everything they looked at from beneath gold-rimmed glasses. His manner seemed to Mike too engaged to be involved in city-run education.

"Yes," Mike said, getting it together. "Hello."

"You were having some trouble in the basement?" Remak asked.

"No. No trouble whatsoever."

"You mentioned something to the gentleman working on the lights just outside Mrs. Tate's office."

"I have boxes of books to store there." Mike indicated the boxes that were making it difficult to navigate the office floor. "That's all."

"But you asked him about a door?"

The principal listened but clearly understood none of it, and was probably wondering, as Mike was, why the mayor's task force cared about doors in the basement.

"No"—Mike shook his head too quickly—"no door at all. What are you talking about?"

"I heard you ask the man in the office about a door."

"You heard wrong," Mike said.

"Mike," the principal interjected, "please." She stared at him as though she'd be pleased to stuff him through the window and send him plummeting to the cigarette-strewn alley behind the school.

"That's all right." Remak put his hand up. "We can leave Mr. Boothe be."

Tate nodded stiffly and, leaving Mike with a fleeting glare, escorted Remak out of the room.

On his way home, Mike was grabbed by two kids who swung him around and pushed him up against a brick wall, obviously prepared to perpetrate bodily harm on him, until they realized he was a "mistah." They conferred quietly, eyeing him with detachment as he cooled his heels against the wall. Needless to say, there was always an MCT officer around whenever Mike was shouting at some asshole on the street, but now—

The boys let him go, though through all rational calculation Mike couldn't figure out why. Did they value an education that much?

Across the street, he stepped around the chalk outline of a woman who had flung herself from a roof in an extreme but eminently understandable gesture of cosmic disgust. Around the corner, he watched a sweating mother, one arm filled with groceries, slapping her child on the back of the head, expecting the smack to drive home the point that he should stop crying.

He walked through Queens, under the gray sky, within the grayer shadows of gray buildings, through a light haze of cold rain. Did it ever stop raining anymore? Was the sky coming apart? When the rain stopped, would there be nothing left above and would the vacuum of space suck the entire planet into oblivion? He should be so lucky.

Home was only blocks from the school, the goddamned place that was swallowing his life. Even so, there was ample space between the two for a taxi to nearly run him down. The driver, who had been driving and attending his cell at the same time, screeched to a stop just short of Mike's legs, then cursed at him for the trouble. A disheveled homeless man, unable to make an effort at coherent speech, got in Mike's path and wouldn't get out of it until Mike actually reached out and shoved him to the side.

Mike opened his front door and climbed the stairway, slowly and heavily, weighted down by so very, very much. On his landing he pulled out his keys, only to have the key ring separate and spill keys all over the filthy landing. He glared at them angrily, then gathered himself and managed to pick them up. He had meant to invest in a cellock long ago, but he found that the money for that kind of thing always wound up being spent on beer. He pulled the right key from his palm, opened his door, and stepped in, and there was the man from the Mayor's Task Force on Education, sitting in Mike's shitty little living room in the only good chair he had.

"Mr. Boothe, there's no need to panic," Remak said, holding his hands up, because Mike looked as if he were about to sincerely, wholeheartedly do just that.

"What are you doing in my house? How did you even get in?" Mike decided to play the anger card instead.

"That's complicated," Remak said, standing up. He was shorter than Mike but seemed as if he were taller. "Part of a bigger story."

Mike stood dumbly, caught between wanting to hear the story and wanting to punch this fucker in the face, go into his bedroom, and maybe hang himself with a belt.

"I got in here by showing your landlady my Department of Sanitation ID."

"Department of Sanitation? How the hell did that get you in here?"

"The Department of Sanitation is surprisingly powerful, actually. 'We've had several complaints of an unusual smell emanating from 7C,'" he said in a convincingly officious voice. "That kind of thing."

"So how do you get a job in both sanitation and education, anyway?"

Remak made a tight, humorless smile of surrender and motioned to the table.

"Maybe we could sit down. You look like you could use some coffee or something."

"Is this about the door in the basement?"

"I think so, yes."

Mike dropped his bag on the sofa, shucked his jacket,

and yanked a beer from the refrigerator, making a point not to offer another one to his "guest." He sat down and stared out the window over Remak's shoulder. The only window in the place, it revealed a stretch of dirty city on the other side of it, but the only thing that ever really held your eye out there was that goddamned dome, even as far away as it was. Mike was sure that one day he would look out there and find the dome growing bigger, until it swallowed the people, the buildings, everything.

"There are hot spots in any city," Remak said as Mike took his first swig of beer. "Places that experience higher instances of violent crime due to a number of sociological and demographic factors. Inner city neighborhoods like—"

"This one. I get the idea." Mike was one more long-winded sentence away from tossing this guy out and downing all the beers in his refrigerator.

"All right. There are other sorts of hot spots, too. We call them Down Zones. They're not subject to higher rates of violent crime per se, but to many other incidents of a generally nihilistic nature. Crime, sometimes, but also suicide attempts and traffic accidents. Businesses in the area fail more often, and people who work in these areas are prone to cycles of depression. Areas with underfunded hospitals would be an example of Down Zones. Neighborhoods around poorly maintained cemeteries would be another, or inner city schools with a generally apathetic student body."

"Sounds familiar. What do you care?"

"I work for a group that studies these places, these Down Zones."

"Why?"

"We believe that their existence is indicative of a larger phenomenon."

"And that would be?" Mike had finished his first beer very quickly and plunked it down hard on his table.

"It's elusive." Remak seemed displeased to have to admit it. "It's a web of so many interconnected factors that it can be difficult for a layman to grasp. These factors are part of a larger theory of social interaction called the Global Dynamic. The Global Dynamic can predict human behavior by—"

"This is thrilling."

"All right." Remak did not seem chided, but he did move on. "The neighborhood around your school played host to twelve suicide attempts, sixteen traffic accidents, fourteen reported acts of random violence, and thirty-one domestic disturbances in the last two days."

"It's a crappy neighborhood."

"It *is* a crappy neighborhood," Remak said. "That's why we were watching it in the first place. But those statistics are more than *double* the number of such reports compiled for that neighborhood over any given two-*week* period in the last twenty-seven years. This is categorically unprecedented within the Global Dynamic rubric."

"So the world is going to hell."

"You're a difficult man to talk to," Remak said. "Are you always like this?"

"What's this got to do with the basement door?"

"Exactly."

Mike looked around the room for something more.

"Exactly what?" He threw his hands up.

"Over the last two days, something happened. Something opened up and poured out more apathy, more hopelessness, more despair, more amoral hatred than your neighborhood has seen in twenty-seven years. Whatever it was, frankly, seems to have affected you as well, though that's hardly any wonder."

"What the hell do you mean by *that?*"

"Well, you work right in the most hopeless, apathetic place in the entire neighborhood."

"Mm-hmm."

"I came to study the issue," Remak said. "Your comment about the door was the only thing out of the ordinary I saw or heard all day."

"There is no door."

"You said—"

"I know what I said. But there isn't a door there. You can go down and have a look for yourself."

"I did, actually, and I couldn't find the door. I need you to bring me back to it."

"Me? No. I was thinking about quitting just so I wouldn't have to go back in that building. You think I'm going to march right back down into the basement? Look. There was a door, and when I went back, there wasn't any door. That's what I've been trying to tell you." Mike leaned against the table, closer to Remak. "There. Isn't. Any. Door."

"No one else knew what you were talking about, so no one else has ever opened it. But you did. For some reason or other, it opened for you once. It may again."

Mike stared at the wall.

"Whatever is on the other side of it," Remak said, "may answer a lot of questions. It could be that—"

"*Fine.* Let's go."

Remak's intent eyes went dubious.

"You say you need me and only me," Mike explained. "You say this is all about why things suck. Fine. Let's go."

"Let's," Remak said.


Lights were on in the school halls. They stayed on all night, every weekday, weekend, holiday, and snow day. Even during the summer recess, lights stayed on in these halls. It gave the impression of occupancy, supposedly making potential burglars and vandals—and there were many of these, quite a few among the student body itself—less anxious to ply their so-called trades.

However, for much the same reason, the doors were locked. This didn't stop Remak, though. His cell somehow possessed the cellock codes, and he ushered Mike quietly in.

Mike didn't care for the way the school felt just now. It was never his favorite place, never filled him with optimism or pride, but now, with lights on but the halls empty, it vibrated with the disembodied bad will of all who had treaded its tiled floors, infected by their apathy.

The door to the basement was also locked, but Remak's cell had the code for that, too. When Remak pulled the handle, though, it came off in his hand. He turned to Mike as though he might have some explanation, which in fact he did.

"This place is crap."

Remak nodded, having gotten more or less the reply he expected. He put the knob on the floor and pushed the door open. They stepped through, flicking on the inadequate lighting, which served to do little more than highlight exactly how dark the basement actually was. Remak did not lock this door behind him, but he did step in front of Mike.

That relieved Mike, because this was Remak's show and Mike would just as soon let this assclown take whatever spray of machine-gun lead, lash of hellfire, or blast of death ray they doubtless had coming. But it also annoyed Mike, because what was he, a little girl? This was his school's goddamned basement after all.

They walked down the dark, humid hall, stepped over the upturned box of books, and stopped short of the maintenance closet, directly in front of the rectangle of blank wall in question.

"Right here," Mike said, indicating nothing with a pointed finger. Remak looked at it and then back at him. "I came down, and there was a door. Gray with a shiny metal handle. It was a little bit open, so I pushed it. Like I told you on the way here, what was behind it I have no explanation for. Why it's not here, the same."

Remak was nodding and pressing his hand to the wall.

"Well," he said, stepping back and shrugging. "Try opening it again."

"Opening what?"

"Imagine there's a door there and try to open it."

Mike breathed out and shook his head, but stepped over, envisioned a door, *the* door actually, and—feeling very silly about it—mimed reaching out, turning a door handle, and pushing a door inward.

Naturally, nothing happened. Slit-eyed with annoyance, Mike turned to Remak and, over Remak's shoulder, saw with a start that the other end of the basement hall was filled with figures. They were silhouettes only, backlit by the dull light.

"Jesus freaking Christ," Mike said.

Not hesitating for an instant, Remak spun and saw the figures. He grabbed Mike's arm and pulled him back the way they had come. They turned the corner, and coming down the hallway toward them were more figures, clogging the passage.

Remak's hand went into his jacket and came out with a gun. The figures behind them were advancing now, too. Mike could make them out as they passed beneath a pale yellow pool of light. They were students, every one of them. But they were virtually silent, and they walked with a calm and a sense of community that none of these kids had ever experienced in their lives.

Remak also saw that they were students and pulled his gun away just as the figures were upon them. Remak put the first down with a chop to the neck and the second with a stomach strike. Behind him, Mike grunted and flailed. The figures made no noise at all.

One caught Remak across the jaw; another grabbed an arm. His useless gun hit the floor. He threw one off and put stiff fingers into a solar plexus, then one had him by the head and others were going for his legs. He cracked one across the nose, chopped another's arm away as it reached for him.

Mike shouted, groaned, then stopped making any noise at all. The figures kept coming, washing over them like a silent, irresistible tidal wave, until Remak and Mike were swept away by darkness and into oblivion.

# PART 2

# THE MOUNTAIN

MAL OPENED HIS EYES and the first thing he saw was the last thing he was expecting: a tree. The limb, dry and lifeless, hung over him in the foreground of a flat, pale sky. He raised himself on his elbows and found himself merely one of an array of bodies littering the ground. Only one other person was awake, sitting with his hands planted on the ground, ready to push himself up, but still blinking the daze out of his eyes.

He was smaller than Mal, but compact, wiry-quick and whipcord strong, and beneath wire-rimmed glasses, his sharp eyes began collecting every detail. Just the sort of opponent

Mal hated fighting. The man was wearing slacks and a sports jacket, torn in places.

"Remak," the man said to him. "Jon Remak."

"Mal." His voice came out rough, and he felt the tightness in his throat where the thing had grabbed him . . . if that had really happened and was not the figment of some nightmare imagination.

Remak extracted a cell from his pocket, examined it, and almost immediately put it away. Mal searched for his own and was surprised to find it. He was not surprised, though, to see the words "no signal" scrolling joylessly across the screen.

"Mal," Remak said, "do you know any of these other people?"

There were four others in a small enclosure of trees so thick on three sides as to be impenetrable. The trees opened up on one side to a cliff edge, and down beyond that, a flat granite plane, cracked and unwelcoming, spanning a long way across to another mountain, granite-gray, short, and squat.

The sky looked more like a ceiling, low and without depth or color, just a blank wash of dirty white. The trees around them gave a sense of greens and browns, but they were vague, muted, as if they had been put through the wash too many times. Even the short, prickling grass Mal was sitting on, growing out of hard, packed earth, felt stiff and brittle, more like twigs than plants. There was a disturbing

JESSE KARP

stillness here. No breeze trickled through the dead branches or blades. There wasn't a single sound of life here, either— no birds, no crickets—just his own breathing and the rustle of Remak coming to his feet. The entire place communicated a sense of being used up, and filled him with unease.

"I know him." Mal nodded at Brath, who was prostrate some five feet away. "And I've seen her." He pointed at Isabel as he came unsteadily to his own feet. "You?"

"Him," Remak said, indicating another figure. The still form was an adult, big and a little overweight. But as they turned their attention to him, Mal saw that he was not actually still at all. He looked as though, alone and unconscious, he was under attack.

He looked, in fact, as if his brain were being eaten by a dream. His eyeballs flicked madly back and forth beneath his lids, and his jaw worked and clenched as something seemingly alien in his head appeared to tear into his gray matter, feasting through the channels and on the electrical flashes of his synapses, threatening to gorge itself on his mind. The big body was becoming smaller, tightening into a fetal ball.

"What's wrong with him?" Mal said. "Is he having a seizure?"

"I don't think so," Remak replied.

Their voices appeared to have an effect. The mind within the struggling body seemed to grab hold of the voices and use it to pull himself free of the sucking maw inside his head. With a heavy, leaden resistance, the man's eyes opened.

Remak let the madness leave the man's eyes. Once he shook his head and sat up, Remak addressed him.

"Mr. Boothe," he said, his hyper-focused eyes studying the man through thin glasses."Are you all right?"

"Screw you, Remak. What the hell have you gotten us into?"

Remak looked at Mal, eyes half-hooded. He turned around and walked away.

The guy roused himself as if he were coming out of a bad hangover, rubbing his temples and working his jaw. He touched places on his body gently, and Mal recognized the aftereffects of a fight.

"Stay down until you're sure everything works okay," he advised the man, who scowled up at him as if he had had enough punk kids spouting off at him in his life.

Mal watched him find his cell and, as soon as he saw there was no signal, cram it back into his pocket and look around at where he was.

Mal looked about at the others still on the ground. Brath, his dangerous face odd to see in repose, wasn't stirring yet, but Mal could see he was breathing. There were two others, both girls and both roughly Mal's own age. Isabel had dark hair and a deep olive complexion, and even asleep, her face looked hard and defiant. He could see part of a tattoo creeping up her hip where her shirt was pulled up. The last one looked softer, as if there was some kind of peace for her in sleep. Her hair was jet black and in a ponytail that flopped out from under an old Mets cap. She was in jeans and a sweater, rumpled but clean, comfortably worn and not inexpensive. Mal's eyes were fixed on her, and even when he heard a soft moan from Isabel, Mal had a hard time pulling them away.

"She's waking up," Mal said, pointing at Isabel, whose eyes were beginning to flutter. Remak, returning from his investigation, came over.

"Take it slow," Remak said to her as her eyes opened. "My name is Jon Remak. We're trying to figure out where we are."

She came up on her elbows, made a face at Mal, and took in the world around her. Even confronted with this bizarre place, her eyes were more angry at the strange trees than scared of them.

"You were better off asleep, right?" the big guy said as her eyes passed him.

She pulled out her cell, checked it, and scowled.

Inside two or three minutes, Brath roused and Mal helped him to his feet. He stood up and started flexing his arms and legs, exchanging names with Remak.

Finally, the other girl woke with a start. Mal kept checking on her and so was the first to offer her a hand. She steadied herself against a tree and looked around, clearly confused and scared, but somehow managed to summon a soft smile for him. For some people, smiles were instinctive. Mal knew it but had a hard time believing it until now. Her eyes were vivid blue, almost like strobes, definitely the brightest thing in this place. Even now, they made her face, heavy with worry and confusion, somehow bright and hopeful.

"Whoa," the big guy said, pointing at Brath, who had pulled his gun from under the leather jacket and was checking the clip. He took his time to make sure it was done right before he snapped it home and looked up at the others looking at him. From the stoic expression on his face, there was no explanation forthcoming and no sense that he owed one.

"Is it fully loaded?" Remak asked after an instant of uncertain silence.

"No. Five rounds. Clip holds six, but I think I got one off, before"—Brath waved his hand at the place around them—"all this."

"That's hard to figure," Remak said.

"Yeah," Brath agreed. "Just our good luck."

"I'm not sure. I had a gun, too, but I don't have it now." The two looked at each other as if something was unsettled between them. "Look"—Remak's face was tight, not liking having to say it—"maybe you should let someone else hold your weapon."

"No chance."

"Why leave you with a gun and not me?"

"I suppose you want to hold it?"

"That's not necessary. Why don't you let your friend Mal hold it?"

"No. Sorry, Mal."

Mal shrugged.

"Who did you fire it at?" It was the other girl, not Isabel but the bright-eyed one, pushing away from the tree she'd been using for support and rubbing her upper arm as if she'd discovered an ache there.

"What?" Brath said.

"Who did you fire the one shot from the gun at before you ended up here? It wasn't Homeland Security agents, was it?"

"Homeland Security? No, nothing like that. No, it was"—he looked at Mal—"big. And fast."

"And strong," Mal said.

"How did you get here?" she asked.

"How did *you* get here?" Brath shot back.

"All right," Laura said. "It looks like none of us knows why or how we're here, but maybe we each know, like, a part of it. Why don't we go around and say who we are, how we got here?"

"Okay," Brath said. "Him first."

"Fine. My name is Jon Remak."

"He works for the CIA," the big guy said.

"No, actually." He didn't even look over. "I don't work for the CIA. I work for a cooperative of interests. They study anomalies in group behavior, incidents of crime, suicide, things like that. I was sent to a school in a neighborhood undergoing a sudden, extreme rise in such incidents. I was trying to get a look at a door, which someone said had appeared but had never been there before."

"A door?" Mal said. The idea of doors made Mal's stomach hollow.

"Yes," Remak said. "Before we could find it again, a group of students attacked us. I mean, dozens of students, working together like a trained army. They worked toward a clear goal and didn't get in each other's way. We lost consciousness. Now I'm here."

"Who was with you?" Isabel asked. "When you said 'us,' I mean."

Remak looked at the big guy, and then so did everyone else.

"I'm not telling you people my name," he said.

"Why not?" Brath asked, his voice even, letting his eyes give the attitude.

"I don't know any of you. I'll tell you how I got here, that's all."

"Why don't you just tell us your first name?" the bright-eyed girl said, and just in asking it, she made it sound reasonable. "I'm Laura."

"Mal," said Mal, feeling an urge to show his support.

"Isabel." The three syllables conveyed an extreme sense of being unimpressed.

"Nikolai Brath." His accent showed on his first name, and he raised his sharp eyebrows at the big guy, who stared back with naked distaste. It was a personal thing now.

"Why don't you just make up a name?" Laura suggested. "Just so we have something to call you."

"I've already got something to call you," Brath mumbled quite loud enough to be heard.

"My name's Mike," he finally said, straight at Brath.

"How did you get here, Mike?" Laura asked him.

"I was delivering some books to the school basement—"

"You're a teacher?" Brath asked him, his disdain for the idea clear.

"Yeah, I'm a teacher. I brought some books down. There was a door there that hadn't been there before. Never been there before, I swear to God." He clearly doubted it himself, even as he was saying it. "This guy found me"—he pointed at Remak—"and we went back to look for the door. It wasn't there anymore, and we couldn't find it. Bunch of students came along, and they beat the living shit out of us. They didn't seem like students, though, exactly. My students, they're loud and rude even when they're not trying to beat you up. These were quiet. Like Remak said, they marched toward us like robots or something."

The remote look of the students sounded uncomfortably familiar to Mal, like that of the kids in front of Tommy's place. But there was more than that.

"What about the door?" Mal said.

"What about it?"

"Did you open it? What did it look like?"

"It was metal, I guess; gray and metal. It had a shiny handle."

Mal nodded. "And when you opened it, you saw a white room with lots of other doors in it."

"And a guy in a suit, who saw me and started to come toward me before I slammed the door in his face."

"How did you know about the room behind the door?" Laura asked Mal.

"It was in a basement?" Mal went on with Mike, who nodded. "There was a boiler room down there, down a short hall?"

"Yeah," Mike said impatiently. Remak's eyes were intent on Mal.

"I saw that door. I think I was in that room," Mal said, having a hard time hiding his uneasiness. "My brother called me, sounded like he was in trouble. I found his girlfriend—" He stopped himself, his hand shot to his back pocket, searching for the photo of Tommy and Annie. It was there, thank God. It gave him some inexplicable measure of relief. At least they hadn't taken that away, hadn't cast this precious thing into doubt.

"Mal," Laura said gently.

"Um, right. His girlfriend told me he worked for this guy sometimes, and she showed me where they met. It was a big building in midtown. Midtown Manhattan, that is."

"Is that where you live?" Remak asked. "And your brother?"

"No, Brooklyn," Mal answered. "But they got me—me and Brath—in Manhattan. Is that where they got all of you?"

Isabel nodded.

"I was in Queens," Remak said.

"Queens," Mike grumbled. "I don't go into Manhattan since they put up that giant dome full of goddamned poison gases."

"Long Island," Laura said. "I live on Long Island. I was

at home when . . ." She waved her hand as Brath had before at the impossibility around them.

"So I went to this building in midtown," Mal went on, "all mirror from bottom to top. Do you know the one?" He told them the cross streets.

"All the buildings up there look alike," Mike said. "Who looks up at them, anyway?"

"Yeah, I'd never really noticed this one myself. Anyhow, I went in." Mal described the place to Remak's obvious fascination, and told how he went up in the elevator to the thirty-second floor. "I opened one door, and it looked like it went into a hospital or something. The other one opened into a basement. There was a hallway, and it was humid in there. I lived in a basement near a boiler once, and it was humid like that."

"Did you close that door?" Remak asked.

"I . . ." Mal went over it in his head. "I think so. I threw it shut and ran out."

"But it might have bounced from the frame—it could have remained open," Remak said. "You didn't *see* it closed."

"No. I didn't." He tried, but couldn't make it not true.

"You dumb bastard." Mike scowled at him. "It's your fault I'm here. The door disappeared after I shut it. If you'd shut it, I wouldn't even be here. You dumb bastard."

Mal took it, wiping all expression from his face.

"Take it easy, Mike," Laura said.

"Easy? Who the hell are you to tell me that? You're a child. Do you see this place? We're never going to get out of here!"

"We're all scared and upset," Laura said, not fighting, but reasoning, making a plea. "Mal obviously didn't mean to bring you here. I think there's a lot more going on than just that door."

"If that's why you're here," Mal said, "then I'm sorry. I wouldn't have gotten anyone into this"—his eyes cut across to Brath—"if I'd known . . ." He shook his head.

"You got out of the building, Mal," Remak said, "and you got your friend Brath to come back with you."

"Pretty much." Mal glanced at Isabel, then quickly away from her. "I almost went to the police, but what was I going to tell them?"

"What about your brother's girlfriend?" Laura asked. "What happened to her?"

"She was gone when I came out." Another subject that put a pain in his gut, another life he was responsible for ruining now. "I guess I'm looking for her, too."

"Well done," Mike said.

"Hey," Brath said, pointing at him, "shut it."

"Bite me, you crime-lord wannabe."

"Please!" Laura shouted. "*Please.* Can't we just get through this? Nikolai, Mal came to you?"

"Right." Brath slid his eyes away from Mike. "He brought me back to the building. We met her on the way," he said, pointing a finger like a gun at Isabel. "We went into the place, rang for the elevator. Someone came off it, like I said: really big, really strong. That was it."

"So he kicked your ass?" Mike said.

"What about you, Isabel?" Laura cut in, before anything more could come of Mike's remark.

"I was making deliveries for a guy," Isabel said, then she stuck her chin across the circular group they'd formed, at Brath and Mal. "Batman and the Boy Wonder over here caught up with me. He pulls open the package, and there's nothing in it. So I followed them back and waited outside for a couple of minutes, and when they didn't come out, I went in anyway. My mistake. Guy in the suit was standing there in the sort-of lobby. I saw him, he saw me, now I'm here."

"What package?" Remak asked. "What do you mean there was nothing in it?"

"It was a small padded envelope." Brath intercepted the question. "Like nine by twelve. There was shredded paper in it, that's all."

"Shredded paper? Where were you taking it?"

"A playground," Isabel said. "I was supposed to leave it on a bench in a playground. The packages were always soft and mushy like that, so I knew they weren't, like, bombs or

JESSE KARP

something. Bombs would have set off subway scanners any-way, right?"

"All the packages you delivered were like that one?"

"Same size, same shape, same weight. I never looked in one before."

"Where did you deliver them to?" Remak pressed relentlessly.

"A lot of places." She squinted one eye, compiling a list. "Schools, banks, hospitals, libraries, fast-food places."

"What about the man who gave them to you? Same man every time?"

"Yeah. Wore the same dull suit, kind of plain looking." She thought about it, searched for more detail, but couldn't seem to find any. "Really plain looking."

"Did his voice sound familiar to you?" Mal interjected, remembering the voice he'd heard in the lobby giving direc-tion to another courier. "Did you recognize it at all?"

"I don't know. A little, maybe. He sounded like every adult who ever said they were trying to help me out." She chuckled at that idea, as if her life were filled with promises that had never been kept.

"How did he approach you for these jobs?" Remak pressed on.

"I'm part of a program where they find work for you, sort of tell you what you should be doing."

"It's called parole," Brath sneered.

"Yeah"—she glared at him—"well, as long as we're talking about it, my parole officer keeps throwing jobs at me where they treat me like shit or don't even pay me enough to keep my cat fed. It's, like, designed to push you back into what you were doing before and then, bang, you're back in jail. Well, fuck that. That's not me anymore. I'm not going back to jail, and I'm not letting this brilliant system put me there. I can do better. So I'm going around businesses in my neighborhood, seeing if they need any help, just cleaning up or making deliveries or whatever, and one day, I'm sitting at a McDonald's and this guy in a suit comes up and offers me this delivery job. I took one job. He's not Mr. Personality, but he doesn't treat me like a slave. He won't tell me what's in the packages, but like I said, I can tell they're not bombs or drugs or anything. So I'm working for him for a while when this guy comes along and screws me up again."

Brath held her eyes briefly, then turned away, no apology on his lips or face.

"Whatever," Isabel said to the back of his head.

"And you'd never seen this man in the suit before?" Remak asked. "Can you describe him?"

"He was average height," she said. "He didn't have . . . I mean, he looked . . . he was just sort of plain looking."

"The color of his eyes?" Remak said. "His hair?"

"Jesus," Mike said. Mal had to admit, there was something about Remak's calm that gave the sense of a scientist looking at them through a microscope. "Are you done getting her life story, for Christ's sake? Do you ever run out of questions?"

"Actually," Laura spoke up, looking at Mike with a chagrined expression, "I was wondering why all of us ended up here but"—she turned to Mal—"your brother's girlfriend didn't, Mal. I mean, she was taken around the same time, right? Why isn't she here with us?"

"I figured," Mal said, dredging up some meager optimism, "that is, I was hoping, maybe, she got away."

"I wouldn't count on it." Remak shook his head, not seeming malicious, just coldly realistic. "And you, Laura? How did you wind up here?"

She looked up a little sourly, as though she'd hoped to be skipped over for that one.

"You're the last," Remak pressed.

"I was home alone. My parents were away for the weekend," she said, her voice suddenly shaky. Mal felt his heart beating in his chest at her hurt. "When I called them . . . I don't know how this is going to sound."

"Nothing could be stranger than what's happening to us, Laura," Remak said. "And it could be important."

"I called them," Laura said, nodding, as her voice grew

smaller, "and they didn't know who I was." She stopped, either for a reaction or to collect herself. "Had, like, no memory of me at all. I went to confront them, and they still didn't recognize me; didn't even recognize themselves in old home movies."

Mal barely knew what to make of that. He could see how painful it was for Laura, but there were times when he had *wished* his mother would forget him.

"What do your parents do, exactly?" Remak wondered.

"My father works for an architectural firm. My mother doesn't work anymore, but she used to teach graduate art history."

"Go on," Remak encouraged her. He clearly preferred listening to speaking.

"I went to my school, to speak to friends, but they didn't know me there, either. I wasn't even in the school records." She angrily swept a tear from her cheek. Mal tried to put himself in her position. How many people in school even knew his name? Right now, how many cared that he was gone?

"I know all about identity theft," Laura went on, "but what the hell is this? I went back home and two Homeland Security agents were waiting for me. They wanted to arrest me. No, that's not all. They pulled a gun on me. I wasn't doing anything at all. Nothing threatening, that's for sure.

The agent pulled a gun, and then they shot me up with something." She rubbed at her arm again. "And I woke up here, just like the rest of you." Her eyes cast about, searching for an explanation. "But why a forest? Why here?"

"The real question is," Brath said, "did anyone mention what was going on to anyone else, anyone who might come looking for us?" Brath's ice-chip eyes were losing interest with this process.

"Just him." Mike put his thumb toward Remak.

"My mother and her husband know my brother is missing," Mal said. "But that's all."

"People know where I was dispatched," Remak said, "but I hadn't reported anything yet. I hadn't *found* anything yet."

"Just my parents." Laura said it as if it were a joke. "I don't think they're going to come looking for me."

"No," Isabel said. "I didn't have a chance."

Brath, his eyes suddenly dull with lack of interest, pulled his gun from behind his back and shot Isabel in the head.

The force flung her backwards, and Laura, standing just beside her, stumbled backwards, too, from shock or survival instinct.

"Jesus!" someone shouted.

"Oh, my God!" another voice cried.

Mal hadn't been hit by the bullet, but his head split apart. What was Brath doing? This was beyond even the worst of what had happened so far. Mal's arms and legs were paralyzed from the shock.

Brath turned the automatic on Laura, who, through plain bad luck, happened to be next in line. Mal wanted to move, *needed* to move, to protect her, to stop Brath. Suddenly, Mike was in front of her, between her and the gun, throwing his arms around her, tackling her to the ground, and covering her with his body.

The gun didn't go off again. His mind nearly spinning off its axis, Mal saw Remak chopping down at Brath's wrist with stiff fingers. The gun sprang free, but Brath struck Remak in the face, sending him backwards, and this struck Mal into full awareness. He moved in toward Brath, who dodged away and went for his gun.

Suddenly Mal's eye was drawn beyond Brath to Laura as she pushed at Mike's chest, trying to get out from under him. Mike rolled off her, his face an incongruous mask of bitter shame in the midst of this frenzy. She scrabbled away without even looking back at him and snatched the gun off the ground just as Brath made a grab for it.

She had the gun and scrabbled backwards on her knees as he loomed over her. Mal caught up to Brath, grabbed him by the shoulder, spun him around, and looked into his face, trying to see something, anything he could recognize.

"Hit him!" Mike nearly screamed it.

Brath threw a punch into Mal's gut, and it smacked home with a muffled thump. Mal buckled and coughed, but threw up his elbow to fend off Brath's follow-up strike, then swung his own fist around. It cracked off Brath's head with a report like a rifle shot, and Brath's knees buckled. Mal put another pile-driver fist into the same spot and caught Brath by the shoulders to let him down to the ground gently.

Remak ran over and saw that Brath was out. Then he turned, and Mal followed him to Isabel, lying in final repose. The bullet had hit her in the forehead, just a few inches over her left eye. Her eyes weren't wide in terror; her jaw wasn't slack with shock. Her face had the neutral expression of someone involved in a conversation. She hadn't even had time to look shocked.

It took Remak less than a second to determine that she was dead. He stood up and turned away from her without closing her eyelids. Wasn't that what you were supposed to do? Remak just left her eyes, defiant in life, calm in death, gazing at the void of sky. Mal stared at the eyes, thinking he should close them. But he couldn't look at her a second longer, let alone touch her.

"Is everyone okay?" Laura's back was to the body and her voice was a little bit desperate.

She got nods all around.

"You moved very fast," Mal heard himself say, from a million miles away. "You stopped him."

"I couldn't figure out why they let him keep the gun," Remak said. "Five bullets in it, five of us. And he didn't check his cell when he woke up. I made sure I was next to him." He looked down at Isabel. "But I didn't stop him fast enough."

"Thank you," Laura said, and Mike looked up, because he was still on the ground next to the body. He blinked dumbly back up at her. "Thank you for doing that," Laura went on, keeping her eyes very stiffly on Mike and not what was beside him. The gun was hanging in her hand, too heavy, too big.

Mike got to his feet, went away from the body.

"What the living hell was that about?" he said directly to Mal. "Why did he do that?"

"I don't know. Brath would never . . . I mean, if he was working with whoever is doing this to begin with, why wouldn't he have just shot me as soon as I came to him for help? For that matter, if we're supposed to be dead, why didn't they just kill us while we were unconscious?"

"They wanted to know if we'd spoken to others," Laura said hollowly. "That was what Brath asked right before he did that. Once they knew we hadn't spoken to anyone, he could . . ."

"So they can hear us out here?" Mal asked.

"I can't see into those trees," Remak said, shrugging. "A directional mike. Why not?"

"Brath wouldn't . . ." Mal couldn't seem to complete a sentence. "Wouldn't murder people like this. Wouldn't lie to . . . He's my friend."

"The evidence is hard to debate, Mal," Remak said. "Maybe your friend wasn't exactly who you thought he was."

"He would have to be someone else entirely," Mal said. "Is that what you're saying? This isn't really Brath? It *is* him. I know him as well as I know anyone in the world."

"I don't know," Remak said.

"I know." Mike stepped forward. "At least I know what we should do next: make sure he doesn't wake up and try again." He turned to Laura and stuck his hand out. "Give me the gun."

Her face went sick, brow creased, lips and jaw looking as if she were going to lose her lunch. She started breathing in a weird way, deep and slow.

"Give it to me." He reached his hand toward the gun, and she reflexively pulled it back.

"No one's killing anybody," Mal said.

"Too late." Mike pointed at Isabel, without taking his eyes off the gun.

"Here." Laura shook her head, holding the gun out to Remak by the end of the grip, her arm straining to hold it as far away from her body as possible.

Remak accepted the gun and checked the clip. He carefully extracted Brath's belt from around the unconscious body. He exchanged his own belt with it and attached the gun to the magnetic strip in back, then divested himself of his own, empty shoulder holster.

"There were five bullets," Mike suggested, "and there were five of us, not including him. Maybe once he shot us all, someone was going to come get him."

"That's possible, I suppose," Remak allowed, considering it like a shiny little diamond that might be fake, "but what good does it do us?"

"Maybe if you just fire all the bullets, that will do the trick. Or maybe if you kill him instead"—Mike pointed at Brath—"that would bring someone."

"No," Mal said with a dangerous quiet.

"So what, then? Stay here and die of old age?"

"We have to get out of here," Mal said. He looked off the cliff at the squat mountain across the granite plain. It had a dense forest on top of it just like this one, sticking up like a bad hairpiece.

Remak walked to the edge and looked across.

"It's hard to tell how far it is to the base of that other mountain," Mal said. "There's not much on the ground to judge by." The ground didn't have any trees on it. It was just an expanse of cracked gray rock. It was so featureless, it was hard to tell even how far down it was.

"What about them?" Laura asked, pointing at the two fallen bodies without looking at them.

"We're going to have to leave them," Remak said.

Mal was staring at Brath, searching for some way to protest, but the sense of it was irrefutable. What would happen when Brath woke up? What if he attacked them again? What if he attacked them while they were climbing? He let it go with a sorry nod.

"Don't you think we should . . ." Laura searched and gave up. "I mean, should we just leave her here?"

They all looked uncomfortably at one another. Finally, it was Remak who said it.

"I don't think we're equipped to give her a burial, and time may be a factor. We need to be reasonable about this. How is a burial going to help her, and how is it going to help us?"

Again, they looked at one another desperately. It could take them hours to dig a hole here, if that was even possible in this hard, dry earth without a shovel.

"How are we going to get down from here?" Laura finally said, giving them all permission to move on.

"Well," Mal said, "there's an outcropping not too far down the way here, and there are others below that. I don't think it's a very tall mountain."

He glanced at the others and, seeing no reason to drag it out any further, lowered himself to the ground, swung his feet over, and started down.

Mal held the edge, and the scars on his knuckles whitened under the strain. Remak knelt down to grab his wrist if it should be necessary. Mal looked below him and let go. He sailed down along the rock face for two seconds and landed hard on his feet, grabbing out at the uneven jags to prevent himself from tipping backwards and falling. The outcropping was uncomfortably small.

Mike came next, grudgingly accepting help from Remak on top and Mal below.

"You next," Remak said to Laura.

"Go ahead," she told him. He stood and watched her as she forced herself to look at Isabel.

"All right," he said. "You come right behind me."

She nodded, and he went. Mike pressed against the wall, clearing the way. Mal raised his arms to help, but Remak didn't need it. With his athletic build he managed to climb down most of the way, dropping only the last foot or two.

Laura was last. She hovered at the edge, then lowered herself slowly. Mal told her he was ready, she could let go anytime. She held on a moment longer, as though committing Isabel's face to memory. What else could she do for her, the poor girl?

When Laura set foot on the outcropping below, her eyes were wet.

# THE JOURNEY

IT WAS SLOW GOING DOWN the mountainside. Some of the irregularities in its face required them to make short drops, just a foot or two below dangling feet; others demanded some climbing before a person could drop to the next outcropping safely. At one point there was no outcropping beneath them, forcing them to make a fairly hair-raising fifteen-foot lateral traverse before they came to a position with a clear route down.

Mal, able to hold on a little longer and drop a little farther than the rest of them, always went first. On occasion they could see his face as he moved along the rock or landed hard below and his expression became briefly fierce, as if the rock were his enemy and he was not merely moving across it but engaged in combat with it.

Laura thought she would be the slowest among them, though, as it turned out, Mike proved to be the one with the hardest time negotiating the descent and the one who kept demanding they wait an extra few minutes before they move on. This clearly did not please him, and he remained sullen and quiet for most of the journey, except to grunt at a hard impact or shout in anger or fear once or twice as he felt that his hand or foot might be slipping. Laura, for her part, had gone to the climbing wall at the mall for what felt like every weekend of her twelfth and thirteenth years and was not completely out of her depth. On top of it, Mal seemed to be watching her more intently, keeping a steadying hand on her just a little bit longer.

Gradually, the wall became a slope. At first it was too steep to go down without using both hands and feet. Her hands were aching beyond reason, stiff and abraded and uncooperative. Mike winced when he flexed his fingers, and even Remak massaged his hands intermittently. Only Mal, whose hands had suffered the same rigors, worse in some cases for testing out the routes, seemed indifferent to the damage they'd sustained.

She could not, even in the midst of all this, stop herself from stealing glances at Mal, which she only hoped were not as obviously admiring as they felt. He was slim at the waist and broad across the shoulders and the chest, his torso a V of rising power. He was solid, too, as if right under his flesh he were made of metal. His face was almost a boy's still. The features were young, almost innocent, but the face had been slugged pretty good, judging by the bruise around the left eye. Actually, it looked as if it had taken more than its fair share of slugging, and not just from fists, either. It looked weighed on, the eyes always bracing for the worst. Scars cut across the bridge of his nose, cheekbone, and chin. His dark eyes lit for an instant when he caught Laura looking at him once.

He was not, however, quite enough to make her forget what was happening. Luckily, just when the pain of grabbing and pressing and rubbing up against rock was no longer tolerable, when Laura felt as if she was going to let tears come out with an angry scream, the grade of the slope softened further. It was now possible to walk, taking careful measure of one's balance, slowly down the mountain.

And so, the pain in her hands receded just as her calves began to burn. When they came to relatively even ground, it felt as if they'd been going for hours upon hours, yet the sky was still cloudless and too low, white and gray with no sign whatsoever of the sun's position, but still dropping a tired, gloomy light on them all.

"Hey," Laura said, her voice tired and rough, "what time is it?"

Mal instinctively looked at the watch on the wide leather band around his wrist.

"Broken." Mal held up his wrist and shrugged.

"Ten fifty-five a.m.," Remak said after consulting his own little digital wrist machinery.

"That means"—Laura looked back up the mountain—"if we've been descending for about two hours, it was only, like, eight-thirty when we woke up."

"It's light out. Sort of," Mal said. "Anyway, the light hasn't changed at all. Or the weather."

"It should be cooler than this in the mountains," Remak said, scanning the environment with disapproval. "In the morning, at this time of year, there ought to be a strong wind. If we're anywhere near New York anymore."

It was true. Laura was sweating and hot from the climb, as they all were, but there was no relief here from the elements, no more wind here than there was in a room with no doors or windows. She'd been in the mountains before, camping with her parents, and it was always too cold and too windy for her mother's comfort.

Her mother.

"Why did they put us here, exactly?" Mike demanded. "In a goddamned wilderness?"

Remak shook his head with a bewildered expression that seemed to please Mike.

"There has to be something special about it that would make it desirable for them," Remak conjectured. "It's well removed from where we were. Our bodies would be harder to find intentionally, I suppose, though we could be stumbled upon by hikers. The distance hardly seems convenient. So why go through the trouble to put us here, specifically?" He looked around at the flat gray expanse for an answer.

They had tacitly agreed to take a rest here, finding seats on the bumps of the rocky ground.

"Did you say your watch was broken?" Laura asked Mal.

"Yeah." Mal nodded, looking as if it was one more burden he could hardly bear. "Just taking after my mirror and my bag."

Laura felt her face go agog at his answer.

"Me, too," she said. "All sorts of things have been breaking on me, and for no reason. My cell, a cup I made when I was a kid. It's been happening all week. What about you two?"

"No." Mike shook his head as if to say how stupid this all was. "Wait. Yes. My key ring came apart, too, before I opened my door and he was there." He turned a sour face on Remak.

"A doorknob broke off, though I was with Mike when

it happened," Remak said. "When did you notice the first thing break?" he asked Mal.

"My mirror, the night I got home from the gym. It was fine when I left, broken when I got back."

"What happened in between?"

"Nothing that could have broken it." He stopped, but went on again before Remak pressed him further. "But Tommy called me that night, asking for my help, while I was gone."

"You?" Remak looked at Laura.

"Um, a few hours before I called my parents." She thought on it briefly. "Actually, they were supposed to call me much earlier, so I guess it happened right after they . . ." She searched for another word, couldn't find one, and finally surrendered to it. "Forgot me."

"Anything since we woke up here?" Remak said, beginning to check himself.

Everyone gave him- or herself the once-over, then answered with shaking heads.

"What about it, Remak? What's it supposed to mean?" Mike said, tired of the man's fascinated manner.

Remak shook his head and shrugged.

"I don't know. But it's not normal."

"Not normal." Mike smiled despite himself. "That's huge. Thanks."

After a rest and politely turning their backs for one another to relieve themselves, they went on. The ground was not on a slope here, but it was cracked and uneven in places and it would be easy to twist an ankle or trip. Laura was in jeans with a light, loose shirt and had tied her loose sweater around her waist, her father's Mets cap shading her eyes. She had sneakers on, and Mal, in loose cargo pants and a T-shirt that strained at his chest and shoulders, wore tough leather boots with heavy soles. Mike unfortunately had been in loafers when he had returned to the school with Remak, and he slowed the entire group down, cursing and stumbling along. He wore the khakis and casual button-down shirt that was the uniform of the modern urban teacher.

When they had first begun their climb, seeing Remak in the suit and tie had made Laura think of James Bond, a government agent invading enemy strongholds, fighting on catwalks, and leaping from moving vehicles, all in his perpetually immaculate tuxedo.

Remak was not James Bond. He had discarded his tie and jacket almost as soon as they'd started climbing, revealing the gun at the small of his back. His white shirt and blue pants were now anything but immaculate. They were dirtied, scuffed, torn in places, with rock powder ground into them. The shoes were no better, dull and scratched. He had also removed his glasses for the climb, the lenses through which he examined the world. All four of them were dirty and sweating and scuffed, but Remak, in what was left of that suit, seemed the most like a castaway, without dignity, the trappings of civilization slipping away.

They walked and stumbled for a little more than two hours, plus a half hour stop to rest in the middle. Eventually, the squat mountain with trees on top that was in front of them became larger and larger, and the squat mountain with trees on top that was behind them got smaller and smaller. When the ground started to slope upward again, Laura slowed to a stop and Mike happily took the signal.

"Mal, Jon," Laura said. "Why don't we break here?"

Mal, many steps ahead for the entire journey, stopped, turned around, and walked the few steps back to them. The four formed a vague circle and sat down heavily on the hard ground.

"I don't know when it's going to get dark in this place," Remak said, "but why don't we see if we can get a little sleep here?" There was eager agreement to that, and they awkwardly attempted to arrange themselves comfortably on a ground that made it all but impossible.

"Do you think we should keep a guard up or something?" Mal asked.

"I'll go first." Remak nodded tiredly, stiffly returning to his feet.

"I'm okay," Mal said. "I'll go first. You get some sleep."

"Sure," Mike said. "So you can ogle your new girlfriend all night."

Mal looked away without responding, and Laura made a tart face at Mike, though, frankly, it was not the worst idea she'd ever heard.

Remak nodded and looked back down for a spot with no lumps.

"We were going to go see the school play this week," Laura said after a few moments of windless silence, searching for some evidence that another world still existed somewhere. "My best friend, Rachel, is in it. They're doing *Bye Bye Birdie,* and my dad had been in a production back in high school. He'd played Birdie. Some nights, after he had too much wine with dinner, he'd sing that song about being sincere and pretend to try to get my mom to faint."

"We were going to close the gym early on Tuesday," Mal said, "and have a party for this guy Norman. He's turning ninety, but he still comes in every day and does a half hour with the jump rope and the five-pound weights. He does it slow, but he does it."

"You work at a gym?" Laura asked.

"Yeah, after school. Not like a sports club or anything. It's a small place, for ex-boxers and up-and-comers to train, programs for kids, that kind of thing."

"Where is it?"

"Jericho's Canvas, way downtown, on Greenwich and Edgar."

"Jericho?" Remak asked. "Is that your name?"

"Yeah."

"Are you related to Max Jericho?"

"He was my father." Mal let it go as if he were confessing something.

"Really?" Mike said, sitting up a little. "Max Jericho was your father?"

"Yeah."

"Who's Max Jericho?" Laura asked, her bright eyes perking up with interest.

"Best amateur boxer that ever lived," Mike said, lying back down, trying to show that he wasn't *that* impressed. "Maybe."

"Some sports writers used to say he could have gone toe to toe with Tyson if he'd had the chance," Remak said.

"What happened?" Laura asked Mal.

"He wasn't very"—Mal tilted his head from side to side—"cooperative."

Laura looked at him a little longer, then settled herself back as Mal rose up and started treading a few steps off.

She was going to ask him about school, who might miss him there, but her mind was tugged away, thinking about

Isabel, her eyes open, unsurprised, their defiance gone. Talking and angry one second, and then Brath, and then not talking or angry or even human anymore. It made her think of the dream she'd had on the train coming back from Manhattan, the weird suffocating dream. She was going to mention the dream then, but just in the act of thinking about it, sleep found her again.

When they started up again, Remak informed them that his watch read 7:24 a.m. The sky, the light, the temperature, were all the same.

It was much easier going up this mountain than down the last one, despite the fact that Mike's legs were so stiff that the calves and thigh muscles seized up several times in the first hour and they had to stop a few times to let them loosen as he grumbled and sulked about it. This mountain seemed to be about the same height as the last one, but its slope was far more gradual, at least on this face.

Here it was just walking. Walking and walking and walking forever, with a rest here and there, until the last thirty minutes or so required them to make intermittent use of their raw, throbbing hands.

They made it to the top and looked back at the other mountain. Just like that one, the one they were on was mainly flat but sprouted a tight, impenetrable forest of trees. They might have gone off in one of the other directions along the journey, but there had been nothing there, just sprawling granite with the occasional rise of squat mountain as far as the eye could see. At one point, Remak announced that he saw, or thought he saw, moving figures impossibly far in the distance. But when they all stopped to look, the movement had vanished, or had never been there to begin with.

They also could have traced the base of this mountain to the other side, but the slope, as they could all see, was gentle and thus would be easier going than the last. The thinking was that atop the mountain, they might be able to see something of significance.

So they were up here, with no choice but to try to skirt the forest and get around to the other side of the mountain. They moved in single file along a ledge that was so narrow in places that Laura's throat clenched up and her stomach muscles quivered. At one point along a particularly slim stretch, with limbs and branches and dry, pale brambles trying to force them off into space, she actually found her hands gently shaking.

They were all hungry and dreadfully thirsty, but none of them mentioned it. Remak had them all sucking on pebbles, to keep saliva in their mouths. Mike, whose cracked lips had started to bleed, didn't find the pebble helping much and didn't hesitate to announce it. Laura could hardly disagree. In fact, the pebble felt odd in her mouth, not quite soft, but not solid the way she would expect a rock to feel.

Mal, out in front as usual, had come to a small niche in the trees, affording them an amorphous clearing of some ten feet around to stop and take a rest in.

"There's another opening, a bigger one, I think," Mal said to them after leaning out from the edge and scanning what lay ahead of them. "Like where we woke up on the last mountain. That should bring us around to the other side, anyway. But it looks like rough going."

Tired faces gazed back at him.

"I'll see how it is," he said, always stepping up first, not bragging, just accepting that he was the one who was going to do it. "If there's anything there worth looking at, I'll see if we can make the going a little easier."

"Wait," Laura said. "The forest is thick, but there are some openings low down here. I think I could crawl through."

"I don't think that's a great idea," Mal said.

"You shouldn't do that," Remak told her.

"Fine," Mike said.

"No." Laura knelt down on aching thighs, squinting into the depths of the brambles. "I can get through here."

Remak came over to study it, Mal following the operation with concern on his usually somber face.

"Laura," Remak said. "You can't see all the way through. The path may curve off in the wrong direction, or cut off in a dead end."

"It's got to be better than making Mal climb along the edge over a drop that could kill him." She looked at Remak seriously. "Don't you think?"

He stood up, glanced at Mal, and adjusted his glasses silently.

"Okay, then." She tugged on her thick sweater, tucked her Mets cap onto her head, and got down on her hands and knees.

"Be careful. Seriously," Mal said, causing Mike to roll his eyes.

She squirmed into the gap, and dry branches refused to snap as she forced her way through, instead flicking back and stinging her through the protection of her sweater. It was difficult going. The long, thin sticks pricked at her, pulling at her sweater and gouging holes into it. Even the leaves, dry and sharp like the edges of paper, caught in her ponytail and tugged stubbornly at her head. She put her hand up to protect her face as she shimmied along, but more than once a branch flicked back and slashed a red mark on her cheeks.

Then, finally, her hand came through to the clearing. She struggled until the top of her body was clear, and then dragged her legs out and came staggering to her feet just inches from the edge of the cliff. Blinking sweat out of her eyes, she finally surveyed the opening she had come into and was hit with such a force of shock that she almost stumbled back off the cliff and went tumbling to her death.

Isabel was there, her body lying exactly how they had left it on the other mountain. It was, in fact, the same clearing in every way: the size and shape of it, the pale grass Laura had woken up on, the outcropping Mal had begun the descent with. And across the way, over a long expanse of cracked granite, was another mountain, with trees jutting from its top. The mountain they had just come up. The mountain they were on now.

Laura stood, tight and still, afraid to move for fear of disturbing the space around her and shattering the universe apart. It was so shocking that she almost didn't register the single difference between the clearing now and the clearing the last time she had seen it: Brath was gone.

# THE PRISON

"IT'S CALLED A self-contiguous tesseract," Remak said. They were all in the smaller clearing again. All their faces were turned toward him, and each showed a teetering inability to encompass what Laura had told them on her return.

"A tesseract is a cube," Mike said, shaking his head, seeking to dismiss Remak, even in the face of a screaming void of alternatives.

"It's a theoretical cube, actually," Laura said, reeling off information as if by rote. "A shape that extends into a fifth dimension. Inside is a space larger than the construct can physically contain in four dimensions." She looked around at an array of astonished faces.

"My first boyfriend was a science geek," she explained, unsure whether to laugh or cry at the memory dredged up from another life. "He did a huge project on them. It was all I heard about for weeks, and I had to keep running him through it for the presentation."

"It's bigger on the inside than on the outside?" Mal's somber eyes had gone a little wild, searching for a way to understand an enemy beyond his grasp.

"Yes," Remak said, once he was sure that Laura had no more to add. "I've heard of research being done to create a tesseract, ideally something portable. Something the size of, say, a briefcase, which you could store an entire battalion's equipment in. I understand that there's a current school of thought that says black holes are tesseracts, that whole other universes exist within them." He pushed on into the imponderables, every inch the scientist.

"So you're saying that we're in a black hole?" Mike asked angrily.

"No, no, that's just incidental."

"But"—Laura put her hand up, as though this were a classroom and Remak the teacher—"we *are* in some kind of enclosed space, like a room, aren't we?"

"Not enclosed, exactly. Somewhere on Earth, there's an

aperture, and this aperture opens into a space that coincides with a fifth dimension. But the space doesn't extend infinitely. In this case, it appears to be self-contiguous; that is to say, it folds back around on itself, meets its own edges. It's only"—he squinted and shrugged—"maybe six miles across, maybe less."

"And that's why we're on the same mountain again," Laura said, "because the end of this place just leads right back to the beginning of it."

"More or less. Its boundaries are only conceptual. It's enclosed in the sense that you can't continue to walk over new ground forever. Maybe 'finite' would be a better word than 'enclosed.'"

"Who cares what word you use?" Mike said. "You're only guessing, anyway. You don't *know* what this is. We could all be hypnotized somewhere, or drugged, and none of this is really happening at all."

"No. Too much interaction for that." Remak shook his head. "Too much time going by. There's no sense of compression or dilation. This is a real place, and we're really in it. And it also explains what's so special about this 'goddamned wilderness,' as you called it, and why they put us here in particular. Once we were dead, authorities could scour the entire planet and still never find us."

"At least it has a name," Mal said.

"So what?" Mike said.

"If it has a name," Mal said, suddenly looking back at him hard, "then it's known, it's understood. We're not fighting God."

"Not just that," Laura said. "He said there's an aperture somewhere. If there's a way in, there's a way out."

They all looked at Remak, waiting for him to point it out to them. Instead, he looked as if his collar were suddenly too tight.

"There's an aperture, yes. But I have no idea how it's sealed, or even if it can be unsealed. I don't know what it would look like, or if it would be visible at all. And considering it only needs to be large enough to fit a person through, a finite space of about six miles suddenly becomes a lot larger than it seems."

"What about Brath?" Mal said. "He's not there anymore." He put his thumb toward the nearby clearing where Isabel's body still rested. "Laura said she looked over the edge and he wasn't climbing down."

"I didn't see him between here and the next mountain, either," Laura added, and then shook her head and moved her hands uncertainly. "The other *this* mountain," she corrected himself.

"There is that," Remak allowed. "Provided he isn't out of sight somewhere, that may mean that he can come and go or that they can take him and reinsert him at their convenience."

"If they can do that," Mal said, "then they know we're still alive. If just keeping us in this prison isn't good enough, then why not send back an army with machine guns to get us?"

"Resources," Remak said. "Or value. Maybe we're just not worth that much trouble. For whatever reason, whoever they are, they have access to something like this"—he waved his hand around him at the forest and the mountain and the sky—"but they don't have the facility for something like that. Furthermore, I'm fairly confident that they can't see us or hear us in here now."

"Why?" Mal wanted to know.

"In a normal forest, you can set up microphones that transmit to wherever you are, or you can use aircraft. Not here. You wouldn't be able to transmit into or out of this space, as our cells can attest, and I know there aren't any aircraft flying by. Whatever information they have they've either gotten from Brath or they're going to get from Brath."

"Wait." Laura was shaking her head. "The aperture. Why would the door be down there somewhere? Wouldn't it be as close to where we woke up as possible? I mean, why come through in the middle of the field down there, then drag all of us up the mountain and leave us in that spot?"

"That's"—Remak gave it a second—"true." He looked down at the hard ground, searching the dry, lifeless grass with careful eyes.

"And there was no one in the clearing when Brath left," Mal threw in. "So, if they send someone back through, he'll expect the area to be clear."

There was suddenly an energy pulsing through the group of them, their bodies recharged with purpose.

Getting back to the first clearing was a hair-raising maneuver. Only Laura was small enough to make it through the woods, so moving around the slim ledge around the side was their only choice.

Mal went first, his feet with only a slim lip to tread, and the handholds that stuck out poking and gouging at him. Often he had to put all his weight on his arms and shoulders, his body just hanging out over a long drop. And he had to assist Remak and Mike, guiding each one of them, establishing hand- and footholds. In some instances, he had to give up one of his own handholds and steady his companion traveler, supporting both of them with only the strength of his one arm. The tree limbs were surprisingly stubborn and wiry for such lifeless-looking things, as though this was to be their state for eternity. Like an old photograph, everything in it was dead, but also changeless and preserved forever.

Mal's arms and legs ached fiercely by the time the rest

of the group met Laura in the clearing. They stood milling about, each anxious to stay clear of the vicinity in which Isabel rested, motionless and terrifying.

"I don't know what this is going to look like," Remak said, "or what direction it's going to come from or when—"

"Or if," Mike interjected.

"Or if," Remak allowed.

"The best we can do is wait," Mal said. "And watch as much of the area as possible."

"And supposing"—Mike again—"a door does open and people do come in and they all have machine guns?"

"We make a stand here," Mal said with no budge in his voice. "It's that or wander back and forth until we starve to death. You can go back and wait until the danger is past."

Mike glared back at him.

"I'll stay," he said.

And they waited.

They each stood, their backs to one another, facing either forest or the opening to the empty gray-white sky.

Laura watched the others from the corners of her eyes.

Mal flexed his arms and hands, cords of muscle and vein running down them, working the ache out.

Mike heard his stomach rumble, hoping the others hadn't heard it.

Remak, the automatic loose in his relaxed hand, spared brief glances at the time.

"I had a dream," Laura said. "My parents were fighting, like, really, *really* fighting. Like they would have killed each other if I weren't standing between them. And their yelling stopped, and instead of words, black stuff came out of their mouths and their eyes. Just a little at first, like they were crying, and then lots of it, like a flood of black vomit." Laura's voice slowed as her breathing became deep and long and even. "The black stuff came out like a tidal wave. I was . . . drowning in it. My parents were, too. It was, like, alive; squirming, trying to push its way into my mouth and nose."

"Did you die?" Mal asked, his voice almost inaudible.

"No." Laura looked up at him as if from far, far away. "No. I swam away, managed to break the surface. But I had to leave my parents behind. Underneath." She drew breath in and let it out in an aching sigh.

"When did you dream this?" Remak said, his body half turned away from his quadrant. "Right before we woke up here?"

"No," she said. "On the train. Yesterday. I mean, whatever day Homeland Security came to my house."

"In your dream," Remak said, "was swimming away hard?"

"Not the swimming itself. But"—her eyes flickered

toward Mal for no reason—"leaving my parents behind. Not hard, exactly, but sad. So, so sad. I would never have done that, really. But I did in the dream." She winced, and found she didn't want the attention she was getting. "You had a dream, too, didn't you?"

"Yes," Remak said. "Right before I woke up here. I dreamed that I was in a hallway, guarding a door. A man I didn't recognize came up and wanted to get by. He was very insistent at first, and then, when I wouldn't let him by, he became physical."

"But you kept him out."

"Yes. It was my duty."

"We all had dreams," Laura decided, looking at Mike and Mal.

Mal nodded.

"I was in an apartment," he said. "Something was trying to smash down the door. I wouldn't let it through, though."

"Was it hard to keep it out?" Remak asked.

"Yes. It felt like the hardest thing I've ever done, maybe."

"When did you dream it?"

"A while ago. The night after I went into the building with the doors."

Laura looked at Mike.

"I was in a long, dark hallway," he said. "It was in a

school, I guess, but it went on forever. There were kids there. The hallway was thick with them. They were . . . having trouble, shouting. Screaming, really. Something was tearing them apart. Eating them. I could hear it from far down the hall, beneath their screams, the sound of them being torn apart. I felt responsible. It was my job to do something about it. I pushed my way toward the thing. I couldn't see it, but I could . . . I could feel it." The dream was pulling him back toward it. He stopped himself abruptly.

"And?" Remak encouraged.

"I did my job. I stopped it."

"How?"

"I just did. Isn't that enough for you, you pushy son of a bitch?"

"But you dreamed it right before you woke up here, right?" Remak said.

"Yeah. When I woke up from it, I was here."

"She dreamed, too," Laura said, forcing herself to look down at Isabel. "I'm sure of it. But I wonder," she said to Remak. "Did Brath?"

Mal, waiting with interest for Remak's response to her theoretical question, was the first to see something. He happened to be looking in the right direction, out toward the plain at the gray-white sky. Which was not the plain and the gray-white sky all of a sudden. There wasn't even a cliff anymore, but instead more forest, greener, more alive. Mal hadn't done anything, hadn't even blinked. Just as when Annie had showed him the building. It just came into his head like a lost memory, suddenly returning for no reason, as if the building before and the forest now had always been there and he had simply forgotten to see them.

He opened his mouth to speak but caught his words when he saw Brath coming from between the trunks and branches into the little clearing.

Mal didn't hesitate this time. He was on top of Brath immediately, and before a look of surprise had even crossed Brath's razor features, he had already suffered two blows to the head from Mal's malletlike fist.

Laura saw it happen, saw the sudden burst of determination and anger flash across Mal's grave features. In that one moment, she would have sworn he hated Brath, Brath's betrayal, more than anything in the world.

Remak was at Mal's side, standing over Brath's body, but Mike was caught, staring dumbly at that sudden absence of sky and the sudden presence of more forest.

"I'm not sure this is a tesseract at all," Remak said slowly, looking at the forest suspiciously through the lenses of his glasses.

"What difference does it make?" Mal asked him. "Isn't this the way out? And we'd better use it."

"Wait," Remak said. "Leave your cells here. We can be traced through them," he said to Mike's unwilling and uncompromising expression. "But in here they'll just be dead signals." Remak dropped his own where he stood.

"Mine was broken," Laura said. "It's back at home."

Mal flung his back into the forest behind them, and wasn't sorry to see it go.

Mike, sneering, looked as if he was considered winging his own cell directly at Remak. Instead, he let it fall to the dead grass.

"Let's get going," Mal said impatiently.

Remak nodded and moved into the brush. Mike, without his characteristic hesitation, followed, disappearing quickly into the green. Laura spared another look at Isabel and moved away, and Mal came directly behind her.

They moved through forest, not quite impenetrable, but still difficult going. Poked and scratched, torn and bedraggled, more than they had been from their climbing and hiking, they emerged after ten minutes onto a gentle slope that headed toward rolling hills alive with grass. It was warm here and there was wind, and the sun was in a sky magnificently blue.

They were at the top of a slope, and down from there they could see intermittent houses and, farther off to their right, a collection of buildings that resembled a town.

"Are we still in New York State?" Mal asked.

"I think so, judging by all these sugar maples." Remak was squinting at the trees.

"Someone there will know," Laura said, staring down at the town. "Or there'll be a sign nearby."

"So," Mike said, several steps ahead, "what are we waiting for?"

"We need to know what we're going to do," Remak said.

"Get the hell out of here and go back home." It was obvious, to Mike, at least.

"We need to find out who did this," Remak said. "Who *can* do this."

"Screw that," Mike said.

"Mike," Laura said, with a concern that disarmed him momentarily, "do you think we can just catch a bus and go home, that whoever did this is just going to leave us alone?"

"I don't bother them, they don't bother me."

"All right. Bye," Mal said, turning to the others. Mike bent his lips but didn't move on. He didn't particularly care for this new trend of being called out.

"I need to go speak to my people," Remak said.

"The CIA," Mike supplied, and was ignored.

"Will they know what this is all about?" Laura asked.

"They know something," Remak told her. "And they'll certainly be interested in what I have to tell them."

"I still need to find Tommy," Mal said, touching his

back pocket with the photograph. "I might be able to track Annie down."

"I need to know what's going on, too," Laura said. "What kind of a life I can have back."

"If they're hunting us," Mal said, "then splitting up makes their search harder. I'll go with Laura."

"You're kidding," Mike deadpanned. "Really?"

"If anything"—Remak mixed it around in his mind—"they wouldn't expect us to want you two on your own. This could work."

Laura looked at Mal's calm face. He was no older than she was, but they spoke to him as an adult, trusted him to do something like this. She was still somewhere in between to them, still saw expressions of pleasant surprise when adults heard her say something perceptive or wise. But she could see what they saw in Mal, too: the quiet, unconscious confidence that came with having survived whatever disaster his life had been up to now.

"We meet in Manhattan," Remak said. "Someplace anonymous and crowded. The big movie theater on Broadway and Thirteenth." He glanced down at his watch. "It's eleven forty-five. We meet there at this time, two days from now, no matter what."

He got nods from Mal and Laura.

"Don't use credit cards or bank cards or cells for anything. They're just pins in a map that can tell them where we are," Remak said. "Go. And take care."

Mal looked at Laura and got a nod, and they took off.

Mike watched them for just a moment, then started away as well.

"Wait," Remak said. "You need to stick with me."

"So, let's get the hell away from here, already."

Remak was watching the figures of Mal and Laura recede.

"Wait here," he said, and inexplicably started to turn back into the forest.

"What are you talking about? We have to go."

"We will in one minute. Wait here."

"Maybe," Mike muttered as Remak disappeared back into the dense forest toward the clearing that held only Isabel's body and Brath's unconscious form.

A minute later, Mike heard it echo sibilantly from out of the forest. The sound would never have reached Mal and Laura, let alone the houses far beyond. But there was no mistaking it from where Mike was: the crackling hiss of the gun that had ended Isabel's life, a sound he'd never forget.

Moments later, Remak reappeared, and without looking at Mike or slowing his pace, he hurried down the slope himself.

Mike, his hands suddenly trembling and his legs weak, followed.

# THE FIGHTER

AN OLD MAN WAS WALKING along a dirt path running parallel to the side of a paved road. He made little effort to hide his suspicion when two teenagers appeared from out of the field and asked him what town they were coming into.

"East Woodman," he told them in a cracked voice.

"In New York," Mal said, trying to sound as though he already knew it and was just mentioning it casually.

The man nodded.

"Somewhere we could catch a bus, sir?" Laura asked.

The man lifted a dry, bony finger and pointed back

down the road the way he had come, at the row of eight or nine buildings that was the center of town.

"General store," he said.

Laura smiled and thanked him, and she led Mal off in that direction.

East Woodman didn't have a main street; East Woodman *was* a main street. A garage, a bar, and the general store were interspersed with two houses and two trailers. Past the properties, back in the field, the figures of Remak and Mike were no longer apparent. They were making another approach, or Remak had browbeaten Mike into hiking on to the next town, wherever that was. The mountain they had come down from was only partially visible, swallowed up by thickening forest. Of the tesseract, or whatever that prison was, there was no sign at all.

In the general store, they were informed that a bus stopped out front, destined—eventually—for Port Authority, New York City, every Monday and Thursday, which was tomorrow, at around 1:30.

Laura paid forty-eight dollars for their tickets from the one hundred seventy-five dollars that remained of her emergency money. Mal made an embarrassed attempt to contribute the twelve dollars he had in his pocket only to have Laura wave it away.

"Is there someplace to stay in town?" Laura asked the proprietor sweetly, knowing how this must look.

"Ways down Route Ten," the woman behind the counter said with neither reprimand nor approval. "That way." She pointed for them.

They spent another seven dollars for sandwiches and drinks, which they wolfed and guzzled, seated on the stoop in front of the store, just beside its rusting air pump.

Laura took her wallet out, pulled cash and the hard photo of her parents hugging her in the snow. She looked at the scene and was struck hollow by the idea that, if she died, no one would remember that these people ever loved one another and the love would be forgotten, as though it had never even existed in the first place.

"You look happy," Mal said, looking over her shoulder at the picture. "All of you."

"I lost my past, Mal. That's where I come from. Without that, without them, I don't know where I'm going."

Mal looked down at his boots for some time. When he looked up, he stared straight into her eyes.

"I think you make your own future, Laura. And once you have, no one can take it away from you, either."

She looked at Mal, her bright blue eyes shining with sorrow and fear, and something else, too.

"What do you think is happening to us, Mal?"

"I think there's a secret machinery that makes the world work that we're not supposed to see, and we saw it. And now we're paying the price."

As she looked back at him, her face got hard, determined not to back down from the idea.

"But we're going to go back and get your brother out of it," she said. "And my parents, too."

She put her hand on his shoulder softly. Then she pushed herself up and walked over to the garbage can sitting by the door and took her wallet, filled with plastic cards that connected her to the world and maybe the secret machinery behind it, and tossed it in with the trash.

They hiked along Route Ten, not keen for more walking, but energized enough by the food in their bellies.

Three miles farther on was a dusty motel, squatting alone amidst an expanse of highway and grassy field.

Laura laid out another seventy-eight dollars for a single room.

"Single rooms only got one bed," the gawky counter man, little more than a teenager himself, said with a lascivious tone.

Mal was about to suggest separate rooms, but Laura cut him off.

"That's fine," she said with finality, holding her hand impatiently out for the key.

The room was tiny, but it had a shower, of which Laura gratefully availed herself. When Mal had finished, too, she was sitting on the side of the bed in her loose sweater. Both of them were nicked and scratched from top to bottom.

Mal would have been pleased to sleep on the sofa or in the tub, had the room contained either of those. But other than the bed, there was only a small table and a seat. Laura saw him eyeing the floor and spoke up.

"Mal, I didn't mean to make you uncomfortable, but this is all the money we have, and I don't think I could handle sleeping alone in a strange place tonight. I think we can sleep in the same bed after everything we've been through."

He nodded slowly then he lowered himself into the bed, at first with clear discomfort and then with a gushing breath of great relief.

Laura, amused at how such a large person could compress himself into the merest quarter of an already small bed, set herself down along the other side.

The room was dark and silent but for the hum of the air outside and the occasional thrum of a passing car.

"So," he said, staring at the ceiling. "You're a Mets fan?"

Laura glanced at her father's Mets cap sitting forlornly

on the table. "My dad is. Was. I guess he still is. I just don't know if he's my dad anymore. He gave it to me for my tenth birthday because that's how old he was when he got it." She could see her father's face in that moment, bearing the funny, lopsided grin that Laura sometimes saw smiling back at her in the mirror.

"It's nice to have a family that loves you," Mal said. "It makes you strong."

She wasn't sure if Mal was telling her or asking her. She rolled over so she was on her side and she curled her legs up to her chest and put her hands between her cheek and the pillow.

"What's Tommy like?" she asked. He could feel her bright blue eyes on the side of his face like a strobe light, studying his scars.

"God, I barely know him," he said with quiet disgust. "I left home early and I . . . I never went back for him."

"You know him, Mal," she said with absolute certainty. "He's your brother. What's he like?"

"He was always angry, itching for a fight," he said after a short time. "But once he started them, he fell apart. When he was young, he'd let go at my father, because he knew my father would sit and take it. But he'd never even look the wrong way at Sharon, my mother. When he got older, he was a skinny kid, never got my dad's build. He'd pick fights with bigger kids, and half the time, I ended up finishing them."

"An older brother who had to hide behind his younger brother." Laura said it as if she could feel the shame of it. And hearing it in Laura's voice, Mal tasted that shame himself for the first time.

"God, it made him so angry," he said.

"Not at you," Laura consoled.

"Definitely at me. Much angrier at me than at the kids who wanted to beat him."

"No, Mal," she said with a gentle smile that brooked no argument. "Angry at himself. Furious."

Mal's chest went hollow at the idea. He had been carrying around Tommy's anger for such a long, long time. It was moments before he could speak again.

"My father always said that, in a fight, you have to use your anger. If it uses you, you crash and burn."

"It's kinda the same with life, I think."

"It was for Tommy. And for Sharon."

"Your parents didn't get along," Laura said.

"My mother . . . doesn't really get along with anyone."

Laura looked at him, the scars masking with fierceness something quiet and sad and even innocent on his face. He had his hands under his head now, his tightly muscled arms spread at the sides. The cover exposed part of his chest, which also had nicks and welts, some of them recent enough to be raised and red.

She put her hand onto his chest, touching one of the marks gently. She felt him tense, but she kept her hand on his warm skin and moved it until she could feel the slow, steady beat of his heart. After a time, his hand came down and covered hers.

Laura's thoughts quieted. Ten minutes later, she could still feel Mal breathing shallowly and knew that sleep hadn't found him yet, either.

"Would you tell me about your father, Mal?"

He turned his head and looked down into her eyes, and she felt her heart stutter for an unexpected moment. Then he looked up again and let the memories out.

Mal sat in school, paying less attention even than usual. There was a bandage taped across the bridge of his nose, wet with blood from recent damage. An unusual sight on most eleven-year-olds. Unfortunately, it was not particularly surprising to see evidence of rough treatment on Mal; a bruise, a cut, a welt—his classmates barely noticed it anymore. What was surprising that day, to Mal as much as anyone, was to see his father in school, his bleary, roughed-up face rotating back and forth with confusion as he wandered down the hall peering through the windows in the doors. It was more surprising still to have him come into the classroom, interrupting the teacher, who was at first irate and then, sizing up the intruder, cautiously silent as the fighter put a big hand on his boy's shoulder and led him out of the room, down the hall, and out of the school.

He marched his boy into the subway and eventually to a beat-up old tenement, which Mal didn't recognize. The father took the son up three flights of stairs, unlocked a door with a key from his pocket, and brought him in. He sat down on a thick, dusty chair and stood his boy in front of him, hands on his shoulders, looking him straight in the eyes.

"This is home now, Mal," he said. Max's face was full of dents and dings. Even on days when no fight had come along for weeks, the face was puffy in places, trying to find its original form, unknown for many, many years.

"What do you mean?"

"We're not going back to your ma. That's gonna get you killed." He touched his boy's nose gently. Max had bandaged it himself, from the kit he kept in the bathroom. "You and me both."

The gash had been left across the bridge of Mal's nose last night. His mother had come stumbling back into the house, using one hand to steady herself on the wall and the other to bring a tall bottle half full of sloshing golden liquid to her slurring lips.

Mal had watched her from the seat where he read his book. Schoolwork was by and large ignored, but at the beginning of every week, his father brought home a book from the library, one for Mal and one for his older brother. Max didn't care if schoolwork got done, but those books had better be read by the end of the week or for a month there was no going out to the gym to watch the fights.

Now, Mal looked somberly over the cover of his book at his mother's return. And naturally, she saw the eyes, as she was meant to.

She began screaming at him about respect and how he goddamn well better not be looking at her, lying in wait every night for her return so he could judge her. Then her voice got quiet, and that was when Mal knew trouble, real trouble, was coming. He rose from the chair, intending to retreat to his room, where Tommy waited. Tommy would scream at Max, rail at him, while Max looked down with tired, drowning eyes. But Tommy would never let loose on Sharon. He was good at looking for a fight, except when one was really coming. Tommy knew it was one of his father's fight nights, and he knew what time it was, and he knew he should be in their room then, no matter what. Mal knew to be in his room at these times, too, but he never was.

Mal rose to leave now. His mother had struck him before, once or twice even tried to kick him. He was getting too big, though, and he could take the blows without flinching, and that would only enrage her more. So tonight he would retreat. And, for no reason in particular, tonight Sharon wasn't going to allow it. She admonished him in her harsh near-whisper not to dare walk out on her, and the bottle of liquor shot from her hand and blasted apart on the wall, inches from Mal's face. Had she meant to hit him with it or merely scare him? He never knew. But a shard of glass caught him across the bridge of the nose, deep enough so that the mark would never leave.

Max came home from fighting that night and saw his son sitting in the darkened room, the smear of red across the boy's face lit by flickering city lights through the sooty windows. Max took his boy into the bathroom and dressed the wound silently. Max finished the bandages and let out a long hard breath and shook his head.

The next day he collected his boy in school.

"But what about Tommy?" Mal asked, facing his father in his new home.

"I'm sorry, Mal. Tommy is . . . I don't know how I can explain this to you. Tommy is your mother's. I can't do a thing about that. It's always been that way. You were mine, and she gave you hell just like she gave me. And Tommy was hers. I can't make you understand any better than that."

Mal didn't understand at all. He had never seen his

father give up on anything, *anything*. Why should the first thing he ever gave up on be his own son?

So Mal cried. Wailed like an infant. For the first time in either of their lives, and for the last, Max grabbed his son and pulled him close and hung on to him so tight that it hurt. Mal went on and on with it, and Max never let go. Somewhere in that time, Mal felt his father's chest shaking, too. But it was a hard, tight shake, and Mal looked up and saw through his own tears that his father was not crying. His face was dry. It showed nothing; a blunt, stupid refusal to back down.

Mal saw Tommy in school, sometimes over the next year, more bruises on his face, his shoulders slumping a little bit worse each time. At first, Mal approached him, but Tommy turned away and hurried off to class. Eventually, Mal cornered him in the playground, grabbed him by the shirt, and pushed him up against a wall, demanding an explanation. Tommy kicked and spit and screamed, and Mal couldn't hold him any longer. The year after that, Tommy was gone. Sharon had moved to another place, another school district. Mal listened, waited for word of Tommy. It came: Tommy was getting beaten up, was stealing things, had been suspended, had moved again. Somewhere, in the space between the parents, the brothers had lost each other.

\*     \*     \*

Max worked at the gym all hours, filled it in with spare jobs at the dock, scrounging a pittance from six in the morning until nine or ten at night. On fight nights, it was later still. Mal would generally not see him until the next morning, purple and yellow in spots and maybe limping or favoring an arm, but with a particular set of his jaw and an upward line in his lips that was only there after a fight night. Sometimes he would sit with Mal and tell old stories, myths of men battling monsters until one was dead. That was all Max knew about: fighting and stories of men who fought and killed or died.

Mal would wake up, put the bacon on, and roust his father, and on some mornings his father would have new bruises and welts, even though there hadn't been a scheduled fight the night before. Max just shambled out to the table or off to work, slow and limping, once or twice even blind in one eye.

By the time he was thirteen, Mal was big, like his father. After school, two schoolmates would bring Mal to an old, dilapidated park. There, down a path, under a stone bridge that was rotting with moss and solitude, they entered him into bare-knuckle fights against amateur fighters. Not boys, these fighters, not other school kids looking for a rough time, but men who made a sick and dirty living at this. When Mal won, he got the cash prize, which sat on the ground in a pile held down by a rock until the fight was over. Mal started to come home bruised and battered himself on occasion, but that never bothered Max. Maybe, Mal wondered, it was even a badge of pride. Though he didn't have to wonder for long.

One afternoon, as Mal hunched on a rock with blood trailing a river down his face and onto his bare chest, a shadow fell across him.

"You hit like a pile driver, but you're too hot to throw a punch. It makes your guard too low on the right." His father was looking down at him.

Mal looked back, through a partial red blur. As always, his father's face was unreadable.

"How long have you known?" Mal asked.

"How long? Who do you think told those kids in your class to bring you here?"

"What?" The word stretched out in Mal's own ears as the world around him was drowned out by the suddenly shattering volume of his heartbeats.

"I would have taken you myself, Mal, but I didn't want them to see us together right away. I thought they might make it extra hard on you or something."

Was Mal supposed to thank him? Be grateful or proud, revolted or terrified? He felt none of those things. That was the moment Mal realized he was all alone in the world.

At fifteen, Mal started working at the gym after school. One day, as inexplicably as Sharon deciding to hurl that bottle, Tommy showed up at the gym. He was taller now, but had always been thin and still was. His face, though, had become like his mother's: hard, resentful, unyielding.

"Heard you were working here now," Tommy said, as though they were simply old pals who had a hard time staying in touch.

Mal nodded, in terror of saying the wrong thing and maybe driving Tommy off forever.

"I'm gonna get a job, too, soon as I can; get out of the house. Mom's got a new guy. It's not working so well for me."

"Are you all right, Tommy?" Mal asked.

"Yeah." Tommy looked up, insulted. "I'm fine. Her shit can't hurt me." He was angry now. It toppled out of him, as it always had, like an uncontrollable flood. "You can't hurt me, either, Mal. You ran away." His face was red and he skewered the air between them with an accusing finger. "You and Dad both."

Mal backed down, tried to calm him. He asked if they could meet somewhere, for a sandwich, maybe. Just to talk. Tommy agreed and never showed up.

On the first night of Big Black, the first of those fourteen nights of intermittent darkness and catastrophe, Mal raced through the chaotic, crying streets to the apartment he shared with his father. After all the blows to the head and face, the old man could barely see straight when the lights were *on*. Mal let himself in and immediately heard a sound.

Even over the shouts and roars from the street, it was instantly recognizable as crying. But from his father's room? Was someone already here with him? Mal shot through the darkness and found his father, startling the older man badly as he grabbed him by the shoulders.

"Dad?" he said into the murky shadow. "Are you all right? What's going on?"

He got Max at exactly the right time, in the dead of night, in the dark, with the city falling apart outside. At his absolute weakest, the old man couldn't resist giving an answer.

"I've got cancer, Mally," he said between tears and sucking in air. "It's in my gut. Or that's where it started, anyway. They couldn't do anything about it. Not that I could have afforded it, anyway."

"Jesus, Dad," Mal said, something beneath him crumbling away. "How long do you have?"

"Well"—his father actually looked like he was smiling

in the dim moonlight through the window, tears catching and glittering in the curves around his lips—"they gave me six months."

"Jesus," Mal whispered.

"But that was twelve years ago." Max grinned. "So who the hell knows?"

"What? Twelve *years?*"

"Yeah."

"You've had cancer for twelve years?" Mal said. Even as he did, he realized it had come out wrong. His father had been *fighting* cancer for twelve years. That was why he was still alive.

"Days are painful. It helps to let go a little bit at night. Sorry I scared you, Mally."

Mal looked down at him and laughed. What else could you do?

And a matter of months later, Max Jericho finally went down. It wasn't the cancer. A week before he died, the old fighter had retired from the ring.

# THE INTRUDER

THE NEXT MORNING, the bus came and took Laura and Mal
for a five-hour ride. It stopped at towns here and there, each
one getting progressively larger until they were on a thruway
and through a tunnel and finally onto streets suffocated by long
gray shadows cast off of towering gray buildings.

At Port Authority, the silvery gazes of MCT officers
greeted them. The subway headed downtown was dense with
faceless, preoccupied figures, and Laura found herself hyper-
aware of any person glancing at them for a second too long.
It seemed to Laura as if everyone was gazing at her intently
from behind her back or just out of her peripheral vision.

The last time Laura had come to the city—the last time *before* her life fell apart—had been for an impromptu weekend shopping jaunt with her mother. She had been in one of these vast rat-and-cockroach warrens the city referred to as the subway when the car had ground to a halt and sat there in the dingy tunnel for nearly an hour. She remembered with disturbing clarity the dull looks on the other passengers' faces, more resigned than upset, really. The dead faces, many retreating into the comforting companionship of their cells, waited for the MCT to come through the dark tunnel and haul them all out. Laura had wondered then if no help had come or if the train hadn't started up again, would those other passengers have bothered to get off their asses and hike out? Or had the Con Edison attack robbed them of something so integral that they would have just sat there, tapping away at their cells until they starved to death?

"When did this city give up?" Laura asked Mal, looking sideways at the numb faces around her now.

Mal watched them, too, staring at their cells or at the HDs, or at nothing at all.

"After Big Black," he said, "the lights went back on, but . . ."

"But they never came out of the dark," she said.

"Dark. Yes. Enough to eat us all alive."

She closed her eyes and rested her head on Mal and searched for his heartbeat.

The sign was well faded, but it still said JERICHO'S. They went up the dirty steps and into the big room, where the smell of worn leather and honest effort brought him comfort. They stood at the door, Laura soaking in the atmosphere with a curious expression and a crinkled nose, watching someone pound the bag, another man jump rope, neither of whom had turned to see Mal yet. And there in the office, amidst a fog of cigar smoke, sat a gruff, stubby-looking man.

"That's Stoagie," Mal whispered, his eyes fixed on the man. She could see the anticipation travel down his body like a physical sensation. He grabbed Laura's hand and hurried them toward the office.

By the window was a wall displaying pictures and trophies. It was crowded, and many of the images held a young Mal in their frames. He was ten, shaking hands with Stoagie in front of the gym. He was fifteen, sweating and with a bruise on his face, and on either side of him Stoagie and a man who must have been Max were holding up his gloved hands. He was a little boy, giving his father a sock on the chin, his father pretending to reel backward from it. Laura looked at the younger face—fewer scars, brighter eyes—and tried to find the Mal she knew in it.

Stoagie had come out of the office and was standing outside in slacks and shirtsleeves. Mal had described him on the bus ride, an old coach and corner man. He looked every inch of it, grizzled and mean and invincible.

Stoagie eyed the incongruous young lady and nodded at Mal's approach. Mal had stopped dead, not receiving the smile and gruff hug he had expected as greeting.

"Ben Carmichael," Stoagie said, offering his hand. "Welcome. You interested in our place?"

Mal forced his hand out, cold and numb, and swallowed weakly as he shook the other man's.

"You look like you've done some boxing in your life," Stoagie said. "Whereabouts?"

"Around," Mal said in a tone that was rigid and hollow. Stoagie nodded, waiting for more. Mal looked at the wall near them. "Is it true Max Jericho used to coach here?"

"Sure. Used to own a piece of it. That's why his name's over the door."

"What about Max Jericho's son?"

"Sorry?" Stoagie squinted.

"Didn't Max Jericho have a son?"

"Not that I know of," Stoagie said, "and I knew him for a long time. So, no."

Laura could see that it would have been less painful if he had struck Mal with a sledgehammer in the gut. Mal's hands actually went to his stomach, and she could feel his suddenly labored breathing through the hand she had put gently on his back.

"Who's this boy in the picture?" Laura asked. Stoagie came around and squinted at the images in question.

"That's Max," he said of the picture where Mal was punching his father. "Don't know which boy you mean."

Mal stared at this old man he had known all his life, now a collaborator or a pawn or something even worse.

"I'm a friend of Nikolai Brath's," Mal finally came up with in a voice so weak, Laura barely recognized it. "Seen him around lately?"

"You know Brath?" Stoagie looked mildly interested. "I haven't seen him in a bunch a days, actually."

"I haven't seen him, either," Mal said, and Laura saw his eyes shining with moisture. "That's why I came around."

"Ah." Stoagie stuck his cigar into his mouth and munched it in thought. "Well, if you see him, tell him we're looking for him."

"I will."

And Mal stood, uncertain what exactly to do, until Laura's hand curled around his and she led him toward the stairs. The men there watched them go, but no one said a word.

\*       \*       \*

"I'm so sorry," she said to him when they were back on the subway. She was holding his hand as tight as she could, but his had gone slack. "We need to find someone else, someone at school, maybe."

Mal shook his head. It was a life she could hardly imagine herself, going somewhere every day with no friends, no one to talk to, just whiling away the hours.

"Your foster parents?"

"If they got Stoagie, the Fosters won't know me, either. They barely knew me before all this."

"What do you mean?"

"When my father died, I was supposed to go back to my mother. I could see the problem with that, but it seemed like it might be a way back to Tommy, too, to make up for leaving. And to have at least part of a family again. My *own* family. It didn't matter, though. She wouldn't take me. She filed papers with the court, said I was threatening and abusive."

"They believed her?" Laura was incredulous.

Mal's jaw was tight, fighting the explanation.

"Tommy," he said, "gave testimony backing her up."

"Oh, Mal." She touched his face.

"That was the last thing I ever heard about him, before all this started." Mal's face was a flat blank. "So I went into foster care. It didn't really take. I snuck out sometimes. When I came back a little beat up, they thought I was into drugs or something. They kicked me out after a few months. The next one, the father knew who my dad was, wanted to see if I was as tough. I learned. I learned that I don't have to get to know them or let them get to know me. I learned we don't actually have to *be* a family, that I can stick it out until I'm eighteen. It's less than a year now, then no more school, no more foster parents. I just go and live my life."

She looked at Mal. He didn't put up a fight, he had said. But that's exactly what he was doing. Not with his mother, maybe, but with his own life. He could easily have bunked in the gym, asked Stoagie or even Brath for help. But he stuck it out in foster care and at school, both of which clearly held no interest for him, because to walk away from them would be giving up.

"Then there's only one place to go, isn't there?" she said quietly.

They came to the eastern edge of Manhattan, where the huge gray dome shone dully, like a bug's carapace. Its bloated body, the size of a tidal wave, loomed over everything and looked as if it were preparing to swallow buildings whole. The creature's shadow spread across the surrounding neighborhood, and the air smelled of something nauseatingly metallic. The buildings around Mal and Laura were cracked and decrepit, as though the shade of the thing were eroding them, and they could feel its presence like a physical weight. People had scrawled their despair low down on the shell's surface. *We got what we deserved,* claimed one message in bleeding paint. *The Old Man did this—what will He do next?* asked another fading entreaty.

Mal led her finally to a squatting, dirty building, and they stopped at the metal door with the wire-reinforced window. He stared at it long enough that Laura put her hand on his arm and squeezed it softly.

"Do you want me to come up with you?"

He stood silent, then shook his head once and pushed his way in.

The city was running out of Starbucks. The vast corporate dynamo seemed to have given up on the city as the city had started to give up on itself. Once ubiquitous, these commercial shrines to coffee-worship were now so sparse as to be nearly forgotten. But here, amid the cracking buildings, in sight of the dome itself, Laura had found one, remaining perhaps as an outpost to witness the final decline and internment of the city and its people.

She sat sipping coffee that was too sweet, looking around her. Remak had said to find places that were crowded and anonymous. She had shelled out five dollars and forty-eight cents from their dwindling supply of cash and had to suffer for it, too, because paying cash meant having to type your order and feed your money into the sticky and neglected manual order-station.

Other people beamed their orders from their cells to the express order-station and lined up to collect their drinks. Then they sat around, sipping, engaging with the same cells, looking up distractedly from time to time, blinking at the flickering HDs mounted on each of the walls. Laura stared at one absently, showing a dignified man with perfect hair speaking soundlessly from in front of rows and rows of body bags laid out in the background. A picture of Isabel, a hole over her left eye, burned unexpectedly into Laura's head.

The world was slipping away from them. Now, with their regular food and drink orders digitized into their cells, they could simply use the order stations and didn't even have to bother with the most rudimentary human contact of asking for something to eat or drink. The world was slipping away from these people, all right, and something else was slipping in. They were forgetting to care. When they finally bothered to look up, there would be nothing to keep them going. They'd never even put up a fight, because they let desolation consume them bit by bit without even knowing it.

Shadow poured in the window instead of light. The vast smudge of the dome was nearly all you could see through the window. *If* you bothered to look out at it. Laura's eyes moved from face to face, wanting one of them to look up from a cell and out, to see the darkness infecting them; just *see* it.

She rose and tossed her coffee disgustedly into the garbage. She walked out and went to wait for Mal, unconsciously huddling her body as she walked along the edge of the dome.

At the sound of the bell, Sharon Graham pulled herself away from the flickering faces on the television and, more painfully, from the glistening bottle sitting on the counter.

On the other side of the door was a big man with broad shoulders wearing dirty cargo pants and a dirty T-shirt. He was a kid, really, but his face was bruised and marked like he'd gone fifteen rounds with a pro or three. He was looking at her queerly, expectantly.

"Yeah?" she said, when he offered nothing but his mute gaze.

"Sharon," he said, as though trying to shake her out of a trance.

"Yeah?" She had a buzz starting, a warm light suffusing the edges of her vision. But she would surely have recognized someone who looked like this, and she'd never seen him before in her life.

The look on his face got stranger still, from shock to—almost too briefly to discern it—desperation, to disgust, and hell if she was going to stand in her own goddamned door-way and let some stranger be disgusted with her. She swung the door closed, but his hand came up fast and stopped it dead.

"It's Mal," he said in a hard voice, and when she only squinted back, his body shifted, loosened, lost some of its tension. She wondered briefly and distantly why she would be so acutely aware of the expressions and body language of a total stranger, and particularly in her state. "My name is Mal," he said again, in a softer tone.

"What can I do for you, Mr. Mal?" She hoped the sar-casm came through.

"I'm"—he blinked twice—"I'm looking for Tommy. I'm a friend of his. It's very important that I see him."

"Good luck," she said. "I have no idea where he is."

She flinched back as utter rage reddened his face. He poured into the room, shoving her casually out of his way, and when she felt his strength, she realized if he'd pushed harder, he could easily have broken her against the wall.

"What the hell are you doing?" she shouted after him, her voice both slurred and shaking. "My husband will be home any minute!" What a joke that was. George was about a third this kid's size.

The intruder stopped in her living room, looking left and right, searching for something.

"Pictures," he demanded.

"What?"

"Pictures, photos, an album you have of your family."

"I don't have—"

"Show them to me!" he thundered.

She grabbed her cell from the tabletop, keyed for the album. He ripped it from her hand, glared down at it, then threw it on the floor.

"Older pictures," he demanded. "From your first marriage."

Who the hell was this kid? Her body worked almost mechanically, went to the small closet, removed a thick book with hard photos crammed into it, and held it out before him.

He took it, opened it to a page.

"Who is this?" he said, pointing at a picture of her and Max, long ago, sitting at a table in a restaurant where they used to go to dance after a night at the fights.

"That's my first husband, Max," she told him.

He whipped through more pictures.

"This." He jabbed at another picture. She looked down and saw little Tommy playing with her sister Nancy's two girls from years and years ago. She hadn't seen them, or her sister, in person for more than a decade.

"Tommy and my nieces. They—"

"No!" he screamed in her face. "That's my brother and me!"

She shook her head desperately at him, her mouth agape. Was he saying that she and Max had been his parents? She and Max had Tommy, and that was it for them, *more* than enough. The trouble that kid caused, who would ever want another? The intruder flung both albums away. He pulled a picture from his pocket, Tommy and a girl she had never seen before.

"How dare you give up on him?" he said, his voice suddenly as quiet as death, conveying far more rage and danger than his hollering had.

She was sure he was going to hammer her into a bloody pulp with those terrible, jagged knuckles of his.

"Hello?" came George's voice from the hall, and she was blessedly relieved for just an instant until she saw that her visitor had taken George's arrival as a cue to start looking through the house again. He walked straight by her, ignoring the figure in the hall, and went into the bedroom.

"George." She hurried to him.

"What the hell is going on?" George saw the man and her obvious consternation.

She explained to him what she could while the intruder walked back past her, with George, ineffectually stuttering threats, storming after him. George could yell at the guy and threaten to call the police, but that was about it. Some men would fight even knowing they couldn't win, or fool themselves into thinking they could win. But George was not that kind of man. Sometimes she hated him for it and sometimes she loved him for it, but she never wondered how she ended up with him. Her father had been a quiet man with vast reservoirs of violence tumbling beneath. George was a quiet man with vast reservoirs of more quiet beneath.

"Time for you to get out of my house," George said from a safe distance of nine or ten feet.

The intruder had stopped in the kitchen, staring at the bottle sitting on the counter. He glared at Sharon briefly, then turned back and snatched up the bottle by its neck. George stumbled backwards, putting his arms out in an attempt to protect his wife, as the intruder turned it over, clear liquid pulsing out and splashing on the floor, then flung it as hard as he could against a far wall.

It blasted apart, showering glass and liquor in a wide area. George and Sharon stared, paralyzed, as the intruder walked up to them.

"How could you let this happen?" He burned them with his glare. "You're supposed to protect your children."

He walked away and slammed the door behind him so hard that their ears rang with the harsh echo of it.

# THE COOPERATIVE

REMAK AND MIKE, their faces grim, were waiting for Mal and Laura among the crowds in the movie theater.

"I assume," Remak said when they reached him, "you've discovered that Laura's problem now extends to all of us."

"You, too?" Laura said, her eyes like those of a drowning woman who's just had a potential savior push her head deeper underwater.

Mike looked beaten by it, worn down to a husk. Only Remak seemed beyond pain. He nodded and rubbed the back of his head, recalculating his equation with the new numbers.

She wondered about Remak: Who had forgotten him? Where did he no longer belong? Maybe, Laura considered, that wasn't as important as his reaction. This was all starting to seem like a science experiment to him.

"Are you okay, Jon?" She asked him for her and Mal's sakes as well as his. They were looking to him for their next move.

"I'm frustrated, naturally," he said. "Without the cooperative, our choices are very limited."

"I meant, how are you dealing with it? Where's your head at?"

"What's that got to do with anything?" he said, and before she could press him further, he nodded out the door. "Let's get going."

He walked out with purpose, and they, of course, had no choice but to follow.

Where he led them was to a parking lot rising seven stories from Forty-Fourth Street up toward the soggy gray sky. He spoke to the attendant, and they exchanged information and items. The four of them got onto the elevator and went to the top floor, where the cars were scattered intermittently, several with a rental car logo swooshing across their sides.

Remak took a quick inventory of their choices and went straight to one of them and pulled a keycard from his pocket that opened the doors. They climbed in, Laura getting the front passenger seat by default, though she'd have far preferred sitting next to Mal in back.

Remak, in the driver's seat, scanned the area through the windshield and then took the gun from the small of his back.

"What the hell are you doing?" Laura's eyes went wide, and she felt a shifting in the back seat.

Remak reversed his grip on the weapon and began hammering at the GPS panel in the dashboard with the butt of the automatic. Laura pulled herself away as metal and plastic shrapnel sprang out onto the seats.

"A GPS works both ways," Remak informed her. "A car with a GPS could be tracked as easily as a person with a cell." His arm worked back and forth, but the expression on his face didn't change.

Once he had turned the thing into a jagged cavity, he leaned over, peered inside, and jammed his hand into it. He tugged hard and came out with a small chip, trailing wires. This he tossed out through an open window, and then, as though strapping in for a ride through the country, he buckled up.

"Where are we going?" Mal said.

"That's complicated," Remak said, starting the engine.


They drove. Mike wasn't heeding the other human beings around him anymore. He looked out the window at the trees and fields that flashed by along the side of the highway. The sun, which had appeared after the city was long behind them, was just starting to duck below the horizon, and a bright point of reflection flickered in his eyes as the trees opened here and there to let it shine through.

"I work for a cooperative," Remak said through the hum of the car, "whose efforts are concerned with cataloging the social flow in the world. There are certain details of human life that serve as red flags, warnings of upcoming events. Like when you hear thunder and you know rain is coming. It's a matter of discerning our collective social unconscious and watching it closely. This is a phenomenon we call the Global Dynamic."

He glanced over at Laura in the passenger seat, who nodded back at him, before he continued.

"There are things you might never think to associate with one another, things you'd never even think to compare, that are tied together as tightly as our conscious and unconscious minds. In Middle Eastern nations, the consumption of chickpeas, a mainstay of the Middle Eastern diet, drops sharply before a shakeup in governance occurs, a coup, for example. Western Europeans and Middle Americans tend to let the upkeep of their lawns and gardens slip shortly before financial recessions. In the United States, sales of action figures skyrocket before our country engages in military actions."

"Action figures?" Laura said.

"Yes. The little dolls that children, mainly boys, play with. Their sales are an indicator of when this country's aggression is on the rise. There may not be anything in the papers about foreign trouble; the issues may not have even come to a boil at the highest levels of government; yet the sales of action figures boom. Our attitudes are bound together not merely on the level of individual contact but like a giant body of water that ripples all over even when a tiny pebble is thrown in at one small corner. Few people *know* the aggression even exists yet, but we feel it. All of us feel it. And some of us act on it. We buy action figures. These feelings, these indicators, are called the Global Dynamic."

Laura glanced behind her: Mal listening intently, Mike in a dead stare locked on nothing. She wanted to prod him, let him know something important was happening, but Mike looked as if his mind had taken him so far away that he wasn't really here anymore, just a man digitally inserted into an environment he wasn't a part of.

Behind them, the dome, glimpsed between buildings, edging over roofs, receded as they left the city behind. It had become such a part of what the city was that Laura couldn't even imagine the city anymore without the image of it being slowly swallowed by the thing.

"So we catalog these indicators," Remak said, "and we watch them, and when there's an obvious anomaly, either an aberration from previous statistics or indicators suddenly pointing toward something significant, we investigate."

"And that's what you were investigating this time?" Laura asked.

"Yes." Remak nodded slowly. "The occurrence of desolated response—that is, behavior indicative of apathy or desperation on a large scale such as street crime, domestic violence, and suicide. The occurrence of desolated response experienced a massive spike in the neighborhood of Mike's school." Mike looked up absently, having heard his name, then looked away again just as quickly. "A certain level of desolated response is standard in low-income, high-need neighborhoods, and while the sudden rise was astonishing, it wasn't the only notable element.

"Out of fourteen acts of random violence, five of them had been committed by people of widely varying demographics simply passing through the neighborhood. A teenage girl who had just disembarked from a bus, for instance, attacked her mother. The family, who owned a chain of Laundromats, were quite well to do. Of thirty-one reported domestic disturbances, eight were likewise committed by people who just happened to be in the neighborhood. A stockbroker began beating his wife as they passed through the neighborhood on the way to a restaurant. The traffic accidents actually reflected a higher number of perpetrators among those driving through, especially taxi drivers. Even among the shocking twelve suicide attempts, four of them had been by visitors: two cheerleaders, for instance, from out of town and separated from their group, were waiting for a train and threw themselves in front of it.

"Of course, we know the cause now," Remak concluded. "To some degree."

"The doorway," Mal said hollowly.

"Yes. The building you were in contained some sort of psychic virus. But when the door was left inadvertently open, it escaped through Mike's school and into the outlying neighborhood, affecting everyone who lived there, or was just passing through."

Laura could see Mal's face without turning to look, could see the guilt twisting deeper into his eyes.

"What do you mean, 'psychic virus'?" Laura said, thinking of the darkness crawling into the Starbucks, how it seemed to actually infect the people within.

"It's a hypothesis," he said. "A convenient name for a pathogen that thrives in the environment of human synaptic transmissions. Its form is unknown, but it has the capacity to alter human perception and information storage. It could even, conceivably, control its host's actions."

"That's exactly what this is!" Laura said with more vehemence than she was expecting.

"Possibly." Remak glanced at her with interest. "Much of the Global Dynamic is founded on similar thinking, that ideas multiply and transmit in a viral fashion, though documented proof is difficult to come by. I had been hoping to bring the information we had to my superiors, but when I tried this morning, well, you can imagine what happened. I'm lucky to be here and not in some basement interrogation room."

"What is this cooperative you work for?" Laura said. "A cooperative between who?"

"The cooperative is all funded by anonymous individuals and entities, collaborating interests outside the standard sociopolitical superstructure. We don't take a cent from government or industry; it's in our mandate. But we do recruit from government and industry, for our analysts, investigators, and theorists. Any field operative may be required to analyze, interpret, and act on any intelligence gathered. Multiple areas of expertise are required even before recruitment: economics, advanced mathematics, logic, strategic systems, game theory. Then the training: tactics, close-quarters combat, firearms, counter-insurgency, demolitions."

"You?" Mal asked.

Remak nodded.

"I used to work for the IRS."

"Sorry." Mal leaned forward. "The IRS?"

"They're not all accountants, Mal." Remak smiled only

a little. "Some of their operations require more field know-how than military operations."

Mal nodded and sat back, trying to decide whether or not that could possibly be true.

"The cooperative was created to pursue avenues opened by the Global Dynamic, a theory developed by one man, culled from years of research in the corporate field. You see, after 9/11 there was an upsurge in government interest in the Global Dynamic. My cooperative predicted something like Big Black months ahead of time." Remak let out a long breath. "But governments work from a philosophy of definite, provable necessity: does this *need* to be done for things to keep working? Corporations, on the other hand, work from a philosophy of investment: will attention *now* profit us later?

"The kind of thinking—about social structures and interactions—that led to the Global Dynamic existed long before 9/11 and Big Black, and corporations saw its efficacy long before the government did. Corporations were collecting numbers on such social interactions decades ago for marketing purposes."

"So this one man," Laura said, "the one who developed the Global Dynamic, he worked for a corporation. Who is he?"

"I don't know his name. No one does. He's kept it well hidden. Even my superiors never knew it, though he was our primary consultant for many years and, I believe, a major benefactor of the cooperative. He was once a lower-echelon administrator, a corporate librarian for a company based in California called Intellitech. They collected raw data on human interactions and responses to a vast array of stimulation and input the world over. The company was founded by two graduate students with degrees in the field, and consequently, Intellitech's efforts in this area were far in advance of its competitors. Various departments accumulated the data, but this librarian was the first to collate it all.

"He saw ramifications, and he created the Global Dynamic rubric. It was a predictor of human behavior that was to be a great boon to human knowledge and understanding. But Intellitech saw other possibilities for it, far more . . . profit oriented. Any corporation would.

"They weren't just interested in how to read the Global Dynamic, but in how to push it one way or another. In essence, how to *make* people think and feel according to the corporate agenda. Corporations were interested in how to get an entire city or state or nation to move in a desired way by faking this Global Dynamic, by creating the symptom and, in effect, having the symptom create the disease."

"Like launching a massive increase in action-figure marketing," Laura tested, "and *causing* the military action to follow in its path."

"Exactly." Remak nodded. "Reverse-engineering the

Global Dynamic. Imagine what an arms manufacturer could do with the ability to manipulate a nation's aggression by, say, contracting a toy manufacturer to launch a multimillion-dollar marketing campaign for a particularly militaristic new line of action figures. There's no more producing the goods and waiting for the demand. With this kind of control, you can manufacture the demand as easily as the product itself."

Heavy silence fell on the car.

"In any event," Remak continued eventually, "the Librarian broke off from Intellitech, began using the Global Dynamic to serve other causes. As I said, he was once a great help to our cooperative. He was like an information dynamo, a living computer. He had always been private, though. His name was never disclosed. And, a few years ago, he cut himself off completely, with no warning, no explanation. He went away, wouldn't consult or advise; he just kept taking reports, collecting information. He still does. Reams of data go in; nothing comes out."

"What happened?" Laura asked.

Remak gave a small shrug and touched his glasses.

"We think he figured something out, saw something coming that none of the rest of us could, and it was so terrible, he removed himself."

"What do you think?" Laura persisted.

"I think," Remak said, "I'm going to ask him myself."

# THE LIBRARIAN

"I THOUGHT NO ONE KNEW where the Librarian was," Mal said.

"No one *knows* where he is," Remak responded, looking through the windshield and scanning the large house and sprawling lawn cut by the long shadows of twilight. "But there are educated theories. The one I favor was corroborated by another agent, who claimed to have traced the route of certain electronic files transmitted to the Librarian."

"Traced them to here," Laura said, her eyes gazing somewhat mournfully over the still and tranquil expanse, not altogether dissimilar to her own town.

"For isolation, it's rather an ideal choice," Remak said.

Laura could hardly argue that. Given the condition of the GPS, they'd had to stop at a gas station to find a paper map. Laura had been flabbergasted to discover that such quaintly antiquated things still existed, and she'd had a crash course in how to navigate by them, as Mike was categorically useless, gazing out the window dimly as though the world were diminishing while he watched. It had taken them long enough to find the minuscule town of Pope Springs, Remak's first landmark, and then another hour to track this house down based on his complicated triangulation methods.

"So . . ." Mal hesitated, and silence filled the space. "Do we just knock on the door?"

"Yes," Laura said resolutely.

"Absolutely not," Remak said at the same time.

They looked at each other, and something crossed Remak's usually placid face. Was he impressed that she was stepping up, or irritated?

"I'm going to reconnoiter," he said. "You wait here."

"Listen." Laura put her hand on Remak's arm, and Mal felt an unexpected pang of jealousy. "You need him to trust us, right? Suppose you snoop around and he catches you. How's that going to look to him?"

Remak looked back up at the house, a gothic construction of wood with curtains drawn over all the windows. It presented a distinctly unwelcoming picture.

"Yes," he said, at the very least always able to see good sense. "You're right." He held his eyes on the house a moment longer and opened his door even as Laura opened hers.

He stopped. "What are you doing?" he asked her.

She looked at him and back at Mal and Mike, neither of whom had moved to exit the car.

"Uh," she said, "going with you."

"Laura"—he looked at her sharply—"this man is a recluse and probably for very good reason. He's not going to—"

"What's less threatening," Laura countered, "a scary stranger by himself or a dude with an innocent-looking young girl?"

Remak removed his glasses and rubbed the bridge of his nose.

"All right," he said quietly. "Let's go."

"All of us," Mal said from the back.

Remak froze at the door again, his chin falling to his chest and his eyes closed.

"She's not going into that messed-up-looking place without me," Mal said.

Remak was uncharacteristically speechless. He looked at the two of them: Mal's flat resolution, the tiny smile crawling up the corners of Laura's lips.

He shook his head in resignation and finally got out of the car.

"Mike," Laura said. "Mike! Let's go."

Mike snapped to attention and looked around as if for the first time, then slowly departed the car with the rest of them.

They crossed the gravel road from the place beneath a shaggy tree where the car was nominally obscured. They trailed the curving dirt driveway up to the house, their shadows casting weirdly elongated monsters across the grass of the lawn.

"Hang back," Remak said to Mal and Mike as they neared the door. "Please."

Remak and Laura went up a short flight of four stone steps and stood before a large wooden door with an antique knocker on it. Laura's hand came up, but Remak's hand shot out and got to it first, lifting and banging the heavy thing three times.

They waited in a chilly breeze, the sounds of the first crickets beginning to ring in the evening. Remak knocked again.

After a minute, they exchanged glances and Laura shrugged. What now?

"Sir," Remak said to the door, "my name is Jon Remak. I . . . I'm associated with the cooperative. I'm here on a matter of some urgency."

He looked around the doorframe, at the lintels of the roof, anywhere there might be a camera.

"Please," Laura said to the door, knowing her tone was a beseeching one, knowing it always convinced her parents to tack an extra hour on to curfew. "We have nowhere else to go."

No response.

"Maybe this is the wrong place," Mal said from behind them.

"Please," Laura said again, and now there was no mistaking the ache in her voice. "No one knows who we are. No one remembers us. We need your help."

There was an anxious moment of silence, then a click.

Laura looked at Remak, whose attention was now riveted on the door. Feeling as though she'd earned the right, she pushed it.

There was a large if minimally appointed foyer. A table on one side and a large couch on the other flanked a flight of old wooden stairs traveling up to a dark balcony. Remak stepped in first, then the rest came. The door closed behind them, sealing off the outside world. The interior of the house was a set piece, furnished and well-ordered, but like an artifice, untouched and empty of more than just people.

"What are your names?" A voice reverberated through

the room. It was so clear and vibrant that only electronic alteration could have achieved it.

"Remak. Jon Remak."

"Laura Westlake."

"Mal Jericho."

"Mike," he said when Laura nudged his shoulder. "Just Mike."

"You've come here"—the electronic voice filled the room—"because you approached this cooperative and they turned you away?"

"No, sir, not precisely," Remak said. "I'm a field analyst. Used to be a field analyst. I was . . . kidnapped, for lack of a better word, during an inquiry. When I escaped and returned to make my report, no one remembered me. I wasn't even on their files, or so they claimed. I understand that's hard to—"

"No," said the voice. "Not at all, unfortunately. And you, Laura. Who forgot you?

"My parents." Her voice was all but dead.

"I'm very sorry," the voice said. "Jon, you and Laura may come up. You'll forgive me, but I need to limit my exposure."

"No," Mal said, a gentle but heavy hand falling on Laura's shoulder.

"This is our only opportunity, Mal." Remak's voice was low and harsh. "You're going to have to trust me now."

Unconvinced by Remak's demand, Mal allowed his arm to fall to his side only when Laura touched his hand and nodded at him.

Remak and Laura turned toward the stairway.

"Up the stairs and through the door at the left," the voice directed them.

Together, they climbed the stairs, and the door clicked as they came to it. They pushed it open and disappeared into shadow.

Mal watched and, at the last sight of them, scowled.

"This seems like a bad idea," he said up to the shadows. He turned and looked at Mike. "What do you think's going to happen up there?"

Mike looked at him without expression for a moment, then, taking a deep breath and setting his shoulders, he rejoined the world around him all at once.

"They'll be tortured and killed. But don't let it get you down, kid. We're all gonna be dead inside a few days."

Mal's eyes burned into him.

"You've been a zombie since we left the city, and now you come out with that? What the hell's wrong with you?"

"Are you joking?" Mike said, with something of his old acid. "What's wrong? Are you blind and deaf and retarded?"

"Do you see Laura shutting down? Remak?" Mal demanded hotly. "Are they any better off than you?"

"You're goddamned right they are." Mike nearly shouted it back at him, his voice reverberating up the empty walls. "Know why? Because they *care.* Yesterday, Remak puts me in a grocery store and tells me to wait while he checks with his people. When he comes back, he tells me that no one remembers us, that we're somehow disconnected from our entire lives, anyone we ever knew and loved. So I make a few calls from a paycell and guess what? He's right. And I'm thinking, 'Holy shit, this is hell.' But when I'm over the shock and I'm thinking it through, about what it means to me specifically, I realize: it doesn't matter at all. I never met my old man; my mother has nothing but grief for me. My students, I don't miss any of them. I haven't got any friends worth a damn." Mike leaned closer, nearly into Mal's face, though his voice didn't lower. "My whole fucking life, it was so empty that when someone took it away from me, I don't even miss it.

"Remak and Laura had their lives taken away, but they want them back. I had mine taken, and I don't care. My mother was right all along: I don't matter at all."

His eyes burned into Mal from inches away, challenging him to find a solution to that.

And Mal couldn't. Was his own life so different? He had essentially been alone, even before his father left him. So he glared back at Mike, never willing to be the first one to walk away.

Eventually, Mike's eyes cooled and he walked away with a sneer. Mal watched his back as Mike stalked to a window, yanked the curtain away, and turned his gaze on the empty, darkening lawn outside.

Remak and Laura passed into a long hallway of rich, dark wood. There were two doors along one side and a single door on the other, and at the far end, across from them, another door. Laura looked up at Remak and they proceeded forward until, as they came to the single door, it clicked sharply in the murky silence.

Remak pushed it open.

"The doors here are heavy," he whispered to her. "Reinforced with metal inside."

Metal, indeed. They came into a room that was flat gray metal from the floor to the walls, whose corners were vague with shadows and crawled upward into darkness. In the middle of the room was a single gunmetal table, spotlighted with a pale yellow glow.

"There are chairs against the left wall," the electronic voice said from out of the dim reaches. Remak found two, made of a harsh metal that matched the table, and pulled them up. He gestured for Laura to sit and then did so himself.

Unprompted, Remak began speaking to the anonymous space around them, recounting their last few days. It was not particularly cold in here, but Laura felt herself beginning to shiver, a cold sweat pricking the nape of her neck. When he finished, the room returned only a silence that seemed to vibrate from the shrouded corners. When the disembodied response finally came, it was like being haunted by a phantom.

"There are two kinds of evolution," said the voice from the depths. "There is Darwin's evolution, the mutation and adaptation of genes. This is a physiological process, occurring when an animal, a gene-carrier, interacts with environment. This change, of course, occurs over thousands of years."

The voice was coming from somewhere in front of them, but with the majority of the room cloaked in black, the Librarian might have been in the same room, hidden in the darkness, or somewhere else through the unknown halls of the house.

"And then there is cultural evolution." The voice vibrated out of the black. "The process by which our *minds,* rather than our bodies, adapt as they interact with environment. It is what our minds soak up from the world around us, from other people, from what we see, what we are told. Now, it takes millions of years for a flipper to become a leg. But our minds, our perspective, in a sense the very nature of who we are, can change in an instant, in the amount of time it takes to hear and process a word or interpret an image. Do you understand? Just as the dangers of our environment—persistent attacks by a predator species, eating a poisonous plant—will evolve us over a millennium, *ideas* will evolve us, too, over the course of months or minutes or seconds."

Remak nodded. To Laura, this sounded similar to the rudiments of the Global Dynamic as she understood it.

"Darwinian evolution is genetics," the Librarian's voice went on. "The units of transmission are genes. They move in the physical universe, the strongest ones surviving, passed from generation to generation. What, then, is the transmission unit of cultural evolution?

"In 1976, a biologist named Dawkins at Oxford University gave these units a name. He called them memes. They are conceptually alive, just as genes are. Like genes, memes are born in one person and are capable of implanting themselves in other people. Unlike genes, however, they move over physical space, but not in the physical universe. Memes are living ideas, moving from brain to brain in the space of a glance or a synaptic impulse, the most contagious life form ever to exist. These memes, these living ideas, are the carriers of human culture."

If the Librarian was watching them, there was nothing to see but the faces of two people turned to stone.

"Once upon a time, memes were revelations," the Librarian told them. "The invention of the wheel, or Einstein's theory of relativity. Religion—possibly even God Himself—is a meme. And other, more basic things: an unforgettable quote, a way of playing a game or making a clay pot. When human beings had less access to one another, culture grew more slowly, and the memes were simpler, more significant ideas.

"Not so, anymore. Now memes are catch phrases from movies, tunes you can't get out of your head, a cereal commercial jingle, an empty political slogan, a garish fashion. The birth and transmission of these living ideas is no longer a natural process, an inherent by-product of human life. Now corporations produce them in limitless quantity, flooding the entire world with them, suffocating the meaningful memes, the important ones, the ones that nourish life and thought because they've had generations to grow and flourish organically in our minds. Corporations manufacture hollow ideas, or deformed ones, and they're winning the battle through sheer numbers.

"Of course, the capability to do this is fairly recent. The Internet is the greatest propagator of memes in the history of human thought by a factor of millions. Writing was crucial, radio a vast step forward, television a powerful leap beyond that. But in just a single glance at a standard commercial web page, more than twenty-five distinct meme transmissions occur. Currently, there are on the order of 39.7 billion individual web pages on the World Wide Web. Multiply that and imagine the virulence of the memes, the number of empty ideas slipping into minds that aren't even aware of them. With the improvement of imaging technology and Internet capability in standard cells, people are exposed to this virulence every moment of every day. They now crave the stimulation, to the point that its absence feels undesirable. They are, in effect, addicted to meme transmission, and they don't even know it."

Through the electronic barrier, Laura could hear the Librarian take a deep breath before continuing. Laura, for her part, was holding on to her breath tight. She felt what was coming in the trickle of sweat down her spine. Beside her, Remak was as motionless as death.

"Now, not all memes are undesirable. But consider that most web pages are initially reached via search engines, their complicated algorithms determining which memes we are most likely to be exposed to. And who determines these algorithms? Who, in effect, decides what ideas we are going to have? The corporations, of course. Just as they determine what we see on television, the music we hear, the news that reaches us. And what do you imagine would be their motive in determining what memes we're exposed to?"

"Profit," Remak said, and the word echoed in Laura's ears like a death sentence.

"Rather. My former employer, Intellitech, was the leader in this field of inquiry. They wanted the ultimate competitive edge: an idea that could transmit spontaneously. That is, an idea that moves from mind to mind *without* a standard means of communication, in a sort of inadvertent mental telepathy. Imagine an idea that transmits merely by proximity, or via a cell conversation, through voice tone or facial expression. How long until an entire city had this idea lodged in their brains by doing no more than coming too close to a stranger on the street? How long before the entire world is thinking it, simply because someone spoke to a relative on a cell halfway around the world? True viral marketing.

"For this you would need the ideal meme: an idea that combined maximum latent profit with unprecedented level of transmission potential."

"Hopelessness," Laura said, barely more than a whisper because she couldn't catch her breath. The empty look on her parents' faces, the murderous void in Brath's eyes, the shudder of despair that ran through Mal's body when Stoagie didn't recognize him; what else could give birth to those horrors? Laura could feel the weight of it pressing the air from her body right now.

"Yes, Laura. Hopelessness. And, truly, it was the only way for Intellitech to go. Hopelessness existed already, of course. We have always been so susceptible to it. The media has been trading in it for centuries. It creeps into our heads like a hungry spider and begins feasting.

"But Intellitech wanted it more powerful still. They targeted teens to begin with; they had to. Teens are the largest consumers of media and transmitted culture and are thus the highest meme-transmitting demographic.

"Intellitech already controlled search technology, and they flooded search engine hits with websites that would promote this meme's transmission. Their tentacles slid out. They began aggressively acquiring a cross section of media properties to accommodate their plans. So, HD channels were flooded with images that would carry the hopelessness meme most potently; they began producing music with words and tones that pushed the meme. Finally, there was nowhere left to turn that the meme wasn't present.

"Then came their 'focus groups,' thinly veiled psychic torture chambers. Teenagers were exposed to headlines of disaster and ruin, simulated images of their own families in agonizing pain. They were shown falsified proof that their own reputations, records, lives were being irrevocably ruined. Data-rich smart liquids were injected directly into the amygdalae, the portion of the brain responsible for emotion.

"And then, *then* Intellitech got exactly what it needed: Big Black. The initial destruction was bad enough. But soon after, to have a great black symbol of our own ability to destroy ourselves rising from the skyline of the world's greatest city . . . This broke down the final barrier, let the hopelessness come flooding in like a tidal wave. It was so effective, it seems impossible to me that Intellitech didn't have a hand in it.

"Whatever the case, Intellitech had its success. If that's what you can call it." The Librarian's pauses were filled with a low electronic hum. "In short order, the extraordinary rise in desolated response they had stimulated in their test subjects spread to the doctors administering the experiments, and to the doctors' families and associates. The idea was catching."

"Why?" Laura pleaded, nearly in tears. "Why that? Couldn't they see that it would destroy us?"

"No, Laura, they couldn't. Corporations are vast living systems with one, single evolutionary imperative: profit. Perhaps Jon has familiarized you with the Global Dynamic? Hopelessness promotes certain behavior patterns crucial to marketing. But it is also a by-product of those same behaviors. It promotes the shortest-term thinking and thus increases sales of blatantly harmful substances like tobacco, liquor, and beverages and foods made primarily of sugars and chemicals. It creates violent impulses of resistance at the same time as a yearning to escape into video games, action movies, and fast, no-thought entertainment at the expense of considered, constructive solution-building. It makes parents forget to care what their children do and children forget to care about how they treat one another. It makes us need more and more and more because no amount is ever enough to fix us, to make us happy. Hopelessness creates all of these conditions, but it also *arises* from them. Do you see?"

She did. They both did, and the realization was strangling them.

"They did it," Remak said. "They reverse-engineered the Global Dynamic."

"They did. They intensified the cycle. Hopelessness creates the need for the product, and the product creates more hopelessness. The supply *creates* the demand. An ultimate, endless profit loop. Except, when they grew the meme to its ultimate potential, they pushed it so hard that it evolved and mutated into a new form altogether.

"But, in the end, how could they hope to keep control of it? Even the smallest child can tell you: you can't control an idea. And even in this non-Darwinian evolution, only the strongest survive. Hopelessness is now the strongest, most powerful idea in existence. And it's alive."

Electronic silence stretched out. Perhaps the Librarian was trying to figure out a way to undo the meme for the millionth time.

"I found evidence of the earliest stages of Intellitech's experiments. I left, but continued to monitor them. Of course, it's grown far beyond Intellitech over the years. Consulting the cooperative's collected intelligence, I pieced together the disastrous 'success' of Intellitech's project and the 'escape' of the meme just within the last few years. I saw desolated response grow. The apparently random incidence of it—not just in the areas and groups it's associated with, but across *all* demographics—doubled within the first year. Then *tripled* from that number in the following year. And it's growing outward. The mass killings on the Mexican border, those suicide cults that swept through schools here and now into Canada and Western Europe; how much of that is just us and how much of it is something edging us toward a line, pushing us into darkness?

"I've watched the cooperative's efforts to investigate and curtail these outbreaks, but they only continued to increase. That was when I left and isolated myself. I've been watching us lose the battle ever since. I'm very sorry to say that you are far from the first cooperative field analyst who has stumbled onto something and disappeared. I see the reports come in and then suddenly stop, because the analyst in question is expunged, just as you have been. You're the first who's made it to me, Jon. But the world has been fighting for years what you've been running from for the last week.

"Hopelessness is now the only meme that is no longer a passenger in our minds. It can drive us. It is a race unto itself that has its own best interests at heart, and it is simply trying to execute its nature: propagate itself. It has done this so effectively, become such a dominant component in people's minds that, if everything you told me is true, it has become powerful enough to actually manifest itself physically."

The electronic silence returned, and Laura looked up at Remak, waiting for him to speak, to offer refutation. But when he spoke, his words rang helpless.

"How do you fight an idea that's already in you?" Remak said, and though it was barely more than a whisper, it echoed back from the darkness, a needless taunt.

"You can't, Jon," the Librarian said. "This meme has mutated into something new, just as sea life evolved into the bipedal forms that eventually became humans. And though it seems to have adopted some sort of a physical representation or location, it truly lives in our minds, in a mindscape, just as we live in the landscape. It moves from one mind to another with the same mechanics and ease with which we step from one room to another. If hopelessness can now control people's actions, memories, and perceptions, make them see different things from those actually before them or remember things that never happened . . ." There seemed to be no bearable conclusion to that thought.

"But it can't control *everyone, all* the time," Laura spoke up, refusing to let their chances simply fade into silence. "I mean, look at us. If it could drive everyone else, then all the people we've passed on the street in the last day could have gathered and killed us. It may have millions or billions of bodies—or doorways into people's minds, like you said— but it's still just one force."

"Its influence does not seem to be actively exerted all the time, that much is true." It was hard to tell through the frosty alteration whether the Librarian was being convinced of something or if he was just exploring this for their benefit. "But once it's in you, it's always there. Nascent, perhaps, but never absent. It may not always be driving, but it *is* always riding. And it takes so little for it to slide into the driver's seat."

"The hopelessness doesn't appear to be riding in you," Remak said.

"I saw it coming far enough in advance to limit my exposure," the Librarian said. "Hardly an option for everyone."

"But Mal and me? Jon and Mike?" Laura said desperately. "It hasn't been able to drive us, take control of us. If it could, why are our lives being stolen from us? The meme has to interact with people based on their psychological makeup, doesn't it? I mean, Remak was saying, some people commit suicide, others become like drones. Doesn't it make sense that somewhere along the spectrum, there are people who aren't affected at all?" Laura gained strength from the fact that they weren't interrupting to contradict her. "If it travels through our minds like we travel through rooms, can't a room be cut off by locked doors? What if there are people who can shut the door in their brains and lock out this thing completely? People who are basically immune to this meme?"

The last word echoed away, and there was a long expanse of silence. The electronic hush began to thrum in Laura's ears, and she wondered if the Librarian had abandoned the conversation. A chill struck her spine. What if the Librarian had actually *not* escaped at all by isolating himself? What if the meme was already in him, and that was why he denied that there was a way to fight it?

"Jon." The voice suddenly returned, and its sanitized tone had a different quality now, one of urgency. "There are people in the house, coming through the front and the back."

"Oh," Mike said, still at the window, "fuck me." He pulled his head back as though the window had given him a shock, and looked at Mal, who pushed past him to get a look.

A trail of cars had come from up the road. Pickup trucks, sedans, two-doors; old, beat-up models of every make that came out of Detroit made up the convoy, about seven or eight at first glance.

"I guess we should be grateful that crappy little town is too small to have its own sheriff," Mike said, not sounding particularly grateful.

"Go out and talk to them," Mal said.

"Screw you."

"Slow them down. They're not going to listen to me for a second. I'll go find the others."

The cars were pulling in, not bothering with the driveway, but simply tearing up patches of lawn and stopping midway to the house before they came to a sluing stop and disgorged the invaders. Men of every appearance began marching up toward the house in an amorphous group: well-dressed or in torn jeans and T-shirts, muscular and suntanned, potbellied, bespectacled, shaggy, and balding. They had clearly come together, but they were in no way of a type. Some were empty-handed, others carried bats, sticks, even a shotgun. A group of them had broken off, were heading around to the back of the house.

Mal was about to grab Mike and fling him out the door, but as his sight fixed on the first of the invaders, he saw something that tightened his jaw and sent an angry buzzing through his brain.

It was in their entire faces, an attitude, really, but it collected around the eyes in a particular way. They had the eyes of the gang standing in front of Tommy's door that first night, the eyes of Brath just as he shot Isabel. Eyes that were lifeless and dull.

The sight sent a jolt up his body that straightened him out like a board.

"What?" Mike demanded, trying to force his way in to get a look out the window again. "What?"

The invaders were just a few feet from the door.

"Their eyes," Mal said. "This thing is inside them. It saw us at the gas station, or when we passed through Pope Springs."

Mike stared back at him.

"Get in the corner," Mal said.

"What?"

"Get in the corner." Mal's voice was suddenly quiet and even, loaded with something that belied his outward calm. Mike ran to the corner beneath the stairway and pressed himself into it.

Mal stood at the wall immediately behind the door, so that when it opened, he would be hidden behind it.

"There are people coming!" he heard Mike yell, for the benefit of the electronic voice. But Mal knew that he was, as always, alone.

Something slammed against the door, one, two, three

times, and Mal braced. *Just like in my dream,* he thought. *It's trying to get in.*

There was a crack, and the door swung open straight at him. Mal's foot came up and kicked the door back hard. It caromed from the sole of his boot and smashed back into something that let out a yelp of pain. There were sounds of movement, stumbling, then two came in at once, one with a bat, the other empty-handed.

Mal had leaped before the door, and he caught the armed one flat in the face with a powerful cross. Beneath the dead eyes, the nose flattened, squirting red, and the man flailed back and fell. Mal slipped the second man's attack and came back up with two uppercuts to his ample gut. All his air coughed out of him, and he staggered off to the side.

Two more were already in, and two more were coming behind them, fanning out to surround Mal. Mal snapped out a short, quick jab and followed with a powerful curving hook, connecting with both and sending one invader to the floor. The other, however, landed a clumsy backhand full of knuckles across Mal's turned cheek. Mal came back with a flurry of jabs that took the man out of the fight, his face red and distorted.

But the other two had him, one at each arm, grappling madly, as the rest came flooding in, four more in all, their faces eerie for their empty expressions atop the violent, scrambling bodies.

Mal stomped down on an instep and felt bone crack as the man at his right toppled. But one of the newcomers got a shot into Mal's stomach, a hard fist slapping into layers of muscle. Then a stick came down on Mal's head, and he felt warm blood crawling through his hair. Through swimming vision, Mal saw the stick come up again. This time, he punched up as it swung down, his fist connecting with the wrist of the man wielding it, breaking it at the joint with a sharp snap that Mal felt through his knuckles. The stick spiraled through the air and away and the man leaped back, grabbing his wrist.

Four left.


Remak moved. He got to the door and pulled Brath's slim black automatic out. Laura stared at him in shock.

"What room are you in?" he said to the darkness. "I can get you out of here and take you somewhere safe."

"I'm not in the house, Jon," the voice said. "I'm not even in the state. Get yourselves out. They're coming up the back staircase now. Your friends are holding others at the front door." The lock on the door clicked open.

"Come on," Remak said, his voice harsher without rising at all, his hand out to Laura. She jerked into motion, as though having been held back by an invisible barrier. He grabbed her hand, threw the door open, and ran out with her in tow.

Laura screamed. There were men appearing at the back end of the hall, and even from this distance, she saw the haunting emptiness in their eyes, the void that had been in her parents' eyes the last time she saw them. The first of the men, solidly built, wearing jeans and a plaid hunting shirt, was leveling a shotgun at them.

Remak let go of her hand and grabbed the door he had flung open. Just as the hall boomed with the discharge of the shotgun, he swung the door between them and the men. The sound of metal shot thunking into the wood and striking the metal it was reinforced with carried through the door, and immediately Remak pushed it open again and snapped off a single hissing shot from the hip.

The hunter thrashed, his gun tumbling from his hands, and was flung back as though a rope attached to his back had suddenly pulled taut. He knocked over the man immediately behind him, and the approaching faces retreated behind the door.

Immediately, Laura went into a sprint back down the hall, toward Mal.

"Come on," she said.

"Go, Laura. I'll hold them here," Remak said, pulling the door back for protection.

She skidded to a stop. Leave him here? They needed to—

"*Go.*"

She did, hurling herself toward the door they'd first come through and, as it clicked open before her, throwing herself through it. She was on the balcony, looking down into the foyer.

Bodies were strewn around the front door, either still or writhing on the floor, favoring an injured part. Mal was surrounded by four men, one holding tightly to his arm, the others firing attack after attack at him. Mal slipped, parried, took a blow to his chest. One of the men had a short metal pipe and swung it, only to have Mal's fist come down like a hammer and deflect the pipe into his thigh instead, where it landed with a meaty thwack that made Laura wince and Mal grunt hard.

She started down the stairs and saw, from beneath the steps, Mike come running out, snatch up a wooden stick on the floor, and lay awkwardly but fiercely into the head of the man with the pipe. The man turned just in time to catch another blow across the face that cracked the stick in two and sent him to the floor, inert.

Mike staggered back, his eyes wide, thunderstruck at the loss of his weapon. Mal had taken advantage of the opportunity to grab the neck of the man holding his left arm and swing his head hard into the face of one of the two others. The skulls met with a shocking sound that made Laura want to vomit, and Mal finished by plunging his fist into the face of the man he held by the throat. Both men went down, the second only after Mal released him.

She saw something in Mal that she had thought absent, despite his history, a steady, controlled fire lighting his features. Now she realized it had always been present, only contained. There was a whirlwind in Mal, and it had burst out of him.

Even if she had not seen it in the emptiness in the last man's eyes, it was obvious to Laura that he was being controlled by something. What sort of a fool would throw a punch at an enemy who had just taken out so many opponents?

But the man did. He threw a slow fist before him, and Mal avoided it with a minimal tick of his head, bringing the man down with a merciless fist that seemed to dislocate his jaw.

And instantly, Mal's body faltered. He held his feet, but the injuries to his leg, torso, and head were immediately clear from the way he turned and moved.

"Where's Remak?" Mike shouted at her from just a few feet away.

"Coming." She glanced back up at the balcony. "He's coming."

Some of the bodies around them were beginning to rise, their injuries obvious but not stopping them. Three who still stood but had retreated to corners took tentative steps forward.

"We have to go," Mal said in a rough, hoarse voice.

"Who has the keycard?" Mike demanded, already knowing it was Remak. "*Shit!*"

Laura's frantic eyes saw a chain of actual old-fashioned keys hanging from the back pocket of a man at Mal's feet. She stooped down and tore it off.

"Go," she said to Mike, grabbing Mal's arm. Supporting him would have been a trick, but he carried himself, limping badly on one leg as they careened out the door and down the stairway.

There were five keys on the ring, but only one of them fit a car, and it worked on the third one she tried, a dented blue Chevy adorned with ancient streaks of rust. When the door was opened, she flung the keys to Mike and began helping Mal into the back.

"Uh," Mike said, holding the keys before him, "I can't drive."

"What?"

"*Look,*" he said, incensed by the question regardless of the situation, "not everybody in the whole goddamned world knows how, okay? I failed my test and didn't bother going back—I live in New York City, for Christ's sake. Is that okay with you?"

She snatched the keys back and helped Mal lower himself into the front passenger seat, then raced around and got in.

The car closed and locked, they sat and stared at the open doorway of the house. They could see bodies moving up the stairs. Two faces appeared in the doorway, scanning them with lifeless gazes.

"Start the engine," Mike said from the back, his hand gripping the front seat hard.

"What about Jon?"

Remak fired a shot down the hall into the wall, causing the man reaching for the shotgun to retreat once again. There was a single bullet left.

"There are more men coming up the front stairs as well," the Librarian's voice echoed just behind him in the metal room. "They're injured, but there's a substantial number."

Remak turned toward the door at the front of the hall, awaiting the rush.

"There's a room across the hall from you," the voice said. "There's equipment in it you might be able to use, and another way out. Go fast—there isn't much time left."

Remak didn't hesitate.

"God help you," the Librarian's voice echoed as Remak left it behind him.

Three men were coming out of the house, one armed with a pipe, another with a bat. They favored their injured parts, but they were being driven by a force beyond them.

"We can't wait," Mike said. "Who knows what else is coming this way? Remak has the keys. If he makes it out, he can—"

"I'll go back in for him," Mal said, smearing his head-rest with blood.

A rush of flame burst through the windows of the top floor, followed immediately by a low *whumpf*. Almost instantly, another burst shattered the second-floor windows, the charred curtains flapping outward on the wave of heat. Men were tumbling out of the building now, some stagger-ing, others being carried. Finally, flame rushed out after them from the ground floor as well.

"Okay, go ahead," Mike said from the back.

"Oh, God," Laura said. "Jon."

The three approaching men had not even turned to see the flame engulfing the house. A mere ten feet away, one of them raised his pipe.

"Go! Would you go, for the love of God?" Mike yelled.

The pipe flew from the man's hand and rang off the windshield, leaving a spider web of cracks in front of Laura's face. She stamped down on the gas and swung the wheel so that the car slewed to the side. The man with the bat ran up and swung it down, creating another chaos of fissures along the side window, even as the car thumped into him and sent him careening backwards.

The last man chased the car futilely as it gathered speed down the lawn and onto the gravel road. They raced away, and the sight of the weird, empty men gathering before the burning house disappeared around a bend of forest.

# THE ROAD

LAURA WAS CRUISING as fast as she could along bumpy side roads, avoiding the highway but trying to run parallel to it. They were speeding toward the nearest town with a train station, according to a tattered map that had been in the car. Luck had been with them for a change. The car they'd stolen— yes, Laura realized with a shock: she was a car thief now— was old enough that it had no GPS to track them by, but did have a veritable atlas of old road maps crammed into the glove compartment. Once they got there, they could ditch this thing and go . . . somewhere. Laura squinted to see through the cracks in the windshield. The black night rushed by them, skeletal trees and jagged rocks lit up at the edges of their path.

Silence hung heavy in here. Laura had described the conversation with the Librarian, and without Remak here to usher them through the full understanding of it, each wrestled with it in his or her own mind.

"It isn't over for us, you know," Laura said, and received a snorting bark of laughter from Mike in back. "It's *not*. It hasn't won, yet. We're still here, aren't we?"

"Some of us," Mike said. "Or did you forget about Remak already? It *has* won. We just keep running away from the consequences."

"No," Laura said absently, her mind moving toward something else. "It hasn't, because it's not inside us." She looked at Mal. "Why isn't it inside *us?*"

Mal looked back, short on answers, but holding her eyes as long as he could.

"Teenagers," Mike said acidly, sick of the bond that had formed between the two of them. "Teenagers are what ruined my life."

"You're a teacher," Laura said, turning her eyes back on the rushing road ahead. "And that's your attitude?"

"What the hell do you know about it?" Mike demanded. "What the hell do you know about teaching and what the hell do you know about kids?"

"I teach sometimes," Mal said. "Coach little kids, I mean."

"You're a damned kid yourself. You teach them what, exactly? How to beat the shit out of people?" Mike would not give an inch.

"No." Mal stiffened in his seat. "Discipline, confidence. I treat them with respect and I teach them to show respect."

"Well," Mike said, his shadowed face deepening into a scowl, "I want to personally thank you on behalf of every teacher, every *real* teacher, who was ever ignored or cursed at or attacked with a knife in a hallway. Thanks for getting those really, really important messages through to our kids."

Laura's instinct was to intervene, to defuse this the way she defused her mother's depression, her father's ire, once upon a time. But was there a point here? Would either of them ever give up?

*No.* Laura flinched at the realization. Neither of them would *ever* give up.

"This thing that's after us, " she said, "it lives in people's heads. It makes them think and do things they wouldn't normally think or do. That's why our friends, our families don't remember us. This thing is in their heads, and it took those memories away."

"It's made out of our fear, or our desperation," Mike interrupted her, a disembodied voice from the darkness in back. "I see it every day when I look at a classroom of kids who gave up. I see it in other teachers. I see it in the mirror every goddamned morning. It looks exactly like those people at the Librarian's house did, exactly like Brath did before he shot Isabel. It looks like everybody you walk by on every street in the world."

"No," Laura said. "That's not true."

"It *is* true!" Mike shouted from the back. "You *know* it's true! It's in us right now, and that's why we're all *fucked!*"

"No." Laura's voice was consumed with a preternatural calm. "It's not true. It's not in all of us. That's why it's chasing us instead of just making us want to crash into a tree. It *can't* control some of us."

"Our dreams," Mal said quietly.

"Yes," Laura said. "Our dreams. That was the meme, hopelessness, whatever you want to call it, trying to take us over and not being able to. You, Me, Mike, Jon. And Isabel."

"Why?" Mike said, his voice smaller now. "What makes us so special?"

"Mal," she said with serene self-assurance, "how did you do that, back in the house? I saw a fight once, between my high school football team and another team. One punch was enough to put someone out of it. What's your trick?"

"There is no trick." The green and blue light off the dashboard instrumentation made the yellow and purple bruises on Mal's face glow weirdly, turning them into a partial mask.

"You just take it," Laura said, completing Mal's unspoken answer.

Laura had seen the picture of Tommy and Annie; Mal had showed it to her on the bus ride back from East Woodman. Tommy looked like a thinner, shorter Mal. Where the younger brother's face was somber but unyielding, the older brother's was impatient, lines of anger etched permanently around his eyes. But Tommy looked happy, in the picture at least, standing in the sun with his arm around a girl he loved. Annie was softer, her happiness fresher and without a history. Yet there was a sense in her of something else. Laura knew she must certainly be projecting this onto the picture, but it looked as if there was an undeniable melancholy to Annie's happiness, that she knew even then what was coming.

That image was Mal's goal, the brother he believed he had a debt to. But it was not the reason he was going on. Mal was going on because it was all he knew how to do. He fought with his life every day. Laura had never faced a future without certainty, without family, without a clear path before her, until now. But that was the future Mal stared down every day. What had he said? You make your own future. And Mal kept moving toward it because he simply refused to go down.

"You just take it," she said again. Mal looked at her, confused at the import she put into the words. He might not have understood it about himself, but she could tell Mike had caught on from his silence.

"Jon," she said, "believes he has a duty to solve this. He's, like, a scientist and a soldier. He said it himself when he was talking about his dream. He has a duty to figure this out."

"He *was* a scientist and a soldier," Mike said. "Now he's just dead."

"We don't know that," Mal said.

*"Please."*

"Even if he is," Laura said, "all it could do was kill him. It can never really *have* him the way it did those people." *Or my parents,* Laura thought, and her heart fluttered.

"Killing him isn't bad enough?" Mike muttered. "You talk about fighting, about going on no matter what, like you know it from the movies or something. It's not all cool and dramatic. It sucks ass. It's what happens when everything you care about is gone, when you have to face the worst things about yourself and you still keep going. It doesn't feel impressive and powerful when you're doing it; it just fuck-ing hurts. Do you know that?"

"Yes," Laura said, and her calm had broken, her jaw trembling. "I know that. And I know that you do, too."

She heard Mike shift, set up an angry response.

"Mike," she said, hoping to cut it off. "Why are you a teacher? You seem to despise it and the students. Why are you doing it?"

She looked into the shadowy depths of the back seat, and Mike's eyes glistened back out at her.

"When I was a kid," he said in an even voice, "my mother had a scolding chair. That's where you sat when you were in trouble, so Mom could give it to you real good. Over Mom's shoulder, if you were sitting in the chair, there were all these faces staring back like judges. That was the family wall: all the great Boothes throughout history." He let out a choked, ridiculous laugh at that. "Really, most of the pictures were of my grandfather, as a young man, as a teenager, in the army, his framed medal, family gathered around his grave. Granddad was the great wonder of the Boothe line, the one great success that made the rest of us fuck-ups look that much worse. See, while he was stationed in Texas, waiting for his assignment, a fire broke out in his barracks. Granddad—well, back then he was only a father to two children he saw about two days a year—Granddad rushed in and pulled out three GIs with his own hands. He went back in for a fourth and never came out. We weren't even at war. It was an accident, a fire. So, do you see what the great success of the Boothe lineage was?"

*Sacrifice,* Laura thought with admiration.

"Giving up our own, worthless lives." Mike laughed a high-pitched shrill that threatened to go on and topple him into madness. But suddenly he recovered and pulled himself up just inches from Laura's ear.

"So why do I teach these kids? That was your question? I do it because somebody has to do it," he said. "Anyone can teach smart, ass-kissing suburban kids like you, Laura. Somebody has to suffer and teach the kids who can't be taught. And since my life is a towering pile of crap anyway, why not me?"

Laura saw it: the kids he was talking about hadn't stolen his life; he had *given* it to them. He had sacrificed his life to them, thinking that only in that sacrifice could he give his life value. The realization caught in Laura's throat. She was flummoxed, not out of pity, but out of awe.

The car was quiet and bumpy for a long stretch of the black expanse outside the cracked windows.

"What about you?" Mal said to her. "Why aren't you giving up?"

"I feel like"—she fumbled for the right words—"I don't know. It's hard to say. My parents have given me . . . I feel like I owe something to the world, to make it better. To make it a place where the fear and desperation that Mike talked about can't be used as a weapon. I guess the reason I'm not giving up is for the future."

Mal looked like he wanted to reach out and touch her,

and she wanted him to. But her hands were locked white-knuckled on the jittering steering wheel. And there was another thought that came unbidden into her head.

"What I can't figure out is how it got my parents," she said. "They made me this way, didn't they? They always pushed and pushed to give me a good life. To give me the future I'm talking about. Why couldn't they find strength in that, too?"

"Because they're *those* kind of parents," Mike said. "The kind that make your life into theirs, that hover over every decision like the world is hanging on it."

"You make that sound like a bad thing," Mal said, his question coming from some deep place inside his own head.

"No," Mike said in a voice steadier and more resolute than he had ever used in Mal and Laura's experience; as if for just a moment, he was talking about something he actually believed. "Whatever strength they had before they were parents, it's all concentrated now. Because everything changes when you become that kind of a parent, and it only takes one thing to upset your precariously balanced strength. Whatever this is, a *meme*"—he said the word as if it tasted bad—"it climbed into them and took away the one thing they couldn't go on without: *you*, Laura."

The road blurred before Laura, as she found new tears from a place she had thought was all dried up.

The twinkling lights of a town came into view in the distance.

Laura should have been exhausted, but her eyes were wide with her recent realizations. She was ready to keep going now, even without Remak. It occurred to her, for no reason she could form coherently, that maybe it served them in some way to be without Remak and his precise command of every situation. And she thought of her parents, who had given her something they no longer possessed, this sense of strength that had saved her. Was this how it was supposed to be? Were parents supposed to slowly fade away, bequeathing the best of themselves to their children?

She was ready to keep going. But to where?

"What happens now?" Mike said from the back, seeing the lights of the town approaching and beating her to the question. "We take a train into Canada, climb into the mountains, and disappear forever?"

"That's not what you really want, Mike," Laura told him flat.

"Like hell it isn't."

"No." Mal's voice was hard and final, not unlike it had been right before he had ordered Mike into the corner and lit into the invaders. "We go back to the building, the one with the doors. Whatever's making this happen, that's where it is."

"That is utter genius," Mike said. "You want us to go there without Remak? And when we find whatever we find in the building? Then what do we do?"

Mal's voice was as heavy as a stone when he said it.

"Fight."

# PART 3

# THE GUARDIAN WAITS

"THERE," MAL SAID, pointing unnecessarily—he thought—across the street.

Mike squinted.

"Which one?" Laura said. "With the two women smoking in front or the one with all the plants?"

Mal's finger wavered as though it were the defective aspect of this scenario.

"In between them," he said, studying the other two, bringing his finger back up more certainly. "Right there."

Laura blinked, and then her back went straight and she blinked again. Mike was staring.

"Oh," Laura said slowly. "That one. That's weird. It's like I forgot to look at it."

Mal nodded and looked at the building and the crowds of people walking by it.

"So," Mike said, and let it hang, waiting for someone else to bring the thought to fruition. When no one did, he asked, "Do we just walk in?"

"That's what I did," Mal said.

"And it went so well."

"What else, then? Wait until someone comes out? I don't think"—Mal watched the building in silence for a moment—"anyone ever will."

"What if it knows we're coming? What if it's waiting for us in there?"

"Do you want to go in at night?"

"*Night?* No way in hell."

"We should go in now," Laura said. "If it knows we're coming, it's not going to un-know it by tomorrow. And we can't afford to wait for a week or a month. What difference would nighttime make, anyway? It doesn't sleep or go home for dinner. There won't be, like, less of it on duty. We need to go in now."

Mal nodded and then Mike nodded, and they turned back to the building and waited for one of the others to take the first step across the street.

Tentatively, Laura went first. She weaved between stopped cars, leading the other two at a short distance, until they came up on the opposite sidewalk and stood before the cold, metallic tower.

"You made it," someone said from behind. They turned as one, Mal moving between the other two and the speaker.

"I wasn't sure you would," Remak said, and Laura instinctively lurched forward and threw her arms around him. He hugged her back mechanically, and when she let go and looked into his face, for just an instant—maybe it was a projection of her own fear—Laura thought he wasn't pleased to see them.

"When the house went up," Mal said, "we thought . . ."

"No." Remak didn't go beyond that. He looked away from them and at the building. "I've been looking for this place for hours. I remembered where Mal said it was, but I walked up and down the block and couldn't find it."

"But you see it now," Mal said.

"When you walked up to it." Remak nodded. "I feel as though I just remembered to see it," he added curiously. "It's not just me, either. I've been sitting in the restaurant across the street. No one else sees it, either. Not a single person glanced up to look at their reflection in the door or stopped to take a smoke in front. It's like it's not even here."

"They'd see it if you showed it to them," Mal said.

"Maybe," Remak said. "But even we had a hard time

seeing it, and we haven't been gotten to yet. I assume Laura explained what it is we're facing."

"Should we be doing this out here?" Mike asked, the building looming right behind him.

"Why not?" Remak said. "Do you think it doesn't know we're coming? Do you think it doesn't know we're here? It's in half the people around us, like a disease, an infectious disease of the brain."

"Not the brain," Laura cut in. "The mind. I mean, that's what the Librarian was saying, more or less, wasn't it?"

"There is no mind without the brain," Remak said. "Nothing affects one without affecting the other."

"But the brain is physical; the mind is intangible," Laura said. "A disease, like Alzheimer's or something, affects the brain physically. Are you saying that's what this thing does?"

"Probably not."

"Then this thing is really more like a ghost than a disease. It haunts the mind as much as it infects it." Laura didn't bother to camouflage the challenge in her tone any longer.

"If you like," Remak allowed. "The point is, for whatever reason, the four of us are clear, for the time being. We can do something about it."

"The last time I tried to go up, something big and very, very strong stopped me," Mal said.

"I have an idea about that," Remak said.

"Me, too," Laura said.

"Oh?" His scientist's eyes studied her, and a moment of tension stretched between them.

"This is what we were thinking." Mal broke into the uncomfortable moment and explained.

Remak examined the plan for flaws with the care of a jeweler. When he found one, he offered modifications and when all of them were satisfied, they went over the plan again without embellishment.

Once they were all clear on their parts, Mal stepped in front and led them through the glass and metal door into what now felt to him like another place altogether. Not a different world or a different time, but a different way of thinking, where you couldn't count on any of the laws and truths you knew.

It was the same as Mal remembered it: dank, gray, somehow unfinished, and uncomfortably pregnant with imminent menace. The others looked about them, at the exposed concrete of the floor, the dulled metal of the walls, the polished chrome here and there, the vastness of the place.

"There are the elevators." Mal pointed at the concrete columnlike banks before them. "On the other side is an open space, like a lounge or something."

Remak led them past the elevators and had a look at the emptiness beyond. He nodded at the space where there could be an internal garden or a fountain or some giant corporate insignia in sculpture. It was a space designed to strip away imagination and hope and replace them with a homogenous inertia so that individuality could die. And worse yet, it was that space in blank, generic form, making it all the easier to see how content, any content, any corporate symbol or ideology—which was to say, *all* corporate symbols or ideology—could be slipped in.

He stared, looking hypnotized at the panorama for a moment, until Mal stirred him with a hand on his shoulder. Mike and Laura took their places, and Mal and Remak positioned themselves at the elevator. Remak slipped the gun out and held it loosely at his side, then nodded to Mal.

Mal went over and faced the row of elevators he had used, or tried to use, on previous visits. Just before his finger reached the button, it lit a dull orange, as if it sensed his presence. He took a step back and waited.

Remak loosened his shoulder, planted his feet.

The elevator in the middle dinged. Mal's hands flexed quickly at his sides. The door slid open slowly. He braced himself.

There was an empty elevator before him, waiting for him to board it. He glanced over at Remak and back quickly, expecting something invisible within it to suddenly appear and attack as soon as he looked away.

Remak made no move, no response, but merely waited.

Mal poked his head into the compartment, looked on both sides, pulled his head out. He looked at Remak again, shrugged, and started to step in.

His foot had barely come off the floor when a dark motion darted from the elevator opposite, at his back. That door had opened swiftly and had not dinged.

All Remak could see of the motion was dark and big and fast. It had Mal before the gun had even twitched.

Mal was in the air, his feet kicking, his hands reaching back over his shoulders to find what had him. Now still, the motion became a figure, of a sort; indistinct, not quite solid, but definitely there, like something seen through a rain-slicked window.

The gun was up. The head of the figure was either hooded or just very dark. Remak shifted to his right just enough to find the front center of the hood or the darkness.

Mal felt the force against his neck, straining it, his tendons reaching their snapping point.

The line of fire between the gun and the figure's face came perilously close to Mal's head. It wasn't just aim that was critical, it was timing, because Mal was flailing and his head kept interfering with the shot. There was a chance the bullet would catch Mal square in the temple, perhaps sparing him the shock and pain of a snapped neck.

Remak fired a single, crackling hiss that reverberated metallically up and down the empty space. It found the center of that darkness, and the figure jolted.

The figure didn't pause to consider or calculate. It tossed Mal thoughtlessly away, sending him sprawling out across the rough concrete on the floor behind him, and then it became a motion again.

Remak was already moving from a standstill to a dead sprint, pumping his arms and cutting the distance to the front door with all his might.

There was Laura at the door. She saw Remak and the motion behind him, an indistinct blur that made her stomach flutter. What she felt wasn't just fear but a particular kind of fear, without reason or hope: that of a child caught before a speeding car with nowhere to escape. She closed her eyes, turned her head away, and pulled the door open.

Remak watched as the door opened to the world they had come from, the people passing by and not looking at them. It was something like a nightmare in which you were close enough to freedom that if you extended your fingers you could touch it while seeing all the people who couldn't help you.

Two feet from the border between here and there, Remak's feet were pulled off the ground. It wouldn't be more than a second before he was dead, either from a splintered spine or from something done to him that would take his mind from him forever.

Mal, also at a dead run, the motion sending jolts up his injured leg, launched himself like a stone from a catapult. He vaulted into the figure's back, and for an instant, just an instant, it felt like a wall made of rock or steel. He knew it would break his bones—until the instant his momentum had carried him, the figure, and Remak through the doorway and outside. Then suddenly Mal was slamming into nothing at all. The figure was gone, and he and Remak tumbled over each other as, for the second time in about eight seconds, Mal scraped his bare arms bloody against concrete.

They looked up at each other, both a little stunned. People saw them, there on the sidewalk. A few stopped dead and stared at them. A woman came a little closer and asked suspiciously if they were all right.

"Great, thanks," Mal said, rising agonizingly from the ground. Remak helped him to his feet. Mal examined his skinned flesh, blood welling slowly in places. He brushed his chest and torso off and followed Remak back inside the building.

The bystanders watched the two men turn and walk into . . .

The people hurried along their way, the incident already murky and vague in their minds.

Mike waited, his foot jammed into the elevator door to keep it from closing. As Mal, Remak, and Laura appeared, he watched the other elevators uncertainly, expecting something else to come bursting out at any time.

They piled into the elevator, and the door closed.

Remak stuffed the revolver back into the holster and looked up at the buttons. His mouth was open, to ask Mal again which floors he'd been to, but froze in that position, silenced. It was quite clear which button mattered. The top floor, the button by itself, crowning the double rows beneath it, was unmarked. Just looking at it made their stomachs weak, dried their throats.

The four stared at the button and were still.

# MAN IN SUIT

THE BUTTON STARED back at them. It challenged them like an eye staring directly at their fears, at the things in their lives that they buried away and never even looked at themselves.

Laura held Mal's hand. Hers was fully a quarter smaller, but he could still feel it crushing, compressing his bones and tendons with the strength of fear, the same fear that held him numb and shaking. The force must be practically breaking her delicate fingers; he could only imagine what it was doing to the rest of her. Why didn't she look away?

Then he saw why. Her other hand was rising toward the button, moving slowly as if it were dragging a great weight under it. Mal looked at Remak. His fear was a quizzical thing, his head tilted at the button, trying to figure it out. Mal looked at Mike, and Mike was looking down, shaking his head.

Laura's hand rose.

And Mal's hand came up, too. He would not make her do it alone. Her above all.

Their hands were up, their fingers extended, the button before them, its only true weapon what they carried in their own heads. And when he felt her squeeze his other hand, when he knew it was time to close his eyes and lurch forward, when they had decided but before they could move, the button glowed hazy orange all by itself and the elevator hummed smoothly around them.

Their arms fell back to their sides, the muscles aching and twitching. Now there was also the feeling that there wasn't enough air. Mal felt a trembling first in his stomach, and then he could see it in his hands. Someone was crying, and he looked up, expecting it to be Laura, but it was Mike, gripping his face, still shaking his head. Laura was making fists, pressing them into her legs, making an effort at steadying her breath. He could see muscles in her throat clenching. Remak's eyes were closed, and he breathed deeply and steadily, mechanically, forcing his body to obey.

There was a loud sob of fear, and Laura clutched Mike to her. They embraced and shook so hard, Mal could practically feel it from where he was. Mal reached around and hugged them both, as though to protect them, but really to protect himself. He reached one of his powerful, bloodied arms out and grasped Remak, and pulled him to them as well.

Remak opened his eyes and let out a wail that they all knew from their own hearts.

And the door opened.

Remak was the first to pull away from the embrace; he straightened his back and turned around to face the door. The others, hearing nothing from him, came apart from one another slowly, rubbing tears from their faces and following his gaze out the door.

There, in an office, was a man in a suit.

And truly, it was *a* man in *a* suit. All you could say of the suit was that it was a suit—cloth cut into a recognizable shape, that shape being "suit." It had no particular color, no particular style. It was much more the idea "suit" than it was actually a suit itself.

So, too, was the man. Even when you were looking straight at him, it was impossible to describe him. He wasn't old, young, tall, short, thin, fat, dark, light, handsome, ugly. Like the suit, he was just a familiar shape that served a universal purpose, to move and, perhaps, to speak.

The office, unlike the space downstairs, had no exposed surfaces of plaster or masonry or drywall. But it, too, was a blank form onto which any style could be placed. It was "office" and nothing more or less than that.

The shape of the man looked at them in the elevator. They knew he did because things they recognized as eyes were directed at them, not because there was any indication of acknowledgment or impatience or humor or pity in his face, because there was no expression there at all. How could there be when there was no true face for those expressions to play upon?

Remak, standing straight, not wiping at the dampness on his cheeks, stepped out first. The others followed him, their fear, at least the unreasoning fear that had built and built, gone now. Remak opened his mouth to speak, but Mal was suddenly alongside him, moving as if he were stepping into a ring.

"What are you?" Mal said.

"What are you?" Man in Suit said. "You ask me to justify my being. What is your defense for your own?"

"We are the evolved and evolving species *homo sapiens*,"

Remak countered, "unique and unprecedented. You are only a genus of a species, just another form of meme."

"No. I move myself, sustain myself, communicate, thrive in a unique way," Man in Suit said. "I am Idea. The others are only notion. They are my prehistory, I am their future. And yours."

The voice, the familiar voice he had heard in the lobby days ago . . . Mal finally recognized it—its tones, its dips and rises, its emphasis, both warmly human and distinctly artificial. It was the voice Mal heard in his head when he saw a commercial on the HD, offering him a deal, or words scrolling by on his cell, advertising exciting benefits. It was the voice that offered him happiness if he would drink the latest sports drink and perfect health through the latest pharmaceutical, that told him about the newest car that would make him a success and the guaranteed diet that would make him attractive. It was the voice of empty promise that encompassed, that inundated, that drowned human life. And looking at it now, Mal decided, this was the only face it could have.

The face, Laura decided, like the rest of the figure, was just the idea, the concept of face. The mouth moved, but no lines ever appeared to lend support when the voice suggested anger or superiority or humor. The face, in fact, was so smooth that it had clearly *never* made those lines. It didn't *look* like a machine face programmed to move in certain prescribed ways; it just *felt* like it. The smoothness, the vacuity of it was more alien to Laura than the weirdest plant, the most bizarre ocean life, the most unrecognizable mineral deposits she had ever seen.

Mike, standing the farthest back, listened to Man in Suit talk about his—*its*—own significance, its individuality. It made him think of all the faces he had looked out on, projecting an education at, every day. Those faces stared back in uniform apathy, at best ignoring him, at worst hating him for his efforts. And those same eyes were looking at him right now, out of Man in Suit's face. Not just looking *at* him; looking inside him, into his head.

"What is this place?" Mal said. "Why can't people see it?"

"The outside, the shell, is something that people made a long time ago," Man in Suit said. "But your Big Black came, and fear drove the people who occupied it away, out of the city. The shell stood empty and faded, and now it is one of the forgotten places. It is in your world, but not in your minds. People can't see it anymore because it no longer has significance for anyone."

"And there are other such places," Remak said, understanding now.

"Many. You were in one before, a place in the forest that people stopped going to and so it ceased to matter, and so I claimed it. It disappeared then, and abandoned, it started to lose things that made it real: color, smell. It will cease to exist at all eventually, and the world will be that much smaller. You think that the world exists apart from your apathy, your inadvertent disdain for things, but it doesn't. They are bound together. Your minds are far more powerful than you know. Your conception destroys things even as it creates them. As evidence, witness me."

"Why did you do this to me?" Laura thrust it out like an attack, surprised that she even had the ability to speak to the face of this thing. "Why take my parents, ruin our lives? Who are we to you?"

"I didn't single you out," Man in Suit replied, the most obvious answer in the world. "I do it to hundreds of people every day, each with their own weaknesses and traumas. I slowly defile and subvert what gives them purpose, and I do not even need to force myself into their minds. They put me there. Parents like yours in particular are quite simple. Their hope hangs on the slender thread of their children. Ronald and Claire Westlake are no one at all to me. It was just their turn. Eventually, I will have done it to everyone."

Frozen, Laura didn't know what drove the spike of fear deepest into her: Man in Suit's goal or that he had so easily, so casually renewed her sense of helplessness by simply invoking her parents' names.

"That's the outside of the building," Remak said, oblivious to Laura's tragedy, needing all his precious information, "the shell, you said. What's the inside, the doors that lead so far away?"

"The inside of this place is me," said Man in Suit. "And I grow rapidly, expanding through those doorways."

Mike realized, with a cold certainty that froze his chest, that they shouldn't have come here. By coming into the building and, thus, *into* Man in Suit, they let him into themselves just a little bit more. Mike could even feel it, wiggling in his brain, not a voice yet, not quite, but growing so that it would soon be a shout that blotted everything else out. His eyes twitched with icy fear toward Remak.

"And where do the doorways lead?" Remak pushed on.

"To where I am already, where I am beginning to be felt the most sharply and I can grow."

"A metaphor." Remak almost laughed, and for Laura, that was perhaps the most disturbing thing she had seen yet, the weird half-smile on Remak's face in the midst of this nightmare show-and-tell. "The doorways are a metaphor of what you are, how you travel from mind to mind. But your metaphor takes solid form."

"Still," Man in Suit went on, "there are not enough to propagate myself as quickly as I would like. That is why I employ agents."

"The MCT," Mal said.

"No." Man in Suit seemed pleased to say it. "Not of my making. You made them, just as you covered the ruined ground with a giant dome that reminds you every day of the event that set you all on this path. Your 'Big Black,' the blow you could not recover from, the event that proved you are losing control of your own lives. And so you retreat into your devices, hiding from the truth. The devices, the agents that I employ—they are simply more ways that humanity does my work for me."

"Agents like my brother," Mal said.

"Yes, he was one; one of very, very many. But Thomas Jericho was beginning to find hope, being pulled away from me by the girl he loved. So I sent others to collect him. But not before he could call for help."

"Why are the packages they deliver stuffed with trash?" Mal said. "Like the ones Isabel carried."

"The packages are for the courier. It is the mission itself that matters. I give them to young people, who waver between purpose and despair. I enlist them in something secret and sinister, something that causes them to question their own actions. And their doubt tips the balance into despair, and in the end, they are mine. The packages," Man in Suit continued, "are filled with stray words of doom, images of suffering. Someone finds the packages and opens them, and then they are one step closer to me."

"Why tell us this?" Laura was through being quiet. Remak was not their spokesman. "Why tell us any of this?"

"I tell you so you understand that you have no hope," Man in Suit answered Laura. "I will answer any question you have, because by merely being honest, I will defeat you. When I first notice you, your world fractures in a small way and things break, things that are close to you or that you value in some way. That is just the stress of my regard. I am everywhere, in everything and everybody, and no one even knows it. I am the secret future of your world and your kind. I will be absolute."

"You haven't taken away my hope," Laura said.

"But I will, because I have what you want: your family and your future. You said so yourself. I can more easily take away the hope of these others, perhaps, and once their hope is gone, yours will only be a sham that you are perpetuating for yourself, because you will be all alone."

"My hope will never be a sham," she said. "I have something that's beyond you. You could never understand it or tap into its power. I have these people, and each one of us is the power of all of us, and that's how it is with everyone alive. All they need is to know, and we'll all stand together."

"Togetherness is transitory. It fractures the instant that purpose is unaligned. Your commonality and multitudes are not strength; they are weakness, because they are only number, not support. You think that once everyone knows, humanity will 'all stand together,' but even the four of you do not stand together."

Laura stiffened, and Mal tensed behind her.

"What?" Laura said, mainly to herself.

"One of you," Man in Suit said, "is a betrayer. He already killed Nikolai Brath without your knowledge."

Mal's face tightened, and his eyes burned between Remak and Mike. Mike, his expression taut with fear, stuck his finger out at Remak.

"He intends to kill me now." Man in Suit didn't let up. "Can you grasp the enormity of this? He will be committing genocide, because I am the only one of my kind. He knows that it means the four of you will be lost forever, that your families will never recover their memories of you. But he thinks that destroying this place, the 'me' that you are in, the me that is this building, will show me to the world and thus destroy me, and he intends to do it now."

Laura turned toward Remak. His gun was out, and he shifted his body to encompass the whole room in its arc. Mal, or even Mike, might have had a chance at him. They were close enough, but they couldn't see beyond their feelings. Their feelings made them hesitate. It was always, in Remak's experience, the one who could act without feeling who could act fastest.

"What the hell are you doing?" Mal said, lurching forward instinctively or intentionally. Remak straightened the gun at him, and he froze.

"How did you know?" Remak said to Man in Suit.

"In this building, you are deep inside me," Man in Suit said, "and I am deep inside you. I can see what you think, own you a little bit, even if I can not have you completely. Yet."

"You're out of bullets," Mal said.

"There was a room in the Librarian's house," Remak told him. "The room I escaped through. It had supplies, equipment. This"—he pulled his ragged shirt open to reveal an array of flat gray packs of plastic explosive strapped to his torso—"and bullets."

"And I'm sure you'd kill us, because Brath was no problem. Right, Jon?" Mal asked, but his voice was already hard, and he knew the answer.

"Mal, Brath was gone. He let that thing into him and gave up hope, and with that went the man you knew. What was left in his place would have been sent after us, because he would always be able to get to you."

"Are you going to?" Laura said. "Shoot us? Blow us to hell? Say it!" Laura nearly screamed it, and Mal took another step forward, putting himself in front of her.

"I'm sorry," Remak said, and maybe he was. "Get out now, fast. None of you have to die."

"He's gone!" Mike shouted, and all their eyes snapped over just long enough to see that Man in Suit had disappeared.

"Was that door there before?" Laura asked.

The door she was referring to sat at the far end of the room from the elevator door.

"Go after him," Mal said to Laura.

Laura's eyes flashed to Remak and to the back of Mal's powerful shoulders and to the door.

"You have to go after him," Mal said.

"But"—Laura's voice was small, weak—"if Remak can destroy the building or something, then Tommy—"

"Go!" Mal's voice, usually so controlled, hit all of them like a pistol shot. "I'll take care of us. You save Tommy."

Laura's eyes blurred. She yearned for an authority figure to make this hideous choice for her.

"Don't," Remak said.

Her eyes fell on Remak. Then, decided, she turned and grabbed Mike's hand and pulled him to the door.

Mal stepped between them, intercepting the line of the gun. If Remak moved himself, swung the gun away, Mal could close the distance.

"Uuuuuh," the syllable of uncertainty stretched out of Mike's mouth. His mind was a thunderstorm now. Something was in there with him. He had let it in, with his fear maybe, or simply by coming in here, because he was the weakest of the four of them. Nevertheless, he was pulled to the door, and Laura yanked it open and threw them both into the darkness on the other side.

# THE WORTHY LIFE

BEYOND THE DOOR was a vast hall filled with ruined instrumentation, unidentifiable, like the components of some immense, secret mechanism. Man in Suit stood at its end, facing them.

"Christ," Mike said to Man in Suit, striding past Laura, who had stopped dead upon going through the doorway. "I am so goddamned sick of you." He leaned down as he walked and hefted a jagged metal bar from the forgotten and useless hunks of machinery that were the inner workings of Man in Suit's ravaged world.

"You are not up to this confrontation," Man in Suit said. "I assure you."

"Mm-hmm," Mike said, and whipped him across the face with the bar.

Man in Suit's head snapped around, and he turned back with wide eyes, thunderstruck. Mike went at him again, bloodying him this time. Man in Suit's arm rose weakly to fend off the next blow, but fell away as Mike battered it down.

Mike lit into Man in Suit with blow after blow, cracking bones and separating muscle as he did. Mal and Remak made it in to see Man in Suit torn and open on the filthy, jagged floor.

"Whoa," Mal said. "Look at that."

Remak stared in stark admiration.

Mike looked down at the little black things squirming feebly from Man in Suit's wounds and flopping wetly onto the dirty floor to die. He continued with the pipe until there was only a smear of red and black, feeling an unburdening in his head that he had never known before. Turning around, he could see from the approval in their faces that the others felt it, too. They stood a little taller; their eyes were a little brighter.

"That was . . ." Mal began, unable to find the right word to end on.

"Astonishing," Remak said. "I think you just saved"—he considered for a moment and shrugged—"everyone."

Laura was staring at him, too, something beyond simple awe in her slightly parted lips.

*Who'd have figured?* Mike thought, looking down at the smear. *All you had to do was beat him up.*

They walked out of the building to find people in the street staring at it, somehow aware of the thing that had finally left their private thoughts and given them back a sense of promise.

Mal and Laura stepped aside, knowing who these people needed to see. Remak hung back, watching the people approaching Mike, not crowding him, not crushing him with their praise, but silently coming forward and touching him gently, as they might a messiah. What he had done for them was beyond mere words.

A television crew had made it here already, perhaps having been called to the scene when the building had appeared. They accosted Remak, who began a lengthy explanation. Mike saw reporters talking to Mal and Laura as well. But they couldn't reach him yet, surrounded as he was, and he was glad. These people needed him too much. He heard his three companions saying his name, though—saying it an awful lot. And it was the first time that he'd heard the

Boothe name, his grandfather the war hero's name, and it didn't echo in his own ears like a taunt.

Exhausted and energized at the same time, Laura suggested that she and Mike slip away. She was understandably anxious to find her family and make them whole again, but there was something she desperately wanted to do with him first. But, heck, she was just a kid. Mike let her down easy, and when he had, she seemed even more in awe of him.

It took Mike about a month to drop twenty, twenty-five pounds, get into fighting shape. Mal offered to help, but as soon as Mike got into a gym it came easily and naturally, now that there wasn't something black in his head holding him back anymore.

He did a lot of television talk shows, because people needed to understand not just what had happened but who Mike was and what sort of a man was capable of doing what he had done. When he walked down the street, people would come up and thank him quietly.

"What you did was so important," they would say. "So important."

They were talking to him about running for office, like mayor, maybe—start small—when one of the five models he was seeing on a regular basis told him she was pregnant with his child.

It was an unhappy shock to begin with. He'd never had kind thoughts for his own parents and thus never thought much of being one. But this wasn't just a matter of having a child. In a sense, this was something for the entire world.

After nine months of running out for ice cream and pickles at all hours, the hero and the supermodel were in the delivery room. The mom-to-be was gasping away, and Mike watched the doctor gently lift a tiny little boy from between her legs.

"It's a boy," the doctor said. Nurses whisked the boy off to a small padded table, where they attended to him carefully. The mother was holding Mike's hand tightly when one of the nurses came over and whispered something to the doctor.

The doctor went over and examined the baby briefly.

"What's wrong?" the mother said.

The doctor looked at her, hesitated, looked at Mike, and made a decision. He stepped to the side, giving the parents a clear view of their baby boy.

"Oh, God," the mother choked out, ripping her eyes away from the child and snatching her hand from Mike's.

"What?" Mike said, stepping closer to look at his boy. "What's wrong?" He couldn't see anything wrong. The boy wasn't even crying, just looking back up at his father thoughtfully.

"I'm afraid your son is . . ." The doctor breathed in, held it a moment, and let go. "I'm afraid your son is completely worthless."

Mike looked from the doctor to the nurses. They nodded back sadly.

"He's never going to amount to anything at all," the doctor said, shaking his head regretfully and making an irrevocable notation on his clipboard. "Completely worthless."

It was too much for the mother. She insisted on blood tests, knowing that she and her family were all accomplished, decent, and smashingly attractive, which made them incontrovertibly worthwhile people.

They rushed the results through, and sure enough, it had been passed down from Mike's side.

"Why didn't you tell us, Mr. Boothe?" the doctor asked reasonably. "After all this fuss, why didn't you come clean that you were utterly worthless in every way?"

People seemed to know all about it without even being told. They scowled at him on the street now, punishing him for his deception.

After all he had done for them. He could barely even

bring himself to be angry at them after a while. In the end, you couldn't hide from your own shortcomings. Whether you saved every human being on the planet or not, worthless was worthless, and the only thing you could really do was just give in to it.

# FIGHTING THE NUMBERS

"I THINK IF YOU HAD any bullets left, you'd have fired already," Mal said, and he was certainly right. It wouldn't have been a shot in the arm or leg, either. Someone of Mal's stubborn resilience would still be able to make trouble, even with a grievous leg wound, perhaps even with a shattered kneecap.

"Are you sure, Mal?" Remak's face was deader than usual, like a warning set in stone. "Better be sure."

Mal was not sure. He seemed to be figuring on what chance he had of beating Remak hand to hand with a bullet in him. Remak, betting his final chip, cocked the hammer.

"Do it." Mal called the bluff. "If you're going to do it, then *do* it."

Remak threw the empty gun at Mal's face and with the other hand pulled from his pocket the triggering remote for the explosives he had strapped to his torso.

Mal slipped by the gun as if it were a slow punch, and his hand shot out and caught Remak by the wrist. The pressure was immediate and extraordinary. Remak's fingers went numb, still locked on the red and gray device, but unable to flex or maneuver.

"Mal, listen to me," Remak said, but Mal's hand only tightened on the wrist until Remak saw his hand turning red, saw it but didn't really feel it. His other hand came up to transfer the device, but Mal's other hand came up, too, and covered Remak's, so that there was a conglomeration of four hands grasped tightly around each other, straining between the two men.

"Mal, this is outside all human experience. You can't win by punching it. But it's here now, solid before us, and that's why we have a chance. We have to destroy this place. Letting that thing live so that we *might* save your brother and Laura's family? That could end up costing the entire human race its existence. It's a simple equation, Mal. Do the math." He was looking into Mal's eyes over the gathering of their hands. "Just do the math."

"We didn't fight our way here because of math. If you don't know that, it's already too late for you."

Remak sagged down, giving up the battle between them, releasing the device into Mal's hands, but in so doing, he forced Mal's weight forward, just for an instant. In that instant, Remak crouched and swept Mal's ankles from the floor.

Mal tumbled, tossing the device as far from him as he could, and rolled back up to his feet two yards away.

The young body was plagued with wounds. Mal's face was yellow and purple from recent blows. At his hairline, there was a thin crust of blood. One of his shoulders hung lower than the other, his forearms were bloody hash marks, and his knuckles were more scar tissue than flesh. A fractured rib or two showed in his breathing, and he limped when he moved.

Remak himself couldn't straighten out the fingers of his left hand, either, and the only sensation he had in that wrist was bone grinding against bone.

Mal lashed forward with a humming right cross, and Remak went under it, spearing two stiff fingers into Mal's ribs.

Mal grunted, wheezed, and stumbled back against the desk and chair that seemed more a part of this generic backdrop than an actual desk and an actual chair. He grabbed the chair and whipped it around at Remak. Remak went flat to the floor, and the chair spun over his head, shattering something behind him. Only when he snapped himself back to his feet did he see there was a window there, now jagged and open to something Remak couldn't see.

Remak circled away so that the window was at his side, and yet he still couldn't seem to get a clear view through it. He did, however, assimilate the data that no wind was rushing in, no noise was rising from the city to prove that cars and people existed out there. There was just a sibilant crackle, like too many voices whispering. It raised some interesting questions: Where exactly was this building? Was it out there, in the world with everything else? Or was it only somewhat there, intersecting in certain places, but mainly occupying someplace else? If this building was, in some sense, a part of Man in Suit's consciousness, then maybe the window didn't lead *out* at all, but actually farther *in*.

A right hook nearly knocked the questions from Remak's head. He darted aside and gouged the nerve juncture between Mal's shoulder and pectoral with stiff fingers. Mal's eyes twitched, but no sound came from him and he shot back with a jab, a jab, a cross. Remak avoided the combination and sent his fingertips for a disabling strike to Mal's thigh. If he could strike deep enough, he could end the fight now.

But Mal shifted just an instant before contact. Remak still landed, but he landed an inch off, striking hard bone, and it sent an electric shock wave up his arm.

Mal was swaying there, dancing wearily from foot to foot, shifting weight and stance back and forth, back and forth. He was near the window, and maybe Remak could maneuver him over another foot or so and upset his weight and put him out.

Remak feinted and took a shot at Mal's arm. Again, Mal shifted at the last instant and Remak scored a strike on Mal's hard elbow instead of into meaty muscle. Dodging Mal's counterattack caused a shift in position, and from the window now behind him, Remak could feel the short hairs of his neck start to bristle, as though charged by some strange, buzzing static.

Four more times they did it: Remak went in, just missed his mark, dodged away before a return blow landed. The window yawned open just a foot from both of them, hissing, airless, but somehow perpetually in their blind spots.

Mal was staggering, every injured part of his body coming into high relief; he was barely on his feet. But that had been his state before the fight started. And here he was, still barely on his feet. Remak went in again, missed his mark again, and dodged again, by a narrower margin.

Remak would find his mark eventually. Eventually. But his fingers were tormented for hitting bone instead of soft tissue, and he couldn't switch to the other hand, because Mal had crushed that wrist.

Remak went in with a spearhand strike, but this time, Mal's fist came down and snapped into Remak's good wrist.

And so the numbers fell into their slots and totaled up, and Remak saw that he was going to lose. He was smart and practiced and skilled and observant and quick and calm. He divided his strength between all these characteristics. All Mal really had was, he would not give up. That was it, his one big muscle. He would not goddamned fall down.

And as the numbers totaled up, Remak succumbed to them, though in so doing was fascinated to observe himself fighting the numbers, struggling to stay up and fight despite the equation that irrefutably stated that he could not win. Maybe, he realized, he could have used more of that sooner.

Mal's fist caught him right in the temple, and Remak blinked, teetered, caught himself, teetered again, and went down, one arm dangling out the window into open space.

Mal went to his knees and nearly fell on top of Remak, his hands wandering over the explosives packed tightly and strung around Remak's chest.

He stripped them from Remak's body and held them heavily in his own aching hands. He hoisted himself upright and turned and looked at the door, through which Laura and Mike had followed Man in Suit.

# WEAKNESS INTO STRENGTH

MAL STEPPED OUT OF THE OFFICE and into . . . the office. The room on the other side of the door was nearly identical to the one he'd just fought Remak in: flat, characterless gray. There was an elevator door directly across from him, even as he knew there was an elevator door directly behind him, the one the four of them had stepped out of. There was a desk, a chair, both standing upright—clearly this was not *actually* the same room; no battle had been fought here. In fact, there was no window, no Remak lying before it. But it was the same generic emptiness.

"More of the same," said Man in Suit. "Soon, the whole

world will be like this: uniform, consistent. Because it will all be made of me, like the people who will inhabit it. They will all be me, too, my flesh. Billions of bodies, one being. Like your friend Michael Boothe."

Midway between them, Mike stood, slack jawed, staring into the middle distance. He flinched sometimes, his shoulders or a muscle in his face. His eyes, God help him, looked dull and vacant.

And in his hands, Laura. She wrestled as she might against a block of concrete formed around her feet or metal shackles around her wrists, furiously but without result.

"As he has come into me, so he has allowed me further into him. And, struggling futilely against him—for an eternity, if necessary—she is lost, too," Man in Suit said. "So, what is left?"

Mal looked at Laura, whose muscles couldn't pull free from Mike's dead grasp. Her mouth was moving, but no sound escaped. Perhaps Man in Suit had taken her words, too. But she looked back at Mal, and her bright blue eyes, blazing like neon against this pallid world, were still filled with fight. And he saw what she was saying, even though he couldn't hear it.

*You are not alone.*

He turned back to Man in Suit.

"Me," Mal said. "I'm left."

"And what are you?"

"I'm the one you're never going to get," Mal said. "You've stripped me bare and I'm still here, so what chance do you have?" Mal took a step forward and waved him on. "Let's go."

"Of you all, your will is the most unsophisticated, the most fierce. It isn't about what other people mean to you, or how you see yourself, or what you owe to an ideal. It's absolutely pure, true to what a human is. Do you know why? Do you know what you have been fighting against all these years? Let me show you."

Something behind Mal moved, and he turned, assuming the door he'd come through had closed, possibly disappeared. But it was there. Except now it wasn't merely an office door, but an elevator door. It stood open to the shaft, and at the opposite side it was also open, revealing the identical office room they had all just come from.

But between here and there, suspended over the yawning shaft, were Tommy and Annie, frozen like statues reaching out toward each other. Reaching out, but coming up just short. Immediately, Mal understood why Annie had not been put with them in the forest before. Looking at them, Tommy's body straining toward her, his fingers stretched to their agonizing limit only to come up a quarter of an inch away, Mal could see that Annie was the thing Man in Suit needed to break Tommy, and Tommy was all he needed to break her. Idiotically, it made Mal happy for his brother, that there was someone he loved so much that they were the difference between life and death to each other. That love, at least, made his life valuable. And, instinctively, Mal's eyes flickered toward Laura, and back.

The two of them, Tommy and Annie, hung there immobile just beyond the doorway, their frail forms nearly swallowed by shadow, silhouetted by the light of the office room beyond them, but held aloft by nothing, over a chasm of black. What was suspending them there? Their love? Or Man in Suit, keeping them alive because he wasn't quite finished with them yet?

"So, here is what you wanted," said Man in Suit. "Your brother. I am going to let him die shortly, as you can see. But he can be saved. They both can. All you have to do is cross the threshold, push them to the safety of the other side. They will be free, and they will, if their hearts are resilient, recover and perhaps even thrive. Go. Help them."

Mal stared at Man in Suit without moving.

"Yes. You will fall and die," Man in Suit said. "But they will live. Not only that, but you will prove by giving up your life that hope has a chance, that human existence can come to more than . . ." Man in Suit looked around him at the ruins.

"I don't believe you."

"Correction: you do not *want* to believe me. But these two are no threat to me, and you are. It is preferable that you be dead rather than they. So they will live, and their hope will be reborn. You just have to give up and die to accomplish it."

Mal could see Tommy from here, hanging, hair a little too long, face trapped in a rigor of tension. And Mal could also see Tommy through a tunnel of years: a boy he used to box with around the living room; who used to steal his little brother's boxing gloves and give them back with a punch in the arm; with whom Mal used to hide, pressed close together beneath the covers as the sound of their mother's voice tearing into their father penetrated the walls. But when Mal left, he had never been able to find the strength to take his brother's hand and pull him out, too. Just like now.

"But sacrifice is not a fight, is it?" Man in Suit asked him. "No. It is a failure to fight. Truly, the ultimate surrender: death," Man in Suit said. "That is why you will not help him. You are fighting what everybody is fighting in the end. Your father fought it, and lost. And if you go in there, *you* lose the fight."

Man in Suit waited. The door to Tommy and Annie remained open.

"And so," he said at length, when Mal had not moved for some time, "what you believed was your strength is, in the end, your weakness. Your sense of fight will kill your brother, and your race, as well. Hope has no—"

Something shot by Mal. Man in Suit reached out to

impede the course of the projectile. His hands went up, but too slowly, too late to intercept it.

Mike tore away from Man in Suit, not bothering to curse him or even look over at him. He shot past Mal, then launched himself through the threshold, toward Tommy and Annie hanging in the dark.

Mike barreled into them, and Tommy and Annie came unglued from their own spots, tumbled back and out from the shaft, onto the gray floor of the office beyond.

And the darkness below swallowed Mike, and he fell down the shaft screaming. But it wasn't a sound of fear. It was a sound of rage and fight that echoed up the shaft and made the office room vibrate. Until, abruptly, it stopped.

But the vibration it set off intensified, and the room began to show cracks and fissures, and through them echoed the sound of Mike's fury.

Man in Suit's face registered something, though it was an expression Mal couldn't describe. It was an expression he had never seen on a human face. And the face and the body began to crack and fissure, like the room around them, and Mike's echo rose to a crescendo and the figure shattered, pieces of it littering the floor. The pieces faded to gray and melted into the surface of the floor, becoming part of the building itself.

And as Mike's echo died, behind Mal Laura screamed, claiming her freedom.

Before the scream stopped, Mal ran forward. The elevator shaft was just a doorway again, and he passed through, back into the office room, falling to his knees and gathering Tommy into his arms. He rocked on the floor, crying to the unconscious boy the way he had cried to his father years back.

"I'm sorry, Tommy." It was all he could say. "I'm sorry."

Laura came up and put her hand on his back. When he didn't turn, she squeezed, and when he still didn't turn, she came around and tipped his head up by his chin and looked into his face. His eyes didn't see her. They didn't see anything but his brother and his failure to act when Tommy needed him most.

"Mal," she said right into his face, "look around you. Tommy is here, Annie is here. You have a chance to save them."

He just looked at her.

"God damn you, Mal!" She grabbed him by the hair and forced his face upward. "My family is still lost, for all I know. You have your brother back. God damn you, don't you give him up now!"

And she pulled at his hair, pulled up, grabbing his shoulders, trying to force this giant to his feet. She struggled, her feet scrabbling against the floor beneath, cursing at him. Then she stopped, her belly full of futile struggles and her face red with effort.

"Mal," she said, going to her knees so she could look him square in the face. "Tommy and Annie have a chance because they have each other. And even if my family is gone, I still have a future. You taught me that. But I want my future to be with you. Please, Mal. Let yourself have a future, too."

She put her hands on his cheeks and leaned forward and kissed him softly on the lips. And she stayed there, until she felt his breathing change on her lips, and he actually did rise. Up to his knees, up to his feet. Tommy was in his arms, held like a child.

Mal looked down at Laura, she back up at him.

"Let's go," he said.

Laura bent down, grabbed Annie and pulled. She was a small girl, but a human being is heavy and her progress was not particularly gentle, made no better by the fact that Laura wasn't exactly interested in taking her time to get out of this cracked and fissured place.

There was a window here that Laura didn't recall, shattered and letting in a weird static, like a billion voices, the voices of everyone alive whispering over one another. But the other side looked like nothing at all, like silence, like absence. And Remak was gone. Thrown out the window? That didn't seem like Mal. Did Remak leave of his own volition, deciding that since he had lost, he might just as well pack it in? That didn't seem like Remak.

Mal was walking toward the elevator they had all come up in to get here.

"Mal," she said, her progress considerably slower dragging her burden. "What happened to Jon's explosives?"

He looked at her, stopped, pulled up his shirt. He had strapped the copious load of explosives to his own torso.

"My left pocket," he said.

She came over, delved in, came out with a small contraption. The detonator, Laura guessed. It was even more alien to her than the twists of machinery beneath the hood of her family's car. But what else could it be? And what had Mal intended to do with it, exactly? Was he just making sure Remak would have to go through him to get it back?

She lowered Annie gently, tore the Velcro strips loose, and took the explosives gently off of Mal and carried them to the center of the room. She laid them down and looked at the detonator. It was perfectly clear. There was a catch, which you pressed, popping a clear hard top, under which was a red button. The catch was snapped and the clear top was bent askew, as though the thing had been under a great deal of pressure, but the red button glared up at her like a challenging eye.

She told Mal to ring for the elevator, then she dragged Annie over and they waited, neither voicing their fear that this place may not be working the way it should any longer.

But the door pinged and the elevator opened, and they went in.

Mal reached a finger from beneath Tommy, to press the lobby button.

"No," Laura said. "The door that you looked through and saw Mike's school, what floor was that?"

"Thirty-two."

Laura pressed thirty-two.

"Mike is—" Mal began, then stumbled. "Gone," he finished.

"I know," she said, staring as the floor indicators lit their way down.

They had been too deep inside Man in Suit, or the situation was too much. Whatever the case, it had gotten Mike. He had grabbed her with the dumb, slack look on his face and the flat dullness in his eyes that she had come to recognize instantly. But as she had kicked and wailed against him and Man in Suit had offered Mal the deal that was intended to break him, Mike's eyes had lost the veil and begun to focus, and his face had slowly cleared. He had looked down at Laura, shocked that his hands were on her. He'd let go and opened his mouth to say something, but no final thought ever issued forth. Instead, he had gazed at her as if she were the only thing in the world he loved. Then he had turned and took off.

Mal's strength had been used against him. But Mike had

used his own weakness against Man in Suit. Mike had taken a sense of worthlessness that had been forced on him his entire life and turned it into selfless sacrifice. He had found strength in his own hopelessness and overcome it. Man in Suit's outlook allowed only for strength that could be subverted into vulnerability. It was his failure not to understand that it could work in reverse, as well. That was the nature of human beings.

The door pinged open onto a room of doors.

"Which one?" Laura said after they had come out.

Mal nodded over to one.

"Open it," she said, pulling Annie along to the doorway.

And sure enough, it was true, just as everything else Mal had told them had been true. The door opened into a space, a dimly lit basement that was larger than the space beyond the door could possibly allow.

"Go," she said.

Mal carried his brother into the other place, and Laura pulled Annie in after. She held the detonator in her hand and looked back into the room of doors.

"Your life was worth something, Mike," she said out the doorway. "Your life was worth everything."

She pressed the red button with her thumb. There was a thunderous roar and a searing flash of fire, and she slammed the door shut on it. And then there was only the cold, dark basement.

# PART 4

# WALKING TOWARD A FUTURE

THERE WAS A WOMAN named Claire Westlake, who lived a quiet and lonesome life. As her husband, Ron, worked during the day and she lacked the enthusiasm for her own work any longer, Claire looked for ways to divide the long days into individual parts, to make each hour endurable, each goal seem within reach. Even the smallest things could be scheduled as events, of sorts: taking out the garbage, fixing herself a snack, unloading the dishwasher. Or walking down the yard to check the mail.

Only packages were hand-delivered anymore, and Claire was expecting nothing. But the thirty seconds it took her to walk down and check was thirty seconds she needn't concentrate on anything else. The box was not empty, however. It contained a single, puzzling envelope. It bore her name and Ron's but not their address, postage, nor return address, either, as if the sender had come to the mailbox and slipped it in. With an unfamiliar sense of curiosity piqued, she tore it open, and she extracted the contents while standing on the grass in the wash of sunlight pouring between the tree limbs of her suburban street.

Within it was a handwritten note on a single card, so unusual to receive in this age of instantaneous electronic transmission, but somehow made more solid, more real because of it.

*"A daughter and her parents lost each other,"* the letter began without preamble.

> *The daughter thought she had nothing without them: no strength, no love, no future. She found out that the parents had given her the power to make those things on her own. But when they did, they lost the power to do it for themselves.*
>
> *A child without her parents becomes an adult. But what do parents without their child become? I think that, like the child, they need to make a future they believe in.*

*You taught me how to fight for everything that matters. You may not remember that. But I will never forget.*

*Laura*

Claire's jaw was trembling and her knees were weak.

The writing was on the reverse of a photograph, the slick surface so unfamiliar to her fingers. How long had it been since Claire had held an actual photograph instead of scrolling by one on her cell? It was a picture of a little girl on a swing, leaning forward and smiling at the camera with bright blue eyes. Those eyes—they made Claire's head light. She didn't recognize them, not exactly. At least not the person they were a part of. But she remembered them because they were the same eyes—brimming with that same curiosity and brightness—that used to look back at her from the mirror.

Tears ran down Claire's face. They came with such intensity that they began to fall on the photo. She brushed the moisture away gently and carefully, as if the image were the most precious thing on Earth.

The words, the picture, were as foreign to her as a world she had never known. But they found a place beneath all the numbness in her chest, where a sense of longing, of something missing had lodged itself.

Laura? Who could this possibly be? She had no memory of a student she'd ever taught named Laura. Certainly it was not Laura Silvers, Paul Silvers's wife. These were not sentiments likely to come from that bitter old shrew.

She walked back in, studying the child in the picture, her mind distracted from the day's rigid schedule of events. She had to show it to Ron when he got home. The words seemed so sad, they should have taken her own despair and multiplied it. But there was something else in them, too; the same thing as in the bright eyes of the little girl in the picture. They were filled with such a sense of . . . what was the word? It was on the tip of her tongue, just tickling at the edge of her mind.

There was a young lady named Annie, sweet-tempered and kind. She worked in a boutique during the day and then, tired but unbowed, got on the subway, went way, way uptown, and worked for another six hours at a clinic. Her fella—it was too late to call him boyfriend, too early to call him fiancé, and the English language didn't have a word for what was in between—was starting trade school soon, to become an auto mechanic, and she was putting him through it and keeping him there. He had just come out of a difficult time, associating with the wrong people and getting caught up in the wrong business. This was their chance now, and she couldn't afford to let either of them falter. She was prepared to work these hours another few years to get them on their feet, then Tommy would support her while she worked her way to a degree in education.

They were long hours, though, and when she was done, her eyes were blurry and she could easily nod off on the train home. It was a surprise, then, that she was alert enough to realize that she was being watched.

It was a cumulative realization. She didn't see the guy one day and say, "He's watching me." She kept seeing him, waiting on the platform of the station she transferred at every day, until it finally added up.

Not one to think the worst of a person or a situation, and certainly not wanting to worry her fella with this, as he could be quick-tempered and leap into things—conclusions as well as trouble—before thinking them through clearly, Annie walked right up to the guy, big and broad and notable for the way his face was both sad and stubborn at the same time. Did he look like Tommy, or was it just the expression?

Surprisingly, he didn't turn away or try to run from her. He waited for her to approach as if he had been waiting for her to spot him and do something about it since he had started watching her.

"What's up, dude?" she said, her chin pointing to the middle of his chest as her head tilted backwards to look up at him. She intended it to sound determined, at least, though not uncharitable. There were a lot of people in this city who were unwell in a lot of different ways, and showing them anger, which was more or less all they ever saw, didn't help anyone.

"I didn't mean to frighten you, Annie," he said, looking down at her with such obvious affection and hope that she didn't even ask him how he knew her name. "I needed to make sure."

"Make sure of what?"

"Make sure you were all right, I guess. I've—I've got this picture. It's . . ."

She waited for a long time on the subway platform for the rest of the thought, but he didn't seem capable of completing it.

"Are *you* all right?" she asked.

He smiled, but it somehow made his sadness deepen.

"I need you to make sure Tommy keeps going, you know? He can turn things into a big fight for himself sometimes, just get angry instead of pushing on."

She nodded, not surprised that he somehow knew Tommy so well.

"I know you can keep him going, even if it seems like

sometimes you can't or even don't want to. But I really need you to."

"I'm going to," she said, and not for his benefit, but simply because it was true.

"Also," he said, "could you just tell him something? Could you say that, ah, that he's not—he's . . ."

"Say it. You can just say it. I'll tell him whatever you need me to."

He seemed to gather it together then, put some height into his shoulders, not sag quite so much under the weight of that unknowable something or other that was sitting on his back.

"Tell him he's not alone anymore."

"Not alone?"

"Yes," he said.

"Why not tell him yourself?"

"No. Not yet. He . . . we both need time."

Annie squinted curiously.

"I'll tell him," she said.

"Thank you. I should probably stop spying on you."

It was a ridiculous thing she was going to say, but it was how she felt and that's what she did: she tried never to hide how she felt.

"You don't have to," she told him.

He smiled again, not so sad this time.

"I wasn't going to." He smiled and looked much younger then, and Annie realized that he was barely older than she was. He nodded and turned and walked to the stairway, where a pretty girl with bright blue eyes and a Mets cap was waiting for him. The girl smiled at Annie and then took the guy's hand in hers. They walked up the steps and off together into their future.

There had been an explosion in midtown some time ago. People walking the street heard it and their necks snapped to as they saw a space in the city that none of them had ever really seen before. For an instant, the bloom of yellow and black was visible, and many started screaming and some started running because, as they would later swear to reporters or relate to friends and family, there was suddenly a building where there had been none a moment before. For its astonishing arrival, it was not such an unusual-looking building; just a sort of generic edifice where Corporations Did Things, with corporate coffee shops in the lobby and banks of mirrored elevators to take faceless people to nameless places.

People screamed and ran, hoping to avoid injury from falling debris, glass, concrete, metal. Firefighters and emergency workers appeared on the scene to find a crowd of shocked and shaken bystanders and, bizarrely, not quite enough building. Confirmed by later investigation, the debris accounted for the outer structure of the building but not for anything that might have been inside it, such as office furniture, interior walls, or, most importantly, people.

There were some inquiries made in the neighboring buildings, where many on the upper floors allowed that they had certainly heard an explosion. On the other hand, none of them could recall in particular what the neighboring building looked like, or what it housed, or even speaking to anyone who worked in it on a cigarette break or a coffee run.

The immediate assumption was yet another terrorist attack, of course. But why that building, which no one could name, no business claimed, no institution spoke for? And why, then, had no terrorist group taken credit for it?

Eventually, the matter of practical disposition was dropped into the lap of a gray-suited man named Meed, who worked for the city. He inspected the scene, did his research, and determined that the lot, zoned for skyscraper construction like the lots all around it, was owned by no one at all. There was a record of the lot, of course, in city files, and of construction by a now-defunct contracting company, but the building had no history of ownership or tenants. It was, in the end, a mystery to be filed away and recounted over dinner with family friends every few years, a story to be retold and perhaps included in an anthology of urban legends someday.

Most practically, Meed determined, what it meant was that the city owned a piece of the most prime business real estate in the metropolitan area, free and clear. Someone else apparently determined this, too, as one morning Meed walked into his office and a man wearing an extremely expensive suit and a cold, sharp expression was waiting there. With the bearing of a lawyer who was doing something absolutely within the confines of the law, he told Meed to shuffle around some papers and arrange for the lot of land to be placed in the name of a certain company that he, the lawyer, represented. Things would, subsequently, go well for Meed.

It was only the first such offer. They came in the form of phone calls, notes, and another visit from a small party of lawyerly-looking men who found Meed outside City Hall one day at a hot dog stand.

Construction of a new edifice would cost enough on its own. Far better to pay a small bribe then the full price of the land. Cut losses, maximize profit, swallow more of the world: death by corporate agenda. Each offer was increasingly lucrative.

Meed was a bureaucrat by trade and by temperament. He detested the chaos of a world that lived outside the rules. Add to that an almost total lack of imagination and a sense of honesty born of the work ethic handed down by his father, who worked in a supermarket from the day he had graduated from high school to the day he died, and Meed proved impossible to influence.

Two hours before a few people in a boardroom decided to kick the pressure up by threatening Meed's wife and two daughters, Meed informed his superiors that the lot was the city's free and clear and could go up for auction.

So there was an auction, and someone bought it. Within a year of this purported explosion, construction began anew.

It was going to be the headquarters of some multi-national conglomerate with a complicated name, the sort of company that people invested in or didn't because their brokers knew something about it, but few people ever really understood, or cared to understand, what it actually did.

It was going to tower up there, just a story or two taller than its neighbors, all metallic and gleaming, infinitely reflecting the similarly reflective multinational headquarters on either side of it. Coincidentally or not, it appeared very much like the structure that had occupied the lot just before it, though nobody knew it, for the last one had escaped their notice altogether. People had been too busy looking down at their cells or blinded by the haze inside their own heads. This one, at least, they could see, if they would just raise their eyes and look.

# ACKNOWLEDGMENTS

They say that writing a book is solitary work. This may indeed be true, but I am here to tell you that *publishing* a book is, in every sense, a collaboration. Among the many people without whom this book would never have reached its current state, I am most deeply indebted to the following.

Jason Anthony, whose keen judgment and invaluable insight shaped the destiny of this book most directly, for the hour upon hour he spent hammering both story and author into shape. Will Lippincot, the most dashing man I have ever met or heard of, for his confident vision and wise command. Julia Richardson, for her faith, for her support and for getting the little stuff as well as the big stuff. Lyall Watson, whose book *Dark Nature: A Natural History of Evil* introduced me to the work of Richard Dawkins and ignited the first ideas that eventually became *Those That Wake*. Gina Gagliano, generous beyond words, for many years' worth of extraordinary competence distilled into some truly indispensable advice. Ian Rustin, for decades of amateur (and extremely astute) editing, who contributed to this book in ways he doesn't even know about and surely never expected. Marilynn Karp, the first person to ever believe in me and, incidentally, this book; whose hand set *Those That Wake* off on its odyssey. And to Maren, because everything good I do, or will *ever* do, begins and ends with her.